GW01271497

PERFECT ATTACHMENT

JULIEN ST. JAMES

Twohungrybowlers.com

This is a work of fiction. Names, characters, places and incidents are products of the author's imagination or are used fictitiously and not to be construed as real. Any resemblance to actual events, locales, organizations, or persons, living or dead, is entirely coincidental.

PERFECT ATTACHMENT. Copyright © 2025 by Julien St. James All rights reserved. No part of this book may be reproduced in any form or by any electronic or mechanical means, including information storage and retrieval systems, without written permission from the author, except for the use of brief quotations in embodied in critical reviews and certain other noncommercial uses permitted by copyright law. For permission requests, write to the publisher, addressed "Attention: Permissions Coordinator," at the address below.

Two Hungry Bowlers Publishing
30 N Gould Street Suite N
Sheridan, WY 82801

FIRST EDITION

ISBN: 979-8-9986541-2-1 (paperback)
979-8-9986541-1-4 (ebook)
979-8-9986541-3-8 (hardback)
979-8-9986541-4-5 (Audiobook)

For my mum who introduced me to Sherlock Holmes and Agatha Christie and then I was off to the races.....

ALSO BY JULIEN ST. JAMES

Love Notes and Sticky Tape

———

As Henri Penuer

Lint Socks and Rock paper Scissors

ACT 1

Discovery

1

DJURGÅRDEN

The call came at 1:17 AM.

Kriminalinspektör Maja Norberg had been awake anyway, staring at the ceiling of her apartment on Upplandsgatan. Stockholm's radiators ticked their eternal percussion while she contemplated the peculiar human need to arrange life into neat eight-hour segments of consciousness—when the mind clearly had other plans. The phone's shrill cry cut through the November silence.

"Norberg."

"We have two bodies in Djurgården Park." The voice belonged to Kriminalinspektör Sergeant Anders Svensson or Sven, tight with that peculiar professional excitement cops develop when confronted with something genuinely puzzling rather than merely tragic. "You need to see this, Maja. It's... unsettling."

Maja sat up, her bare feet finding the cold floor. Through her window, Stockholm slept under a blanket of early winter fog. "What kind of bodies?"

"The kind that don't make sense at all, if you know what I mean. Someone's been thinking too hard about something."

Twenty minutes later, Maja stood at the edge of the crime scene, her hands buried deep in the pockets of her worn pea coat, wondering not for the first time why humanity's capacity for creativity seemed to peak at precisely those moments when it would be better left dormant. The fog had lifted slightly, revealing the true horror that waited in the pale circle of portable lights.

Two bodies lay in the frost-covered grass, arranged with a precision that made her stomach clench. A man and a woman, naked, their limbs positioned in what might have been an embrace if not for the terrible stillness, the unnatural angles. Even from a distance, Maja could see that death had taken them methodically—which was somehow worse than violently. Violence suggested passion; this suggested planning.

She stood there for a long moment, letting the scene settle in her mind. In twenty years of police work, she'd learned that the first impression often contained truths that careful analysis would later obscure. This felt like a message, but written in a language she didn't yet understand.

"Fan också," she muttered, then immediately felt guilty for cursing in the presence of the dead, as if they might somehow be more offended by profanity than by their current circumstances.

Sven appeared at her elbow, notebook already in hand. "Witnesses?"

"None. Dog walker found them around midnight, called it in." Sven's voice carried that flat tone cops develop when trying to process the gap between human potential and human achievement. "No identification yet."

Maja approached the bodies slowly, her experienced eye cataloguing details. The woman's makeup was still perfect, expensive. The man wore the tan lines of formal clothing - a watch, a wedding ring recently removed. These weren't random victims. Someone had gone shopping for exactly the right people, which raised the disturbing question of what constituted "right" in this context.

"Positions," she said, more to herself than to Sven. "Look at how they're arranged."

"Like they're supposed to mean something," Sven said, his voice uncertain. "But what the hell could this mean?"

The killer had worked methodically. Every limb precisely placed, every point of contact between the bodies deliberate. Maja crouched beside them, careful not to disturb the scene. Someone had taken time here, worked carefully. The question was whether the precision served a purpose or was simply the killer's nature. Where their flesh touched, the skin had begun to darken in ways that had nothing to do with normal decomposition.

As Sven moved away, Maja remained crouched beside the bodies. The fog drifted between the trees, and she found herself thinking about the patience this would have required. Most killers were driven by impulse, anger, need. This felt different—calculated in a way that suggested the deaths themselves might have been secondary to whatever the killer was actually trying to accomplish.

The woman's eyes stared sightlessly at the grey sky above. Her face held an expression that Maja had learned to recognize—the look of someone who had realized, in their final moments, exactly what was happening to them. The look of understanding arriving too late to matter.

She stood, her knees protesting after too many years of crime scenes. The killer had left them here like a message, positioned where they would be found quickly. But what was the message? And more troubling—who was the intended audience?

"kriminalinspektör?" Dr. Bergman's voice came from the other side of the bodies. The pathologist had been working quietly since before Maja arrived. "You need to see this."

Maja walked around to where Dr. Bergman knelt beside the male victim.

"Two victims, positioned post-mortem with what I can only describe as obsessive precision." Maja gestured to the bodies. "But look at the contact points. Something's been applied to their skin. Chemical bonding of some kind."

"Chemical burns," Dr. Bergman said. "But controlled ones. This isn't random violence."

"No," Maja agreed. "This is someone with a very specific idea in mind. The question is what."

The portable generators hummed in the background, their mechanical drone replacing the natural sounds of night. The scene felt theatrical, staged for maximum impact. But impact on whom?

"kriminalinspektör?" A young constable approached, uncertainty written across his face. "We found something in the male victim's pocket."

Maja took the evidence bag, studying the small symbol printed on a piece of paper. A circle bisected by a cross, hand-drawn in black ink. Simple, but something about it nagged at her memory.

"Religious?" Sven suggested, returning from his calls. "Occult maybe? Or just someone who likes drawing symbols."

"Maybe." Maja turned the symbol over in her mind. Symbols could mean anything or nothing, depending on who was using them and why. "Have you seen this before?"

Both officers shook their heads. Maja pocketed the evidence bag, making a mental note to run it through the database.

As dawn began to grey the eastern sky, Dr. Bergman continued her examination. Maja watched her work, noting how her expression had shifted from professional interest to something approaching fascination, which was somehow more disturbing than simple horror.

"Time of death?" she asked when Dr. Bergman straightened.

"Difficult to determine precisely. The chemical reactions at the contact points have affected normal decomposition of those areas. Dr. Bergman stripped off her gloves with sharp, efficient movements. "But I'd estimate between midnight and 2am."

"Chemical reactions?"

"Something has been applied to create bonds between their tissue. I'll need laboratory analysis to understand exactly what." Dr. Bergman's voice carried that tone forensic specialists developed when confronted with something outside their normal experience. "kriminalinspektör, in thirty years of pathology, I've never seen anything like this. It's almost... experimental."

Maja felt the familiar weight of a complex case settling on her shoulders. The kind that would consume weeks, maybe months. The kind that would keep her awake at night, puzzle pieces shifting endlessly in her mind. The kind where the answer, when it finally came, might be worse than the mystery.

"Transportation?" Maja asked, feeling the familiar weight of a complex case settling on her shoulders.

"The positioning alone would have taken significant time." Dr. Bergman gestured to the bodies. "They were moved, arranged, then left for discovery. Like a museum display—carefully curated."

As morning light strengthened, Maja studied the precise arrangement. "We're looking for someone with medical knowledge. Someone who understands chemistry, who plans extensively and executes with surgical precision." She crouched beside the bodies, noting the meticulous positioning. "Someone who sees these deaths as components in something larger."

"Maja?" Sven held up his phone. "Missing persons report came in twenty minutes ago. Matches our female victim. Sofia Lindström, age thirty-four. Last seen at a charity gala on Östermalm."

"Östermalm?" Maja's mind immediately began calculating the social geography involved. "So we're dealing with someone who moves in charity gala circles. Or someone who hunts in them."

"That's what we need to find out."

Maja looked once more at the bodies, at their terrible embrace in the growing light. Somewhere, probably brewing kaffe in some apartment across the city, a killer was congratulating themselves on a job well done. Someone who had turned human intimacy into a weapon, who had reduced two people to components in some grotesque experiment. The kind of person who believed their actions served a purpose that justified everything.

"Pack it up," she told the crime scene team. "Every detail docu-

mented. And get me everything you can find about this Sofia Lindström." She paused, studying the symbol again. "And find out what
this means. Check religious databases, occult websites, anything
that might give us a lead."

As the forensics team continued their methodical work, Maja
walked back to her car. The November morning was growing
brighter, but she felt only darkness ahead. This wasn't a crime of
passion or greed.

Her phone buzzed with another call. More cases, more violence,
more of humanity's endless capacity for cruelty. But this one, Maja
knew, would follow her home. It would sit at her kitchen table
during her solitary dinners, would whisper to her in the small hours
when sleep refused to come. It would make her question every
symbol, every careful arrangement, every sign that someone might
be trying to communicate through violence.

She started the engine of the old Mercedes her father gave her
and began the drive back to the station, already dreading the paperwork, the phone calls, the slow machinery of justice grinding into
motion. Somewhere in Stockholm, thousands of people were beginning their morning routines, completely unaware that someone in
their midst had redefined the concept of human connection in the
most horrific way imaginable. Behind her, the crime scene continued
its silent testimony to whatever darkness had visited Djurgården in
the night.

The fog was lifting, but Maja knew it would be a long time before
she could see clearly again. In her experience, the most dangerous
criminals were always the ones who thought they had something
important to prove.

2

POLISHUSET

The fluorescent lights of Polishuset hummed their morning meditation above Maja's head as she arranged crime scene photos across the incident room's whiteboard like a curator preparing an exhibition of human folly. Through the frost-etched windows of the Kungsholmen station, Stockholm's winter dawn crept through the darkness, reluctant and uncertain.

She traced connections between images with a red marker, each line a thread in what she suspected was a web spun by someone who understood that police work, like philosophy, was fundamentally about pattern recognition. The ancient Gevalia kaffe machine gurgled its protest behind her, a sound so familiar it had become part of the station's institutional consciousness.

The antiseptic smell still clung to her clothes from the crime scene. Sharp and clinical, the same chemical scent Bergman had noted at the injection sites. She'd changed into spare clothes from her locker, but some contaminations, she reflected, went deeper than fabric. Some things followed you home whether you invited them or not.

The photos told their story with the stark honesty that only death could provide: bodies in artificial embrace, footprints in the snow. Each piece of evidence felt like a breadcrumb left by someone who understood that the real mystery wasn't whodunit, but why anyone would choose to arrange human suffering so precisely.

"Maja." Kriminalkommissarie Söderberg's voice carried the resigned authority of a man who had learned that Monday mornings invariably brought fresh evidence of humanity's creative capacity for destroying itself. He stood in the doorway, kopp kaffe held like a shield against the day's emerging chaos.

She turned from the board, noting how his eyes moved across the photos with the systematic efficiency that had made him the youngest head of Våldsroteln.

"Two victims, possibly positioned post-mortem," she reported. "Clinical precision in the staging. Everything about the scene feels..."

"Choreographed."

"Choreographed by someone who likes to make a statement, a bold statement."

Beyond the open door, Polishuset hummed with its morning rhythm. Phones rang with fresh disasters, keyboards clicked out reports of last night's violence.

"The press will be circling by lunch," Söderberg noted. "Especially once the victims' identities leak. The Maritime Museum fundraiser was too public. Half of Stockholm's elite could have seen them leave."

"I want hourly updates on this one," Söderberg continued. "Anything unusual, anything that doesn't fit the pattern, I need to know immediately." He paused at the door, and for a moment his administrative mask slipped, revealing something almost paternal underneath. "And Maja? Watch yourself. Something about this feels... targeted."

The late morning sun filtered through November clouds with typical Swedish reluctance. Sven's massive frame hunched over his workstation.

"Hello, Maja!" His voice carried gruffness that came from too many early mornings spent contemplating human nature's darker expressions. "I found something about that symbol."

Finally, Maja thought, pulling her chair closer with a squeak that echoed through the office.

"Fan ta mig..." Sven lowered himself into his chair. "Got this old contact at Kungsmedicinska Institutet. Recognized the symbol immediately." He snapped his thick fingers with satisfaction. "Some fancy student group. Called themselves the Nexus Club. Thought they were going to revolutionize psychology, save the world through better understanding of human nature. You know how university students are."

The overhead light sputtered, casting unstable shadows across the incident board.

"After the university shut them down, the members just... disbanded," he continued. "Some went into private practice, research, whatever academics do when they realize the real world doesn't operate according to their theories." He paused, fingers drumming against his thigh. "But there's this one name that keeps surfacing—Professor Gustaf Nielsen. Their advisor. Was doing some questionable research before it all went sideways. Fear responses, psychological conditioning."

"And Nielsen?" Maja asked.

"Still teaching. Right there at Kungsmedicinska Institutet, molding young minds."

Maja picked up one of the crime scene photos, studying the posed hands.

"Pull everything on Nielsen," she said, her voice taking on the edge that emerged when police work transformed from puzzle-solving into moral imperative. "Research assistants, doctoral candidates, especially anyone connected to that final project."

"I know the drill," Sven muttered, reaching for his phone. "These academic types are always so proper until you start digging."

The antique clock on her desk chimed six times a present from her Farfar—grandfather that she couldn't give up even though it had seen better days and places. Around them, the day shift prepared for departure.

"Go home, Sven," Maja said, noting how fatigue had settled into his shoulders. "Marta must be wondering if you've been absorbed into some investigation."

"För helvete, Maja..." His voice carried the weight of a conversation they'd had too many times before. "Here we go again."

"What?" Though she knew. Of course she knew.

"Marta's already called twice, and you've got that look again." He gestured at her desk, now littered with kaffe cups in various stages of abandonment. "Remember what happened last time? When you forgot that human beings require sleep?"

"Someone needs to work this case, Sven."

"And someone needs to remain sufficiently human to solve it," he replied, struggling with his coat. "God natt. And for fan's sake, Maja, fresh clothes tomorrow."

She watched him navigate the maze of desks with surprising grace for such a large man, his departure leaving behind the quiet that comes when wise counsel has been offered and politely ignored. The night shift drifted in, their faces marked with caffeine-fueled optimism.

The ancient television mounted in the corner caught her attention. Someone had adjusted the volume. The familiar TV4 jingle cut through the office's meditative silence.

"Police remain tight-lipped about the bodies discovered in Djurgården Park early this morning," the anchor reported. "Sources suggest the victims were last seen at the Maritime Museum's annual fundraising gala."

Behind her, footage from the crime scene showed floodlights cutting through pre-dawn mist, the forensics team moving methodically through their work. A flash of worn pea jacket. Kriminalinspektör Norberg conferring with pathologists.

———

Expressen's headline blazed across Stockholm's screens:

HORROR IN DJURGÅRDEN - Elite Gala Ends in Mystery Deaths

In his corner office at Aftonbladet, veteran crime reporter Elger Sandstrom contemplated his kaffe. His sources whispered about chemical compounds that shouldn't exist, bodies posed like installation art, and the curious fact that no one seemed willing to explain exactly what had bound the victims together in their final embrace.

He sipped his kaffe and wondered whether the real mystery wasn't what people did to each other, but why anyone still found it surprising.

3
GÄRDET

The drive to Bergman's temporary laboratory carried them through Södermalm's afternoon ritual of controlled chaos, where Stockholm performed its daily dance between order and entropy. Maja guided the old Mercedes past Medborgarplatsen, where lunch queues formed with Swedish precision despite the November gloom that pressed against windows like an unwelcome confession. The car's heating system wheezed with the dignity of aging machinery, mixing the scent of cardamom from Wayne's kafé with exhaust fumes and that metallic promise of snow that hung over the city like a question no one wanted to answer.

"Fan också," Sven muttered, his phone screen casting blue light across features that seemed carved from the same granite as the buildings outside. "Bergman's sent three more messages. Something about chemical degradation rates." He shifted in the passenger seat, leather creaking with the sound of accumulated decades. "Why'd they have to move the lab all the way out to Gärdet? As if Swedish bureaucracy wasn't complicated enough already."

Maja considered this while navigating past the Fotografiska, where tourists hunched against the wind coming off the water, their cameras capturing a Stockholm that would look different in every photograph, filtered through individual perceptions of Nordic melancholy. The city revealed itself in layers, like the investigation unfolding around them, with each discovery suggesting deeper questions about what people were capable of when they believed no one was watching.

The old military clinic squatted ahead like a monument to institutional memory, its brutalist concrete facade reflecting the weak sun defensively. Built in that optimistic era when Swedish functionalism promised to solve human problems through proper design, it now housed the detritus of bureaucratic reorganization. Each department that had occupied these walls (military medical research, immigration services, various government initiatives) had left traces like archaeological strata, visible in layers of institutional paint and the peculiar smell of places where many people had waited for others to make decisions about their lives.

They found parking in the staff lot, now mostly empty except for Bergman's team and a few cars belonging to people whose purpose remained unclear. Weeds pushed through cracked concrete with the persistence of small rebellions, while a faded sign still warned "Endast Personal" in Swedish and English, which was a linguistic fossil from when the world had been divided into simpler categories of us and them.

"Helvete," Sven said, studying the building. "Looks like something from an old spy film."

The security lock buzzed them through to a lobby that smelled of disinfectant and institutional time, which was that peculiar odor of places where nothing personal was ever supposed to happen. A single fluorescent tube flickered with the rhythm of failing authority, casting shadows that danced across walls bearing the ghostly outlines of removed charts. Their footsteps echoed in a space designed to humble visitors, each sound amplified by surfaces that had absorbed decades of human anxiety.

A hand-written sign directed them to the basement, where

Bergman had colonized the old military medical facility's autopsy suite. The stairwell descended through layers of Swedish bureaucratic history, each landing painted in different eras' official colors: olive drab, institutional beige, sterile white. They were like sedimentary deposits left by various administrations' attempts to improve human conditions through proper color coordination.

"Fan, what a place," Sven muttered, his voice muffled by concrete walls that had been built to contain things that shouldn't escape. "Reminds me of that bunker in Boden where I did my värnplikt. Same smell. Like old secrets and government disinfectant trying to cover up the fact that nobody really knows what they're doing."

Maja found herself wondering about the military doctors who had once worked here, whether they had approached their examinations with the same mixture of scientific method and existential puzzlement that seemed to characterize all attempts to understand why human beings did the things they did to each other. Perhaps there was something absurd about applying systematic procedures to the study of violence, as if logic could make sense of what had never been logical to begin with.

They found Bergman in what had once been the military's primary autopsy room, now transformed into a space where modern forensic equipment shared territory with vintage steel cabinets still bearing their military inventory numbers. The pathologist had adapted to her surroundings, turning a Cold War relic into something approaching scientific usefulness. Banks of computers hummed where army doctors had once conducted their own investigations into the mystery of why bodies stopped working, while sophisticated chemical analysis equipment coexisted with institutional furniture designed to last longer than the systems that had commissioned it.

Bergman stood at a central workstation, her protective gear reflecting LED lights she'd installed to supplement the building's aging fluorescents. She looked up as they entered, her expression carrying that gravity of someone who had discovered something they wished they hadn't.

"Ah, finally," she said, gesturing them closer with a gloved hand. "You'll want to see this. The chemical analysis from the contact points..." She paused, ensuring they were both paying attention in the way that suggested what followed would require their complete concentration. "It's not what we expected. It's much simpler, and much worse."

The central table displayed photographs of the victims' injection sites with the meticulous documentation that characterized Bergman's approach to her profession. Each image was labeled with measurements and timestamps that reduced human suffering to data points, a necessary transformation that allowed the work to continue. Beside them lay chemical analysis readouts, their peaks and valleys forming patterns that seemed to pulse in the institutional lighting like electronic heartbeats measuring something that shouldn't have been alive.

"Look here," Bergman continued, pointing to readouts with the focused intensity of someone who had spent years learning to read the language that dead tissue spoke. "The compound's molecular structure is straightforward industrial adhesive. Medical grade cyanoacrylate, the kind used in surgical procedures." She paused, her voice taking on the flat tone of someone delivering news that was somehow worse for being ordinary. "Modified with a catalyst to accelerate bonding time."

She pulled up molecular diagrams on her laptop, blue light casting shadows across features that had seen enough to understand that human ingenuity was as often directed toward harm as healing. "Someone took surgical adhesive—the kind every hospital has—and modified it to create permanent bonds between human tissue on contact. Not exotic chemistry, just practical application of existing technology." Her finger traced simple molecular chains that looked almost mundane on screen. "The kind of modification someone could do with basic chemistry knowledge and access to industrial supplies."

Maja leaned closer to the screen, studying analysis data that showed the horrifying simplicity of what had been done. There was something unsettling about the idea that such ordinary materials could be turned into instruments of torture. "What exactly does that mean for our understanding of what happened?"

"It means," Bergman said, pulling up comparative analysis from industrial adhesive databases, "that whoever did this didn't need advanced scientific training. They needed access to medical supplies and basic chemistry knowledge. The kind of information you could find in industrial safety manuals." She gestured to tissue samples in labeled containers. "What they needed was the imagination to realize that something designed to save lives could be used to destroy them."

The samples seemed to glow faintly under the LED lighting, though Maja knew this was probably just her imagination responding to information that her mind wasn't prepared to process. "The adhesive created permanent bonds between the victims' tissue," Bergman continued, her voice clinical as she moved between workstations. "The bonds are stable, designed to be irreversible. Medical grade, meant to hold surgical incisions closed permanently."

"Fan ta dig," Sven muttered, leaning against one of the old steel cabinets with the expression of someone who had thought he understood the range of human cruelty until this moment. "You're saying someone used surgical glue to... to stick them together?"

"Precisely that." Bergman moved to another workstation where microscope images showed tissue samples bonded with surgical precision. This isn't random violence. This is systematic application of medical knowledge for torture."

The basement's ventilation system provided a low undertone to the electronic beeping of equipment, while somewhere in the building's depths, old pipes clanked with the sound of infrastructure aging faster than anyone could repair it. The building itself seemed to be participating in their conversation, offering its own commentary on the persistence of human systems beyond their intended lifespans.

"There's something else," She pulled on fresh nitrile gloves and moved to a sealed evidence container in one of the military-issue refrigerators. "We found traces of a sedative in their bloodstreams. Something to keep them conscious but unable to struggle effectively." She placed a vial containing blood samples on the examination table where it caught the light like evidence of betrayed trust. "Basic midazolam. The kind used in every hospital for minor procedures."

Maja felt something cold settle in her stomach that had nothing to do with the basement's temperature. "So they were awake for..."

"For the entire procedure, yes. Conscious but unable to resist. Medical knowledge applied to ensure maximum psychological impact." She looked directly at Maja with eyes that had seen enough to understand the implications without needing them explained.

"Fan också," Sven observed, his bulk casting shadows under lighting that made everything look like evidence of something ominous. "So we're looking for someone with medical training and access to hospital supplies? A doctor who decided to use their knowledge for torture?"

"That's the most likely profile." Bergman pulled up a series of images that documented systematic application of simple chemistry for horrific purposes. "Someone with surgical training, access to medical supplies, and the psychological capacity to use healing knowledge for harm. Most concerning from an investigative standpoint: the precision suggests they've done this before."

The implications settled over them like the building's antiseptic smell, persistent and impossible to ignore. Maja thought of the precision visible at the crime scene, the calculated placement of every injection site, the sense that what they had discovered was the end result of considerable preparation rather than spontaneous violence. "You're saying this wasn't the first attempt."

"The application technique is too refined," Bergman replied, her voice maintaining clinical detachment while her eyes suggested someone who had seen enough evidence to be deeply troubled by its implications. "This level of precision with medical adhesive application, the systematic approach, the knowledge of exactly how much sedative to administer—this represents practice." She pulled up another set of data showing application patterns. "And when I compared the technique to samples from unsolved cases, I found something interesting. Three cases from 2019 to 2021 show similar adhesive residue. Cases that were classified as accidents before full analysis could be completed."

The basement's ventilation system groaned with the sound of old secrets settling into new configurations. Maja felt the weight of the building above them, decades of military medical research pressing down through layers of concrete and institutional paint that had been applied to cover previous layers of institutional paint in an endless cycle of bureaucratic renewal.

"I need everything you have on those earlier cases," she said, understanding that they were no longer investigating an isolated incident but rather the latest iteration of something that had been developing systematically over years. "And Bergman: this stays between us for now. No reports through official channels until we understand what we're dealing with."

Bergman nodded, already moving to secure her samples. "I'll store the tissue cultures in the old military freezers. The temperature stability is better than our modern equipment, ironically enough." She gestured to Cold War-era storage units whose steel facades still bore faded warning labels in multiple languages, relics from an era when the world's problems had seemed more clearly defined. "At least this place is good for preserving things that were never supposed to exist."

As they turned to leave, carrying knowledge that would make sleep more difficult, Bergman called after them.

"Maja? There's one more thing." She paused in the way that suggested what followed would require careful consideration. "The adhesive modification? I found traces of similar alterations in medical literature. Research into rapid tissue bonding, all published by Swedish medical professionals between 2018 and 2020. All from Stockholm-area hospitals."

The fluorescent lights flickered overhead, casting shadows that seemed to move independently across old military tile that had absorbed decades of institutional secrets. Somewhere above them, a door slammed in the empty building, the sound echoing through floors that had housed various attempts to understand human nature through systematic observation.

They left the basement carrying evidence of human ingenuity applied to purposes that made systematic sense only if you accepted that some people viewed other people as experimental material. The building's security system buzzed them out into afternoon light that seemed brighter than it had when they entered, though Stockholm's November sky remained the same shade of gray that suggested winter's approach.

In the Mercedes, driving back through streets where people went about their daily lives unaware that someone was using medical knowledge to torture, Maja found herself thinking about the banality of evil, about surgical supplies turned into instruments of torture. There was something disturbing about the idea that healing knowledge could be perverted so easily.

The radio played quietly, offering traffic updates and weather forecasts that assumed tomorrow would arrive more or less as expected, while in the trunk of their car they carried evidence that some people spent their professional time ensuring that for certain individuals, tomorrow would arrive in ways they could never have imagined.

4
DENIAL

The grey November light crept through Maja's window like an unwelcome confession, revealing the unmade bed she'd abandoned at 3 AM when sleep became impossible. Crime scene photos lay scattered across her nightstand, but it wasn't the evidence keeping her awake—it was the growing certainty that she understood Nielsen's methodology too well. The precision, the documentation, the way he reduced human connection to measurable variables. She'd spent twenty years doing the same thing, just with different intentions.

She pressed her palms against her eyes. When had she started seeing Paul's affection as a behavioral pattern to analyze rather than experience? When had their relationship become another case file in her mind?

Tonight, Paul would be waiting for her at Operakällaren. A reservation made weeks ago, back when the distance between them seemed manageable, when she could still pretend that commitment was simply a matter of scheduling. Now, after yesterday's revelations about Nielsen's research and those sealed cases from 2019-2021, the thought of discussing their future felt absurd. How do you plan a life when death keeps such elegant company?

Loki regarded her from the foot of the bed with the patient disapproval only dogs master, a look that suggested he understood her failings better than she did. Paul's dog, like Paul himself, had become a fixture demanding emotional maintenance she couldn't provide. She could analyze the degradation patterns of human tissue with forensic precision, yet couldn't navigate the simpler chemistry of domestic affection.

"Fan," she muttered, pulling on yesterday's jeans. The wool coat still carried antiseptic traces from Bergman's lab, clinical perfume for someone who spent more time with the dead than the living.

The morning walk felt foreign under her feet. Usually she experienced Stockholm's early hours through her car window, racing toward whatever horror required her attention. Loki trotted ahead with unearned optimism, his leash a thin connection to normalcy she wasn't sure she deserved. The dog's enthusiasm for simple pleasures struck her as a kind of wisdom she'd long abandoned.

Paul had stocked her refrigerator yesterday, another domestic gesture that should have warmed her heart but instead felt like evidence of her inadequacy. Even after eight months together, she remained a tourist in the country of shared lives. Paul, with his architect's precision and patient understanding, deserved someone who could appreciate the blueprints he drew for their future. Instead, he got her, always one case away from complete absence.

Her phone held the weight of two competing worlds: Paul's dinner reservation and Bergman's molecular analyses. Someone had spent years perfecting this compound, testing it, refining it while she'd been solving other murders, building this tentative life that never quite fit. The sophistication troubled her more than the violence: this wasn't passion or desperation, but methodology. Academic curiosity applied to human suffering with scientific rigor.

Back in her apartment, surrounded by case files that pulsed with urgency, Maja felt the familiar pull toward darkness.

Her phone buzzed. Paul:

Looking forward to tonight. Don't let work consume you.

The gentle reminder felt like a lifeline to normalcy, though they both knew which choice she'd make. This was the pattern that had destroyed her previous relationships: the same choice dressed in different circumstances. She could almost script the conversation: her apologies, his disappointment, the slow erosion of hope disguised as understanding.

Loki dropped his leash at her feet, dark eyes full of canine judgment. Even the dog understood the weight of her decision. She typed quickly before courage failed her:

Can't do dinner tonight. The case.

Paul's response arrived with devastating efficiency:

At least you're honest about it.

She stared at the words, understanding what honesty had become between them: not a virtue but a weapon, each truth another small cut. How strange that being honest about her priorities had become its own form of cruelty. Standing in her hallway, yesterday's clothes hanging loose on her frame, Maja studied her reflection with the detached curiosity she usually reserved for crime scenes. Dark circles, intense expression, the familiar armor of professional competence. But instead of the usual self-criticism, something shifted in her understanding. She wasn't a victim of her own patterns, she was their architect. Every choice to prioritize work over Paul wasn't compulsion but preference, as natural as breathing.

She watched herself with the forensic interest she brought to evidence: a woman who could calculate cellular degradation but couldn't figure out why relationships fell apart. Nielsen's research had forced intimacy through chemical bonds. She achieved distance through long practice, choosing cases over people with the efficiency of habit. Both were methodical approaches to human connection, she realized. Nielsen forced intimacy; she engineered its absence.

Another text from Paul:

Loki needs feeding by 6. Don't forget.

The mundane request felt profound in its simplicity. Here was love reduced to its essential function: ensuring something vulnerable survived another day. No grand gestures, no emotional demands, just the basic maintenance that kept life continuing in hostile conditions. Bergman had shown her tissue samples that persisted long after their host organisms died. Perhaps Paul's affection was similar: love that survived in conditions that should have killed it, adapting to scarcity with stubborn biological efficiency.

This recognition didn't bring guilt, surprisingly, but something like relief. She was what she was: someone who found in death's silence what others sought in conversation. The dead demanded nothing but understanding. The living wanted transformation, growth, compromise, processes that exhausted her in ways that murder never did.

The November drizzle matched her mood as she drove toward Polishuset. Stockholm's morning traffic moved with mechanical precision, each driver navigating their own patterns of choice and consequence. Her phone buzzed one final time. Paul:

When this case is over, we need to talk.

She didn't respond. They both understood what that conversation would contain: the same themes explored in different relationships, over different cases. History repeating itself with the inevitability of Nordic seasons, darkness following light following darkness.

———

Sven's car already occupied its usual space in the parking garage, suggesting he'd made similar choices about weekend priorities. They shared this particular failing: the inability to distinguish between dedication and obsession, between serving justice and serving their own need to impose meaning on chaos.

The weight of her gun felt reassuring as she walked through Polishuset's familiar corridors. As the elevator carried her toward the investigation room, Maja felt something settle into place, not peace exactly, but recognition. Paul would spend his evening alone, probably analyzing their relationship with the same methodical precision he brought to architectural blueprints. Loki would adapt to another disruption with canine pragmatism, carrying Paul's simple request like a prayer: feed the dog by six.

The absurdity struck her suddenly: she who studied forced intimacy had perfected voluntary distance. Different methodologies, identical result: two people unable to find the right balance between connection and autonomy. Paul kept choosing to love someone who'd never hidden what she was.

There was something almost funny about it, in a dark way. Here she was, a Kriminalinspektör who studied death for a living, finally understanding that survival sometimes required choosing solitude over connection, understanding over love. Not because love was worthless, but because understanding was her particular form of devotion.

Some patterns, it seemed, were as persistent as those cellular structures in Bergman's lab, surviving conditions that should have destroyed them, continuing their function long after their purpose became obscure. Perhaps that was enough. Perhaps understanding, even when it came at the cost of everything else, still mattered.

The investigation room awaited, promising purpose if not peace. Outside, Stockholm's grey morning continued its ancient rhythm, indifferent to human choices and their consequences, carrying secrets through the city's veins like blood through a body that refused to die.

5
ARCHIVIST

Maja had spent the night in the investigation room, molecular diagrams and university records spread across the conference table like a complex equation she couldn't solve. Dawn crept through the windows of Polishuset, revealing the evidence board she'd been assembling since 4 AM. Four days since the discovery in Djurgården Park, and finally the pieces still didn't form a pattern.

The precinct stirred around her with morning sounds: kaffe brewing, keyboards clicking to life, the gradual awakening of another day's work with human cruelty. Last night's takeaway containers from the Thai place on Drottninggatan clustered on nearby desks like small monuments to procrastination. The sweet-sour scent mixed with brewing kaffe—an oddly domestic backdrop to photographs of the dead.

She pressed her fingertips against her temples, studying the victims' faces on the board before her.

Familiar footsteps approached across the linoleum. "God morgen, Sven," she said without turning.

Sven grunted in response. When Maja turned, the dark circles under his eyes told their own story about the night he'd spent among transcripts and university records.

"The Nexus Club," he said, voice gravelly with fatigue. "More cult than study group.Four core members, all psychology students except their faculty advisor." He set down an empty kaffe cup beside a stack of transcripts. "Amazing how often the study of human behavior becomes an excuse to behave inhumanely."

Maja pulled up a chair, metal legs scraping against the floor. The radiator clicked and hummed behind them.

Sven's thick finger traced down a list of names: "Marcus Björk, Anna-Maria Viklund, Joonas Rask, Nils Håkansson, and Erik Thoressen."

Maja leaned forward, watching Sven lay out photographs.

Marcus Björk, brilliant but unstable, now in pharmaceutical research. Anna-Maria Viklund, the meticulous secretary who understood that power lay in documentation. Joonas Rask, disappeared after graduation. Nils Håkansson, dead of liver failure, but not before leaving behind a manifesto. Erik Thoressen is in the university system.

"The club was conducting unauthorized experiments," Sven continued, rubbing his eyes. "Pushing psychological limits, they called it. Testing human breaking points."

Maja felt a familiar chill. Academic institutions could become laboratories for the kind of curiosity that destroyed rather than illuminated. "The university shut them down when students started having breakdowns?"

"Buried the whole thing to avoid scandal. Standard institutional response." Sven's voice carried the weary wisdom of someone who'd seen universities protect their reputations with the same dedication they claimed to reserve for truth.

"We need to talk to them. All of them." She stood abruptly, chair scraping back. "Start with Viklund. She documented everything."

"Already on it." Sven reached for his coat. "She works the day shift at the hospital."

They drove through Stockholm's morning traffic toward Solstrandsjukhuset. The hospital's stark modernist facade looked grey against the November sky. The hospital's name, "Sun Shore," seemed like Stockholm's idea of irony on a day like this.

Ambulanss waited in their designated bays, red crosses bright against white metal. They parked among other institutional vehicles and walked across wet asphalt. The hospital's automatic doors opened with a soft hiss.

The receptionist glanced up as they showed their badges, waving them deeper into the building's maze. The main corridor stretched ahead, off-white walls and squeaking linoleum underfoot. A cleaner pushed his cart past them, wheels squealing.

The elevator to the basement was old, brass buttons worn smooth by decades of use. As they descended, the mechanism groaned and the scratched panel reflected their faces.

The basement corridor was narrower, ceiling lower, pressed down by the weight of the building above. Pipes ran along the ceiling, dripping condensation that left dark stains on the floor. They passed locked doors marked with cryptic combinations of numbers and letters—hospital bureaucracy's love affair with meaningless codes.

The fluorescent lights buzzed overhead, some flickering. The antiseptic smell faded as they walked deeper, replaced by old paper and dust.

They found Anna-Maria Viklund in the hospital's basement archives, surrounded by filing cabinets. She had changed little from her student photograph, same severe expression. But her eyes held something new: wariness.

"Kriminalinspektör Maja Norberg," Maja said. She nodded toward Sven. "And my partner, Kriminalinspektör Sven Svensson."

Viklund's hands stilled on the file she'd been organizing.

"We'd like to ask you about the Nexus Club," Maja continued, watching the woman's face.

"That was a long time ago." Viklund's voice was barely above a whisper.

"What can you tell us about its work?" Maja asked.

Viklund's hands stilled completely on the files. She said nothing.

"Anna, we're investigating a murder that may connect to your studies back then." Maja's voice carried the patient authority of someone accustomed to reluctant witnesses. "We can talk here or at the station. Your choice."

Still silence. Maja placed a crime scene photo on the desk between them.

"We think that someone's recreating your work. With a few deadly modifications." Maja said

The color drained from Viklund's face as she stared at the image. "No," she whispered. "It can't be. We destroyed everything."

"Did you?" Maja leaned closer. "Or did someone keep records? Continue the research when official channels closed?"

Viklund's eyes darted between them, then to the door. "You don't understand. What we did... what we were trying to achieve..." She swallowed hard. "Some of us wanted to stop when we realized where the experiments were leading. Others said we were too close to breakthrough to let ethical concerns interfere."

"Who?" Sven asked. "Who wanted to continue?"

But Viklund shook her head, tears gathering in her eyes—not of grief, but of fear. "I can't. They'll know I talked. They always know when someone breaks the agreement."

Maja felt familiar ice in her veins. "Who are 'they', Anna-Maria? We can protect you."

Viklund's lips trembled. "You can't protect me. No one can. Not from them. Not from... him."

The pronoun hung in the air between them, and Maja and Sven exchanged glances.

"Him?" Maja pressed. "Who is 'he', Anna-Maria?"

Viklund's eyes widened with terror. She opened her mouth, breath catching, then frantically shook her head.

Sven stepped forward, voice calm. "It's okay, Anna-Maria. Take your time. We're here to help."

But Viklund had retreated into silence, eyes unfocused, body trembling. It was clear they wouldn't get more today.

Maja sighed and placed a gentle hand on Viklund's shoulder. "We'll be in touch, Anna-Maria. Here's my card. Call me when you're ready to talk."

The drive back to Polishuset unfolded in contemplative silence, both Kriminalinspektörs processing the interview. Stockholm's sky pressed down, grey and persistent.

"She's terrified," Sven observed.

"Ja," Maja agreed, watching the city pass through rain-streaked windows. "But of whom? And what exactly did they discover in that club?"

As they drove through the darkening afternoon, neither spoke about Anna-Maria's terror. Some fears, Maja knew, ran too deep for immediate analysis. They had four suspects to locate, but she sensed that understanding what had transformed a university study group into something still capable of paralyzing a woman after ten years might prove more difficult than simply finding the remaining members.

In that basement archive, they'd witnessed something beyond professional discretion, the face of someone who'd learned that certain knowledge never stopped being dangerous.

6

CHEMIST

Back at Polishuset, Maja spread the Nexus Club files across her desk like tarot cards promising revelations she wasn't sure she wanted to receive. Anna-Maria's terror had confirmed their suspicions, but terror, Maja reflected, was often more honest than confession. Fear revealed what people truly believed about consequences, while words could be shaped to protect the speaker from uncomfortable truths.

She studied Marcus Björk's personnel file: current employment at Innovations Park, pharmaceutical research in Kista's underground laboratories. There was something fitting about conducting questionable research in basements, as if burying work three floors down might contain whatever moral compromises emerged from it. Swedish innovation, she mused, seemed to favor depths over heights when ethics became negotiable.

The security guard at "Innovations Park" barely glanced at their badges before buzzing them through. His tired eyes suggested someone who'd learned not to question what passed through these corridors after hours.

The elevator descended to B3, each floor taking them deeper into the building's windowless core. They looked at the list of names on the floor directory and found B3021 fr Marcus Bjork. They walked down the hall and knocked on the door which was open.

When he looked up at their knock, his eyes carried the same unfocus as his student photograph: intelligence without anchor, like a laser pointer dancing across walls.

Björk's hand twitched with precision, knocking a rack of test tubes that rattled but didn't fall, a small symphony of glass commenting on nervous authority.

"We're not here about professional misconduct," Maja interrupted, studying the laboratory with crime scene attention. Neat rows of chemicals lined shelves with their labels facing forward in military precision, equipment hummed with efficiency. Everything appeared organized, yet something felt displaced, like a crime scene staged to appear normal while concealing its true nature.

The recognition hit with impact: pupils contracting in that confession the body makes before consciousness can construct protective lies.

"Jag följer inte nyheterna," he muttered, gesturing at his microscope. "Too busy with research." But his hands trembled with the frequency of someone whose theoretical work had achieved consequences he'd never intended to witness.

"What exactly are you researching?" Sven asked, positioning himself near the door with authority that suggested exit might become negotiable.

"Adhesive polymers. Medical applications." Björk's eyes darted between them and his computer screen, which displayed molecular structures that pulsed with chemical logic. "Non-toxic binding agents for surgical use."

Björk's eyes scanned the chemical analysis with the speed of someone familiar with molecular architecture, and recognition flickered across his features like lightning illuminating hidden landscape.

"Detta är... theoretical work," he admitted, the words escaping before institutional caution could intervene. "Look, we talked about this stuff in theory," Björk said, his hands shaking as he adjusted the microscope. "Just... ideas, you know? Nielsen made it sound so academic. So legitimate."

He stopped, realizing he'd opened a door that years of silence had kept locked. The silence that followed carried weight, the pressure of secrets maintained through institutional protection and personal terror.

"Anna-Maria was terrified when we talked to her," Maja said, watching his face carefully. "Said Nielsen had protocols. Not theories —protocols."

The question revealed more than any answer might have: confirmation that protocols existed, that Anna-Maria possessed knowledge someone feared might surface, that the Club's work had progressed beyond discussion into experimentation.

"Some members wanted to discontinue the research," Maja said, watching him with the attention she reserved for suspects whose guilt was becoming certain. "Others believed you were approaching breakthrough discoveries that justified experimentation."

Björk turned back to his microscope, adjusting controls with trembling fingers that suggested precision had become a refuge from moral complexity. "Vi var naiva—we were naive," he said, voice taking on the quality of someone reviewing choices that seemed reasonable in retrospect but catastrophic in practice. "Thought we could revolutionize behavioral psychology by combining chemical and psychological bonds into therapeutic approaches."

"There were... protocols. Experimental designs that seemed logical within the Club's framework." Björk's shoulders hunched as if bearing weight, the mass of knowledge that had grown too heavy for conscience to support. "But the university shut us down before we could implement testing procedures."

The pause that followed suggested he'd been about to reveal something his survival instincts recognized as dangerous. Maja leaned forward, sensing proximity to understanding.

"I can't." He straightened, lab coat swishing as he moved to a computer terminal with movements that suggested flight disguised as purpose. "I have work requiring attention. If you want answers, talk to Erik. The framework was his creation, his protocols, his vision of therapeutic possibilities. I provided chemical expertise."

"Ingen vet." Björk's laugh carried hysteria's edge, the sound of someone whose boundaries between knowledge and consequence had dissolved. "None of us know his location. He disappeared after the university investigation concluded, but his research... If someone's implementing those protocols using versions of our chemical compounds..."

"Then Gud hjälpe oss alla—Then god help us all." His eyes met hers with clarity that suggested truth had overwhelmed institutional caution. "Because the adhesive represents the initial phase. The real experiment involves manipulation through enforced intimacy. The chemical bond serves as control variable in a larger protocol designed to modify human behavioral patterns."

The centrifuge behind them beeped with insistence, laboratory equipment announcing completion of whatever process Björk had set in motion before their arrival.

"My samples need to be processed," he said, voice acquiring quality that matched his movements. "Unless you're charging me with violations requiring custody..."

Maja exchanged glances with Sven. Communication refined through years of partnership into understanding that they'd extracted information from this source. Pressure might yield details, but would produce defensive silence rather than revelation.

"Vi hörs," she said, sliding her card across a section of laboratory bench that appeared uncontaminated by whatever research transpired in this chamber. "If memories surface regarding Erik's protocols or whereabouts..."

"Sluta gräva—stop digging," Björk interrupted, voice sharp with fear that seemed to echo from sources deeper than self-preservation. "Stop digging into research that should remain theoretical. Some knowledge carries consequences that exceed understanding."

He turned back to his machines with shoulders that suggested dismissal motivated by terror rather than rudeness, the body language of someone who'd glimpsed possibilities he lacked courage to comprehend.

In the elevator ascending toward surface reality, Sven broke their silence with observation born of experience. "Terrified beyond explanation."

Maja agreed, watching floor numbers climb toward daylight and normalcy. "But fear of Erik, or fear of what Erik's research has become in application?"

"Perhaps both represent threats," Sven suggested, voice carrying the weight that emerged when criminal investigation intersected with larger questions about knowledge, power, and human responsibility. "The question becomes: why implement these protocols now, after years of dormancy? What changed that transformed research into experimentation?"

The elevator doors opened to lobby warmth that felt artificial after the basement's honesty. Through glass walls, Kista's towers reflected November's grey meditation on Swedish pragmatism, surfaces concealing whatever ambitions and compromises transpired within their chambers.

Young tech workers hurried past clutching laptops against the cold, their faces bright with the optimism that characterized those who believed technology could solve humanity's problems. Maja watched them with the recognition that their faith in progress would survive until experience taught them otherwise.

"We need to locate Erik," she said, breath fogging in air that carried winter's promise of darkness ahead. "His frameworks seem to provide the blueprint for these applications."

"If discovery remains possible," Sven replied. "Disappeared after university investigation suggests someone with resources to maintain anonymity while continuing research."

Maja thought of the forensics photographs. Bodies arranged with precision, intimate moments transformed into experimental tableaux that demonstrated how human connection could become laboratory protocol. Someone had spent years refining research into methodology, testing approaches that combined chemistry with psychology to achieve effects that exceeded either discipline.

They walked to their car through Kista's landscape, surrounded by monuments to Swedish innovation that seemed fragile. Glass and steel structures housing ambitions that might not survive contact with human nature's darker curiosities. Somewhere in Stockholm's maze of laboratories and corridors, answers waited with the patience of knowledge that had found application. The question wasn't whether they could solve the crimes, but whether they could understand the larger system that had made such crimes inevitable, and whether that understanding might arrive before the Nexus Club's legacy claimed more victims.

In the grey November light reflecting off Kista's towers, Maja recognized they were chasing not just a killer, but the kind of thinking that could make killing seem like logical research.

7
NEXUS

The drive back from Kista gave them time to process what Björk had revealed. Stockholm's afternoon traffic moved with typical November lethargy while Maja stared through rain-spotted windows at the city's careful architecture. Glass and concrete facades that promised transparency while concealing whatever ambitions festered behind them.

By the time they reached Polishuset, the weight of institutional complicity had settled over them. The incident room's fluorescent lights felt almost comforting after the underground laboratory's sterile horror. Crime scene photos lined walls where Stockholm's murders became paperwork.

Maja drew red lines between the Lindströms' death, Anna-Maria Viklund's terror, and Marcus Björk's chemical confessions. Ten years of buried university research had crawled back into daylight, blinking like something disturbed from hibernation.

She stepped back from the board, letting her eyes unfocus. The red lines blurred into a web, and suddenly she wasn't seeing connections but absences—the spaces between facts where truth preferred to hide. Her breathing slowed. Sometimes understanding came not from following the lines but from noticing the patterns in what wasn't there. The gaps in university records from 2019. The silence where publications should have been. The careful choreography of institutional amnesia.

"They didn't just bury the research," she said quietly. "They buried the researchers."

The red lines connecting photographs to peer-reviewed papers told their own story. Someone had approached murder with academic precision.

Söderberg leaned against the window, arms crossed, his iron-gray hair maintaining its perfect composure even as cases descended into chaos. The team arranged themselves around the conference table with police patience.

"Eight days since discovery." Maja studied the board. "Victims killed elsewhere. Sophisticated methodology, pharmaceutical-grade compounds. Someone turned academic theory into very practical murder."

"Connection to Kungsmedicinska solid?" Söderberg asked, studying the photos with the expression of a man who'd learned to find meaning in the meaningless.

"The Nexus Club." Sven flipped through his notes, then paused. "Strange how we name our sins. 'Nexus'—a connection point. As if they knew from the beginning they were creating bonds that would need severing." He returned to his notes with the expression of someone who'd found philosophy hiding in etymology.

"We've interviewed two former members: Anna-Maria Viklund, now managing university archives, and Marcus Björk. Both reacted to questions about the Nexus Club like teenagers caught reading their parents' diary. Equal parts shame and existential terror."

"Fear of what?" Söderberg asked.

"Fear of exposure," Sven replied. "Both insisted their original work was 'purely theoretical,' but their reactions suggest otherwise."

"Björk's current research involves compounds remarkably

similar to what bound our victims," she continued. "The chemical structures are nearly identical."

The city's daily rhythm continued its indifferent dance. Trams carrying commuters who clutched their second kaffe like small prayers against the morning's uncertainties, students with backpacks heavy enough to require engineering consultation.

Normal people living normal lives, blissfully unaware that someone in their city had spent years perfecting methods of human bonding that ended in death. Maja envied them their ignorance. Some knowledge became a burden you couldn't set down, like carrying someone else's confession in your pocket.

"The other Club members?"

"Joonas Rask disappeared after graduation," Maja said, consulting her notes . "No official records since 2019. The same year Nielsen's department underwent what they called 'restructuring.'

"Nils Håkansson died two years ago from liver failure, but left behind materials suggesting their research progressed well beyond university boundaries. And Erik Thoressen stayed in the university system. Mention his name to Björk and the man practically sweats through his academic tweed."

"Media pressure increasing," Söderberg observed, straightening his tie. "The Maritime Museum gala connection creates political sensitivity. Half of Stockholm's cultural elite witnessed the Lindströms that evening, which makes this case highly visible." He paused. "We need concrete progress before Expressen starts writing their own Kriminalinspektör story."

"Additional complications," Maja continued, pulling out Bergman's latest report. "The compound found at the crime scene matches fragments from research proposals dated 2019. All originating from Nielsen's department, all subsequently sealed by court order."

The room went quiet. Sealed court orders meant someone with serious influence wanted this buried .

"Fan," Söderberg muttered. "A research program that never officially ended?"

"The crime scene's precision suggests extensive planning," Maja replied, studying the photos . "Chemical compounds, timing coordination, location selection. Nothing suggests spontaneous violence. Someone with access to sophisticated laboratory equipment and advanced chemical knowledge spent considerable time perfecting these methods.

Söderberg studied the board . "I want comprehensive documentation regarding the Nexus Club. University records, ethics complaints, student files. Anything that escaped official sealing." He paused. "And complete information about Nielsen's current research activities. If these protocols originated in his department..."

"Already initiated," Maja confirmed. "But university administration has constructed barriers. Privacy concerns, academic freedom, intellectual property protection. Every possible institutional shield."

"I'll make strategic communications," Söderberg replied . "Gentle reminders about public safety obligations."

"Time interval between the Lindströms' departure from the gala and estimated death?"

Maja consulted her notes. "They departed the Maritime Museum at 23:42. Security footage confirms their movement to the parking area. Time of death estimated between midnight and 02:00. That white van appeared on Djurgården Bridge camera at 00:17."

"Thirty-five minutes," Söderberg calculated. "Sufficient interval to transport victims to a prepared location, administer the chemical compounds according to established protocols, then position them in the park."

"Larsson, traffic camera analysis?"

"The van's a dead end, sir," Larsson replied . "Stolen plates, abandoned in Södertälje two days later. Cleaned with industrial solvents. Not just wiped down, but professionally sanitized. Whoever did this knows evidence disposal ."

"Professional execution," Sven observed. "Consistent with every other aspect. "

Before anyone could respond, Maja's phone buzzed with an emergency tone. She listened for a moment, her expression darkening.

"Bergman's latest chemical analysis. And the university's legal department has responded to our records request."

Maja accepted the papers, scanning. Her expression soured like discovering your favorite restaurant had been serving recycled food. "They're citing national security concerns now. Something about research protocols being potentially classified."

"Classified?" Söderberg's eyebrows rose with genuine surprise. "Since when does a psychology department conduct research requiring national security protection?"

"Since 2019, apparently." Maja spread the documents across the table like a tarot reading predicting institutional corruption. "The same year those court cases were sealed, the same year Nielsen's department mysteriously 'restructured.' In Sweden, when two unrelated events happen simultaneously, we call it government involvement."

She'd learned to recognize the particular texture of official secrets. They felt heavier than regular lies, carried more bureaucratic weight. How many forms did someone need to fill out to classify human suffering as a matter of national security? Probably fewer than required for ordering new office furniture.

Morning light cast shadows across the crime scene photos, creating a chiaroscuro of evidence and speculation. Outside, Stockholm woke up to another ordinary day while they unraveled how universities could make murder seem reasonable. Another small Swedish miracle of institutional adaptation.

"This exceeds the Lindströms' murders, doesn't it?" Söderberg asked, though it wasn't really a question.

"Yes," Maja agreed, feeling the familiar weight of cases that grew heavier the more you understood them.

"Whatever the Nexus Club researched, whatever protocols they developed, someone decided it merited classification, institutional protection, bureaucratic burial." She paused, looking at her colleagues. "Worth killing to protect."

The silence that followed carried the weight of collective realization. They weren't just investigating murders anymore. They were archaeology students who'd accidentally dug up something the museum preferred to keep buried. And like most uncomfortable Swedish truths, it would probably disappear back under layers of proper procedure and institutional amnesia, filed away with other embarrassing discoveries.

But before they could gather their coats, Maja's phone buzzed with the particular urgency that marked emergency calls. She glanced at the display, then at her colleagues.

"112 dispatch. Suspicious circumstances in Södermalm." She listened for another moment, her expression darkening. "Chemical substances involved. Two victims."

The room's energy shifted like air pressure before a storm. Another possible crime scene. Another demonstration of theory made lethal.

"Address?"

"Götgatan 47." Maja was already reaching for her jacket. "Apparently one victim survived."

The room went silent. Another crime scene meant their killer wasn't finished with his experiments.

"Same methodology?" Söderberg asked.

"We'll know soon enough." Maja checked her weapon automatically. "But yes, probably."

They filed out of the incident room with the grim efficiency of people who'd learned that academic theories could kill. Outside, Stockholm's November afternoon continued its grey business while they drove toward what would likely be another demonstration of how far someone would go to perfect their methods.

The survivor changed everything. For the first time, they might have a witness who could tell them exactly what their methodical killer looked like.

But as they gathered their things, Maja felt the familiar weight of a different question settling over her. There was a peculiar cruelty in survival—to be the one who lived meant carrying what the dead couldn't remember. The Lindströms had escaped into whatever silence death provided. This survivor would have to live with the knowledge of what human beings could do to each other in the name of research.

"A witness," Söderberg had said. But Maja knew better. Witnesses observed. Survivors endured. And sometimes the difference between the two was just another academic distinction that meant nothing when you were the one who had to keep breathing after the experiment ended.

She checked her weapon and followed her colleagues out, wondering if their survivor would thank them for arriving in time, or curse them for arriving too late to spare them the burden of remembering.

8

HENRIK

The drive to Södermalm took fifteen minutes through Stockholm's evening traffic, but felt longer. Maja watched familiar streets pass through rain-spotted windows while considering what they might find at Götgatan 47. Another demonstration of academic precision applied to human suffering, most likely. But this time with a survivor.

The apartment building squatted among its neighbors with typical Swedish restraint. Five stories of pale brick and metal-framed windows that promised nothing more dramatic than the occasional domestic argument. Police cars lined the narrow street, their blue lights reflecting off wet pavement in a pattern that would have looked festive under different circumstances.

Emergency personnel moved with efficiency around the building's entrance. Paramedics wheeled equipment toward the stairwell while uniformed officers directed the small crowd of neighbors who'd gathered in the courtyard, drawn by curiosity about other people's disasters.

"Third floor," Sven said, consulting his notes. "Hugo Wallin from 3B found them around 18:30. Door was open, he went to check."

Poor bastard, Maja thought. No one expects to stumble into someone else's experiment when checking on neighbors.

They climbed the stairs past residents who pressed themselves against the walls with the careful politeness Swedes deployed when tragedy visited their carefully ordered lives. Brief eye contact, murmured acknowledgments, then studied attention to their own apartment doors.

Hugo Wallin stood in the hallway outside 3A, speaking to a uniformed officer with the expression of someone still processing what he'd witnessed. Mid-forties, wearing the kind of cardigan that suggested weekend trips to IKEA and concerns about heating bills. An ordinary man who'd discovered that ordinary evenings could become crime scenes without warning.

"Kriminalinspektör Norberg," Maja introduced herself, showing her warrant card. "You found them?"

Hugo nodded, his face pale under the hallway's fluorescent lighting. "I heard... nothing, actually. That was strange. Henrik and Maria, they usually have music playing in the evenings. Classical, sometimes jazz. But tonight, complete silence." He paused, collecting himself. "The door was ajar. I thought maybe they'd gone out and forgotten to lock it properly. So I knocked, called their names."

He gestured toward the open apartment door where crime scene technicians moved with methodical care. "When I found them..."

"Take your time," Maja said, though she already knew what he'd discovered.

"They were in the bedroom. Bound together somehow. Maria was..." He stopped, swallowing hard. "But Henrik was still breathing. Barely, but breathing. I called 112 immediately."

Through the apartment door, Maja could see paramedics working over a stretcher where two bodies lay partially connected by hardened adhesive—what was becoming their killer's signature scene.

"How well did you know them?" Sven asked.

"Neighbors for three years. Good people. Henrik works. Worked at the university library. Maria taught elementary school in Gamlas-tan. They kept to themselves mostly, but always pleasant. Some-times I'd borrow tools, they'd water my plants when I visited family in Malmö." Hugo's voice carried the bewilderment of people discov-ering that evil could visit anyone. "Who would do this to them?"

Someone with access to pharmaceutical-grade chemicals and twenty years of buried research, Maja thought. Someone who'd decided that human relationships were raw material for experi-mentation.

"Any unusual activity recently? Strange visitors, unfamiliar sounds?"

Hugo shook his head. "Nothing. Their routines were very regular. Henrik left for work at 8:15 each morning, returned around 17:30. Maria came home earlier, usually had kaffe brewing when Henrik arrived. Very Swedish, very predictable."

Predictable routines made surveillance easier. Their killer had probably watched Henrik and Maria for weeks, studying their habits, planning the optimal timing for his experiment. The same method-ical patience most people used for planning vacations.

A paramedic emerged from the apartment, pulling off latex gloves with efficiency. "We're ready to transport," she told Maja. "The male victim isn't stable and may not make it to the hospital."

"Conscious?"

"Barely."

They watched as paramedics wheeled Henrik toward the stair-well, his form still partially connected to Maria's body by stubborn chemical bonds. Someone had turned their bedroom into a labora-tory, their relationship into data points. But unlike the Lindströms, Henrik might survive long enough to become a witness.

Maja followed the stretcher downstairs, past neighbors who pressed against the walls with careful Swedish discretion. Outside, November's early darkness had settled over Södermalm while Stockholm continued its evening routines, oblivious to another demonstration of how academic theory could be weaponized.

The ambulans doors closed with mechanical finality. Through the rear windows, she could see paramedics working over Henrik with urgent efficiency while Maria's body lay beside him, still connected by their killer's perverted chemistry.

"Same methodology," Sven observed, joining her on the sidewalk.

"Yes," Maja replied, watching the ambulans navigate through traffic toward Kungsmedicinska.

"Media containment?" Sven asked.

"For now," Maja said. "But two crime scenes with identical methodology?" She adjusted her coat against the evening cold. "This becomes a pattern tomorrow. Patterns attract attention."

They stood in the courtyard while crime scene technicians continued their methodical documentation. Hugo had been taken to Polishuset for a formal statement, leaving the building to settle back into its ordinary evening rhythms. Lights came on in apartment windows where people prepared dinner, watched television, conducted the small domestic rituals that constituted normal life.

None of them aware that someone in their city had spent years perfecting methods for turning intimacy into experiments.

"Hospital follow-up?" Maja asked.

"I'll coordinate with Kungsmedicinska," Sven said. "First witness who might actually tell us what our killer looks like."

If he survived. If trauma hadn't fractured his ability to process what had happened to him and Maria.

Maja walked back toward her car, past the ambulans's fading tire tracks on wet pavement. This time, they had someone who'd looked into their killer's eyes and might live to remember it.

9
SILENCE

Dawn found Maja outside Solstrandsjukhuset, watching November mist rise from Årstaviken while morning shift nurses hurried past with kaffe from Wayne's. Twelve hours since Henrik's death, and already the machinery of investigation had transformed two lives into case numbers with typical Swedish efficiency.

The hospital's morning shift change was beginning. Nurses emerging from the T-Bana station clutched paper cups, their breath visible in the November cold as they discussed weekend plans in hushed voices. Normal people heading to normal work.

Both victims were gone now. Henrik had lasted one hour after the paramedics freed him from Maria's body, long enough for hope to seem possible before chemistry claimed him too.

She pulled her coat tighter against the November cold, steam rising from her paper cup of kaffe that tasted like institutional disappointment. Medical students hurried past toward morning lectures, backpacks heavy with textbooks that probably didn't include chapters on turning human attachment into experimental data.

Her phone buzzed with another message from Forensics. Same compounds, same precision. Someone had indeed spent years refining their technique, treating murder like any other research project requiring methodical improvement.

Most killers acted from passion or desperation: motives that made human sense, however twisted. This felt different. Clinical. The work of someone who could observe suffering with the same detachment they might bring to studying bacteria under a microscope.

Maja walked back toward her Mercedes, past the hospital's brutalist façade that promised healing while concealing whatever moral compromises modern medicine required. Stockholm's grey November light seemed perfectly suited for investigating how academic inquiry could evolve into systematic murder.

Back at Polishuset, fluorescent lights cast harsh shadows across crime scene photographs.

Marcus Björk's terrified face haunted her thoughts.

Marcus's words: "The adhesive is just the beginning. The real experiment is psychological." Love and terror as variables in some equation.

She spread the Nexus Club files across her desk, assembling fragments of what had once been an academic research group.

Erik Thoressen's research stood out among the former Club members. His theories about attachment and behavioral control read like instruction manuals for emotional torture.

The most dangerous people convinced themselves their actions served higher purposes. At least honest criminals knew they were criminals.

Maja pulled up Erik's academic profile. His dissertation title: *"Exploring Emotional Dependency in Dyadic Relationships: Power, Control, and the Fragility of Attachment."*

"Dyadic relationships." Because clinical terminology made people sound less human.

The university research archives showed Erik's detailed documentation of couple interactions. As she scanned participant lists from his various research projects, recognition hit her.

Henrik and Maria appeared among Erik's documented subjects from two years ago.

They had volunteered, probably answering some university advertisement seeking couples for behavioral research. A few hundred kronor for a few hours of their time, contributing to human knowledge.

Instead, they had provided their killer with a blueprint for their destruction.

Someone had watched them through one-way glass, taking notes on how they touched each other, how they resolved conflicts, what made them laugh. All of it carefully documented, filed away.

Studying love without feeling it: perhaps the most dangerous human trait.

"You believe he's selecting targets based on his old research subjects?"

"I'm certain of it," Maja replied. "Henrik and Maria were research subjects in his attachment studies. I suspect our first couple shared similar connections to his research."

"And you believe Erik's conducting these murders personally?"

"Unknown," Maja admitted. "But someone is implementing his theories with surgical precision. Either Erik himself, or someone with access to his data."

She thought of Dr. Gustaf Nielsen, the shadow figure behind so much of the Nexus Club's original research.

She thought about hierarchies: how mentors shaped students, how knowledge passed from one generation to the next. Usually this was harmless: professors teaching literature, mathematics, history. Sometimes it wasn't.

The compounds were industrial-grade, available through any university medical lab in Stockholm. Their killer moved in circles where such materials were routine, unremarkable. Where chemical bonds were studied rather than feared.

Somewhere out there, couples lived ordinary lives, unaware they were marked for death by someone who'd studied their most intimate moments.

She was still contemplating this when heavy footsteps approached her office.

Kommissarie Söderberg's unmistakable rhythm: a man carrying political weight on his shoulders.

"Maja." His voice cut through her contemplation.

He filled her doorway like an advancing storm system, face creased with the accumulated pressure of criminal investigations threatening university reputations.

"Fan också," she muttered.

"Aftonbladet's publishing '*The Adhesive Killer*' headlines tomorrow," Söderberg announced. "Expressen's calling it '*Stockholm's Dark Academic*.' Press speculation includes phrases like 'serial killer' and 'university cover-up'."

"Helvete," Maja responded, sinking back into her chair. Swedish journalism's favorite morning: academic scandal mixed with violent death. "Too early for that kind of speculation."

"För fan i helvete, Maja, they're suggesting we're concealing evidence." Söderberg's fist met her desk. "University board of governors applies pressure through channels that exceed normal police authority. They resist any connection between prestigious institution and this jävla mess."

As if academic credentials immunized them against harboring killers.

"We've confirmed connection through Marcus Björk," Maja countered. "He verified the relationship to Erik Thoressen's research methods. Henrik and Maria were documented subjects in Erik's behavioral studies."

Söderberg looked at Maja. "Trettiosex timmar—36 hours, the Justice Ministry called. Federal investigators from Rikskrim arrive Monday afternoon if no progress has been made."

As if murder could be solved by administrative scheduling, Maja thought.

Maja stared at the evidence board, calculating. It was Saturday afternoon. By Monday at 1 PM, their investigation would be absorbed into the federal bureaucracy, their local knowledge dissolved into national databases.

"Fan ta dig," she muttered. Thirty-six hours to prove the connection between Erik's behavioral studies and the murders. Thirty-six hours to trace Nielsen's influence through decades of academic manipulation.

10

ERIK

After Söderberg left, Maja sat in the silence of her office watching rain streak down the windows. Thirty six hours to solve murders that had taken years to perfect. Another small miracle of Swedish administrative logic. Outside on Kungsholmsgatan, trams carried commuters home while she contemplated the absurd irony of her situation: she was about to interrogate a university professor about turning research into murder.

Such a conversation would be impossible in any reasonable country. In modern Sweden, it felt like Friday afternoon.

The same university system that had trained Erik Thoressen to study human behavior was now protecting him from the consequences of that training. Swedish institutions had a peculiar gift for creating problems and then insisting those problems couldn't possibly exist. They built fires in their living rooms, then expressed surprise when the house burned down.

She thought about Henrik and Maria: volunteers who'd answered some advertisement seeking couples for psychological research. Perhaps fifty kronor each for an hour of their time, contributing to the advancement of human knowledge. Except the knowledge had been filed away like ammunition, waiting for someone to find a target.

The most Swedish aspect of the whole affair was how thoroughly documented it would be. Their killer probably had proper permits for the chemicals.

Maja pushed back from her desk.

"Sven," she called toward his desk where he hunched over case files. "We need an immediate conversation with Thoressen. No more delays."

Sven looked up, reaching for his jacket. "About time we discussed his research directly," he muttered, falling into step beside her.

"Academic peer review. Annoying but irrelevant to his actual work."

They drove through Stockholm's afternoon traffic in comfortable silence.

The most dangerous evil: justified by intellectual sophistication.

"Intelligence as moral exemption," Maja agreed.

Minutes later, Maja stood before Psykologiska Institutionen. The Psychology Department's concrete facade rose against autumn's grey sky.

Inside, the department entrance carried familiar academic scents: kaffe from the student fikarum, anxiety from approaching exam periods, and mustiness of buildings where knowledge accumulated faster than wisdom. Maja's boots squeaked against linoleum as she climbed worn stairs past bulletin boards advertising seminar schedules and Lucia celebration reminders.

She found the designated door: "Dr. Erik Thoressen, Docent, Beteendevetenskap." Through the frosted glass panel, movement was visible. A figure bent over his desk.

Her knock produced sharp percussion against wood veneer.

"Come in."

The office beyond represented a perfect specimen of academic habitat: chaos organized according to principles comprehensible only to its inhabitant. Journal articles stacked in precarious towers; a neglected potted plant drooped in a window that admitted grey light. An ancient IKEA desk disappeared beneath papers documenting years spent studying people.

Years spent reducing people to data points.

Behind this academic debris sat Thoressen, appearing exactly like his faculty photograph: wire-rimmed glasses and carefully neutral expression.

"Kriminalinspektör Norberg," Maja announced. She nodded toward Sven. "And my partner, Kriminalinspektör Svensson."

"kriminalinspektör," he said, glancing up from what appeared to be student papers with the mild irritation of someone interrupted during important work. "How can I help you?"

Maja and Sven entered the cramped space.

"We're investigating the recent murders in Södermalm," Maja said, settling into the single visitor's chair while Sven remained standing. "We understand you conduct research on couple dynamics."

Erik's expression shifted to one of academic interest mixed with appropriate concern. "Terrible business, that. I read about it in DN. Though I'm not sure how I can be of assistance."

"Your research involves studying couples," Maja continued, notepad balanced on her knee. "Observing their interactions, documenting behavioral patterns."

"That's correct," Erik said, removing his glasses to clean them. A gesture that seemed calculated to buy thinking time. "Though 'observing' makes it sound rather clinical. We prefer 'collaborative investigation into attachment patterns.'"

Academic jargon as armor. "How many couples have participated in your studies over the years?"

"Oh, dozens. Perhaps a hundred." He replaced his glasses with deliberate precision. "We maintain strict ethical protocols, of course.

All voluntary participation, informed consent, complete confidentiality."

"Like a medical study," Sven observed. "Except you're studying love instead of disease."

Erik's smile faltered slightly. "Love is considerably more complex than disease, kriminalinspektör."

"Is it? Both can be fatal under the right conditions."

The observation landed with uncomfortable precision. Erik's academic composure flickered.

"You've documented numerous couple studies over the years," Maja continued, watching for micro-expressions. "Including Maria and Henrik, the couple discovered murdered last week."

Erik paused, his hand freezing halfway to a stack of papers. The silence stretched just long enough to suggest recognition before he recovered his composure.

"Henrik and Maria..." he said slowly, as if accessing a mental file. "Yes, they participated in a study examining conflict resolution patterns in established relationships. Lovely couple. Very committed to each other." He paused. "You're not suggesting their participation in our research is somehow connected to what happened to them?"

Something flickered in Erik's eyes: curiosity about how much the police actually knew.

"We're exploring all connections," Maja replied. "Can you tell us about the nature of their participation? What specific behaviors did you document?"

Erik's gaze sharpened.

"I'm afraid that falls under research confidentiality," Erik said, leaning back in his chair with the authority of institutional protection. "Even posthumously, our participants' privacy must be respected."

"Even if it might help us catch their killer?" Sven asked.

Erik's eyes moved between them, calculating. "kriminalinspektör, surely you understand that academic research depends entirely on trust. If participants believed their most intimate moments might someday be shared with law enforcement..."

"Dr. Thoressen," Maja said, her voice taking on a harder edge, "two people who trusted you with their private lives are dead. Killed in a way that suggests intimate knowledge of their relationship dynamics. You can discuss this with us, or you can discuss it with federal investigators who will have access to court orders."

The threat had its intended effect. Erik's academic composure cracked slightly, revealing something sharper underneath.

"You're fishing," he said, but his voice had lost its earlier confidence. "You have no evidence connecting our research to these tragic events."

"We have Marcus Björk in custody," Sven said quietly.

The name hit Erik like a physical blow. His carefully maintained academic demeanor dissolved entirely for just a moment before reasserting itself.

"Marcus," Erik said, testing the name. "I haven't spoken to Marcus in years. Not since the research group disbanded."

"He mentioned the Nexus Club," Maja said. "And Dr. Nielsen."

At Nielsen's name, Erik went very still. When he spoke again, his voice carried a different quality. Warier, more calculating.

"Gustaf Nielsen was our mentor. A brilliant researcher who understood that conventional ethical constraints often prevent genuine scientific breakthrough." He paused, seeming to weigh his words. "But the Club disbanded because some members lacked the intellectual courage for truly innovative work."

"What kind of innovative work?" Maja pressed.

Erik smiled, and for the first time, it reached his eyes in a way that made Maja's skin crawl.

"Understanding human attachment isn't an academic exercise, kriminalinspektör. To truly comprehend how people bond, how they depend on each other, how they break apart, you need to observe them under actual stress, not laboratory conditions."

"Real stress," Sven said. "Like watching your partner die slowly from industrial adhesive poisoning."

Erik's mask slipped entirely for just a moment, and Maja saw something genuinely dangerous underneath: the cold curiosity of someone who had stopped seeing other people as fully human.

"The question," Maja said, "is whether you're conducting these experiments personally, or whether someone else is implementing your theories."

"I think," Erik said, standing abruptly, "that this conversation should continue through proper channels. The university has procedures for law enforcement inquiries."

The retreat into institutional protection confirmed Maja's suspicions.

"Dr. Thoressen," Maja said, also standing, "if you're protecting research that's being used to kill people, you're an accessory to murder. Academic credentials won't protect you from that."

Erik said nothing, but his eyes followed them with the focused attention of someone making mental notes. As if they, too, had become subjects worthy of study.

As they left Erik's office, the university corridor stretched ahead. Noble architecture sheltering ignoble research.

"He's protecting someone," Sven observed as they descended toward the main entrance.

"Nielsen's still pulling strings, even if he's not doing the actual killing."

Maja nodded, troubled by what she'd seen in Erik's eyes during those unguarded moments. "He knows more than he's saying. But he's also genuinely curious about our investigation. Like we're part of some experiment he's observing."

Outside, Stockholm's November afternoon pressed against them with the weight of approaching winter. The sleet had turned back to rain, washing what little daylight remained from the sky.

They had come seeking answers and found something worse: a man who viewed human suffering through the lens of academic curiosity, who could discuss the deliberate destruction of love and trust as if it were merely an interesting research problem.

"Next step?" Sven asked, pulling his collar up against the rain.

Maja looked back at the university building, its windows glowing with warm light. "We need to find Nielsen. And we need to find him before our thirty-six hours are up."

11

ATTACHMENT THEORY

The drive from the university to Karolinska took them through Stockholm's rush hour traffic, giving Maja time to process Nielsen's threat—or warning, or whatever that had been. Beside her, Almqvist reviewed her notes from their confrontation.

"He knew exactly which buttons to push," Almqvist observed. "That comment about psychological damage, about breakdowns—he's studied us as much as we've studied him."

"That's what worries me." Maja navigated around a stalled Volvo. "We need to understand his theories before—"

"Before he demonstrates them?" Almqvist finished quietly.

The thought hung between them as they pulled into Karolinska's visitor parking. Through the research building's lit windows, scientists were probably conducting perfectly legitimate studies, asking ethical questions, following proper protocols. The same activities that, in Nielsen's hands, had become something monstrous.

Dr. Astrid Lindgren's office was on the fourth floor, tucked at the end of a corridor lined with research posters about memory, trauma, and resilience. The contrast with Nielsen's stark office was immediate—warm lighting, plants, carefully chosen art that suggested healing rather than analysis.

"Detective Norberg," Dr. Lindgren said, adjusting her reading glasses. She was younger than Maja expected, perhaps early fifties, with prematurely grey hair pulled back in a practical bun. "When you mentioned attachment theory on the phone, I hoped I was wrong about why you were calling."

Maja spread the crime scene photos across the coffee table between them. Dr. Lindgren's composed expression faltered as she recognized what she was seeing.

"These couples were found chemically bonded together," Maja began. "We believe someone is using attachment theory as a basis for—"

"Dear God." Dr. Lindgren's voice had lost its therapeutic smoothness. "Someone's actually done it. Made the metaphor literal."

She stood abruptly, moving to her filing cabinet with sudden urgency. "I need to show you something. Five years ago, I was asked to review a dissertation proposal." She pulled out a file, hands trembling slightly. "I rejected it immediately, but the ideas... I couldn't forget them."

She placed the file on the table. The title page read: *"Exploring Emotional Dependency in Dyadic Relationships: Power, Control, and the Fragility of Attachment."* Erik Thoressen's name was printed below.

"You know this work?" Almqvist leaned forward.

"I was on the ethics committee that rejected it. The theoretical framework was brilliant, but the proposed methodology..." Dr. Lindgren shook her head. "He wanted to study what he called 'dependency thresholds'—the point at which emotional attachment becomes pathological. But his proposed experiments involved deliberately creating and then breaking those dependencies."

"Using couples?" Maja asked.

"Using anyone in close relationships. Romantic partners, family members, even close friends. He theorized that by forcing extreme proximity—reducing what he called 'interpersonal boundaries to zero'—you could create artificial but intense emotional dependencies." She opened the proposal to a marked page. "Look at this."

Maja read Erik's precise handwriting: *"When physical distance becomes impossible, psychological distance must also collapse. The subjects will experience boundary dissolution, leading to a shared psychological state that transcends normal attachment."*

"He's talking about forced fusion," Almqvist said quietly. "Not just physical, but psychological."

"That's what terrified me," Dr. Lindgren said. "He understood that attachment isn't just about being close to someone. It's about the choice to be close, the ability to separate and return. Remove that choice..." She gestured helplessly at the crime scene photos. "You weaponize the very thing that makes us human."

"What would victims experience?" Maja asked. "If someone actually implemented these theories?"

Dr. Lindgren sat down heavily. "Initially, panic. The loss of bodily autonomy would trigger extreme stress responses. But Erik's research suggested something more disturbing. He believed that under sufficient pressure, with the right chemical assistance to lower psychological barriers, two minds could be forced to... synchronize."

"Synchronize?"

"Share emotional states. Experience each other's sensations. Eventually, even share fragmented thoughts." She pulled out a diagram from Erik's proposal showing two overlapping circles gradually merging. "He called it 'induced psychological fusion.' The victims wouldn't just be physically bonded—they'd lose the ability to distinguish between self and other."

Maja thought of the victims' positioning, their expressions frozen in that final moment. "And if one partner began to die while they were fused?"

Dr. Lindgren's face went pale. "The surviving partner would experience it as their own death. Not just witnessing it, but feeling it happen to what their mind has been forced to recognize as part of themselves. The psychological trauma would be..." She stopped.

"There's no framework for this. It's the antithesis of everything attachment theory stands for."

"You said Erik's proposal was rejected," Almqvist said. "What happened after that?"

"He disappeared from my radar. But his advisor..." Dr. Lindgren frowned. "Professor Nielsen from Uppsala. He wrote a scathing response to our rejection, claiming we were blocking legitimate research out of squeamishness. He said psychology would never advance if we kept treating human subjects like fragile glass."

"Nielsen supervised this?" Maja felt the pieces clicking together.

"More than supervised. Some of the theoretical sections were clearly his work. The mathematical models, the neurochemical hypotheses about forced bonding..." Dr. Lindgren stood again, pacing to the window. "I should have followed up. Should have made sure the research was truly abandoned."

"Could someone actually create the kind of psychological fusion Erik described?" Maja pressed. "Is it scientifically possible?"

Dr. Lindgren was quiet for a long moment. "With the right compounds to increase neural plasticity, to lower psychological defenses... With subjects who already had strong emotional bonds... And with someone willing to ignore every ethical boundary we've established..." She turned back to face them. "Yes. God help us, but yes. You could force two minds to merge, at least temporarily."

"And the compound that creates the physical bonding?"

"Would serve as both the mechanism and the metaphor. Physical fusion forcing psychological fusion. The victims would be unable to maintain any sense of individual self." She looked directly at Maja. "Detective, if someone is implementing Erik's theories, they're not just killing people. They're destroying the very concept of individual consciousness. They're proving that human identity itself is... fragile."

As they prepared to leave, Dr. Lindgren handed Maja the file. "Take this. If Erik's involved, you need to understand how he thinks.

But be careful—his ideas have a way of getting under your skin. I still have nightmares about some of his theoretical scenarios."

"One more thing," Maja said at the door. "In his proposal, did Erik ever discuss selecting specific types of victims?"

Dr. Lindgren nodded slowly. "He believed certain relationships would produce more dramatic results. Couples with what he called 'high interdependence scores.' People who already relied heavily on each other emotionally." She paused. "Like parents and children. Like romantic partners of many years. Like... professional partners who trust each other completely."

The words hung in the air as Maja and Almqvist exchanged glances. They were investigating a killer who understood exactly which bonds would create the most devastating effects when forcibly fused and then broken.

"Thank you, Dr. Lindgren," Maja said. "You've been very helpful."

"Detective," Dr. Lindgren called as they reached the door. "Erik's proposal included one other element I should mention. He theorized that the ideal observer of these experiments would be someone who understood attachment professionally but hadn't experienced it fully themselves. Someone who could document the effects with what he called 'optimal scientific detachment.'"

"You mean someone like Nielsen," Almqvist said.

"Or," Dr. Lindgren said quietly, "someone Nielsen had trained to think exactly like him. Someone who'd learned to see human connection as data rather than experience it as reality."

As they walked back to the car, Maja felt the weight of Erik's dissertation title pressing against her consciousness. *Power, Control, and the Fragility of Attachment.* He'd found a way to demonstrate all three, using the most fundamental human need—connection—as his weapon.

12
STATUS

Saturday morning arrived with Swedish melancholy that November perfected, grey light filtering through office windows like weak tea, casting everything in shades of institutional indifference. Maja stood before the evidence board, contemplating how academic research had been perverted into a methodology for murder. The irony wasn't lost on her: knowledge pursued in service of understanding human connection had become the blueprint for its destruction.

"Strange how education corrupts," she murmured to herself., then turned to address her team. "What did the adhesive analysis tell us?"

Sven appeared with lab reports . He read from one: "The adhesive's molecular structure is straightforward industrial adhesive. Medical grade cyanoacrylate, the kind used in surgical procedures," pulling up molecular diagrams on his laptop. "But it's been modified with a catalyst to accelerate bonding time," according to Bergman."

"Is it the same as the Lindstroms used?" Maja asked.

"Almost. Bergman says that the catalyst component looks to be modified to dry even faster."

"Tobias, anything from the ethics board?"

Tobias emerged from behind his laptop with the weary expression of someone who'd spent too many hours staring at institutional failures. "Ethics board rejected the original research proposal. Filed under 'insufficient safeguards for human subjects.'" He paused, letting the bureaucratic language hang in the air. "But the research continued. Off the books, naturally."

Maja almost smiled at the predictability of it all. Swedish institutions excelled at creating rules that everyone could circumvent with sufficient creativity. Like building beautiful fences around empty lots.

Bergman arrived with the forensic analysis, her usually composed demeanor showing cracks around the edges. "This adhesive has been perfected over years," she said, spreading photos across the table. "The latest version creates permanent cellular fusion between victims. Look at the precision—same depth, same angle. Someone with medical knowledge applied this with surgical care."

The room absorbed this information in silence. Maja found herself contemplating the grotesque artistry involved—someone had spent years perfecting a method to literalize the metaphor of inseparable love. The academic mind's capacity for transforming beautiful concepts into nightmares never ceased to amaze her.

"Philosophy written in flesh," she said quietly. "Someone's conducting a very twisted seminar on human attachment."

Sven spread the research files across the table with deliberate care. "Both victim couples participated in Erik's attachment studies. But they weren't the only ones." He paused, letting this sink in. "Three more couples from the same research group."

Maja felt the familiar chill of recognition. Erik's words echoed back: the need to observe people "under actual stress." Not random selection but careful curation.

"The studies were never about research," she said slowly. "They were auditions."

Standing before the evidence board, she tried to see the pattern as Erik would have seen it. Young couples, deeply attached, trusting enough to participate in academic research. Perfect subjects for someone studying the extremes of human dependency.

"We need to warn the others," she said quietly. "The remaining couples from his research group. They need protection, but quietly— we can't let Erik know we've identified the pattern."

Hours had passed as they assembled the evidence, each piece adding weight to their growing certainty. By late afternoon, the incident room felt heavy with accumulated knowledge and unspoken dread. They had their pattern, their connection, their suspect—but not yet their proof.

"Two days before Rikskrim takes over," Sven observed as they gathered their coats.

"Then we'd better make them count," Maja replied, but her mind was already moving toward Nielsen. Whatever twisted mentorship had produced Erik Thoressen, they needed to understand its source. In her experience, evil rarely bloomed in isolation—it required cultivation, encouragement, the right academic environment.

"Nielsen," Sven said as they reached the car. "We can't wait until Monday."

"No," Maja agreed, starting the engine. "If Erik is escalating, his mentor needs to explain what he's created."

The city's lights reflected off wet sidewalks like scattered evidence—each point of illumination revealing only small circles of clarity in the gathering dark.

Driving through the city, Maja found herself contemplating the peculiar Swedish gift for institutionalizing evil. Other cultures produced passionate killers, crimes of sudden violence. Sweden specialized in methodical atrocity, carefully documented and properly filed. Their killer probably had receipts for the adhesive, she thought darkly.

The university's lights glowed ahead of them across the dark water, promising warmth and knowledge. From the outside, it looked like any other institution of higher learning. But Maja had learned that the most dangerous predators often wore the most respectable masks.

They sat for a moment in the car, watching students hurry between buildings. Young people pursuing knowledge, trusting in the benevolence of their teachers. The same trust that Henrik and Maria had placed in Erik's research.

13
PROFESSOR

The November afternoon had turned to iron-grey, matching Maja's mood as she drove back to the university. Her old Mercedes protested at being taken from the solace of a parking garage to the coldness of the streets. The machine's version of reluctance, she supposed. Even cars, it seemed, preferred their comfortable darkness to the messy business of human investigation. Institutions resist scrutiny, she thought, whether they're mechanical or human.

Students hurried across the campus plaza, their dark coats and scarves blending into the gathering gloom. Anonymous figures in a landscape of learning, each carrying their own universe of thoughts, unaware of how their trusted educational environment might harbor predators among its protectors. The eternal student condition, Maja reflected: so absorbed in their own dramas that they missed the larger theater playing out around them. Perhaps that was a mercy.

The Behavioral Science building rose before her, its concrete facade even more forbidding than during her morning visit with Erik. Universities, Maja reflected, were curious monuments. Built to

house enlightenment yet often resembling fortresses, as if knowledge itself required defensive walls. Or perhaps, she thought with
dark amusement, because those who wielded knowledge understood how dangerous it could be in the wrong hands.

This time she took the east entrance, following signs for the
senior faculty offices. The institutional quiet felt different here. More
established, more traditional. Unlike the graduate student wing with
its cluttered bulletin boards and vibrant student life, this section
held an almost reverential silence. Name plates on heavy wooden
doors listed academic achievements like battle honors: publications,
awards, years of tenure. The currency of prestige converted into
physical space. Larger offices, better views, greater distance from
undergraduate noise.

As she walked down the narrow hallway, past the department's
seminarierum where doctoral students usually gathered for their
weekly discussions, her eyes drifted toward the office at the end of
the hall. Dr. Gustaf Nielsen's office. The institutional silence was
broken only by the distant murmur of voices behind closed doors, a
particularly Swedish respect for workspace tranquility holding firm
even here. A cultural trait that, like so many, could be both virtue and
vice, creating peace while enabling secrecy.

Before she could second-guess herself, Maja knocked twice on
the door. After a brief pause, it opened, revealing Dr. Gustaf Nielsen
standing in the doorway. He was older than she'd expected, with
thinning gray hair and a pair of round glasses perched on the edge of
his nose. The very image of academic authority, so perfectly aligned
with cultural expectations that it seemed almost a deliberate performance. Like central casting had ordered "distinguished professor,"
Maja thought. The carefully cultivated absent-mindedness, the
precisely disheveled hair. Even his authenticity felt manufactured.
His expression was calm, but there was a sharpness in his eyes, as if
he was sizing her up the moment he saw her, cataloging her presence as data rather than greeting her as a person.

Nielsen's eyebrows arched as he stepped aside. His office struck Maja as a carefully curated display of academic authority. Leather-bound psychology texts arranged just so on bookshelves, papers scattered with deliberate disorder—not too much, not too little, the Swedish way. A pristine armchair positioned by the window. Even the geraniums on the windowsill seemed strategically placed, their neat arrangement a stark contrast to the neglected plants in the hallway.

The office of a man who understood that reputation was performance, Maja thought. Even his clutter had been choreographed to suggest the right kind of brilliant distraction. She wondered if he practiced removing his glasses for emphasis.

A large window behind his desk overlooked the campus, casting long shadows across the room. The positioning wasn't accidental. It forced visitors to look up at him, backlit against the authority of the institution itself. Maja took a seat across from him, her eyes drifting to a framed photograph on the wall of Nielsen receiving an academic award.

"You're aware of the recent murders, Dr. Nielsen?" Maja asked, her tone neutral.

"Yes," Nielsen replied, his expression unreadable. "A tragic series of events. But what does that have to do with Erik?"

Interesting, Maja thought. No protective instinct for his student, no defensive "surely you don't suspect," no academic's natural inclination to lecture her about jumping to conclusions. Just this clinical curiosity, as if she'd asked about a mildly interesting research question.

Nielsen remained calm, his hands folded neatly on his desk. "Erik's work is focused on psychological dynamics in relationships, Kriminalinspektör. It's academic in nature, not something that would translate into... murder."

Maja felt a familiar stirring of dark amusement. The academic's eternal faith in the power of categorization. As if labeling something "academic" created an impermeable barrier between theory and practice, between understanding and action.

Nielsen's eyes narrowed slightly, but his voice remained steady. "Erik's work is rigorous, yes. But to suggest that he's somehow involved in these killings..." He paused, removing his glasses with practiced precision. "Kriminalinspektör, in my experience, knowledge doesn't corrupt. It simply reveals what was already there. The question isn't whether understanding changes how one acts—it's whether one has the courage to act on what one understands."

Maja leaned forward, her fingers interlacing on the edge of Nielsen's desk. "Is it? We have evidence linking the murders to materials from the university. The victims' positioning matches Erik's research themes almost exactly."

Nielsen adjusted his glasses. There it was, the practiced gesture creating a momentary barrier between them. "Kriminalinspektör, in my forty years of academic work, I've found that the human mind often seeks patterns where none exist. It's a natural cognitive bias. We connect dots that aren't necessarily related."

Maja nodded thoughtfully. "Fascinating perspective from someone whose entire career depends on connecting dots. Finding patterns in human behavior, drawing conclusions from limited data. But I suppose pattern recognition is only valid when it serves academic purposes?"

She watched Nielsen's face carefully, looking for the microexpressions that revealed the gap between public presentation and private reaction. In her experience, the most dangerous people were often those who'd learned to perform normalcy so well they'd almost convinced themselves.

"Erik is a brilliant student," Nielsen continued, each word measured and precise. "Driven, yes, and deeply invested in his work." His lips curved into what might have been a smile. "But I can assure you, Kriminalinspektör, that I would never condone violence in any form. My role as his mentor is purely academic."

The careful emphasis on the word "academic" hung in the air

between them. Another talisman against responsibility, Maja thought. The word had become his shield, deflecting questions about the human cost of knowledge.

Nielsen's composure flickered for just a moment. A brief tightening around his eyes that suggested she'd touched something sensitive. The performance was excellent, but not quite perfect.

The truth was there, Maja suspected. Not in what Nielsen said, but in what he chose not to say. After twenty years of police work, she'd learned that guilty people often worked harder at seeming innocent than innocent people did.

"I appreciate your time, Dr. Nielsen. I'll be in touch if I have any further questions."

Nielsen watched her leave, his expression unreadable. As Maja stepped back into the hallway, she couldn't shake the feeling that she had just walked out of a lion's den. Though perhaps that was giving him too much credit. Lions, at least, were honest about their predatory nature. Whatever was happening here, it was bigger than Erik Thoressen. Dr. Nielsen was involved, whether directly or through subtle manipulation, Maja couldn't yet say. But she knew one thing for certain: Erik wasn't acting alone.

"You know what struck me most about that conversation?" Maja said as they walked back toward the exit.

"The complete absence of concern for his student," Sven replied. "Most mentors would be worried, protective. He was clinical."

"Exactly. It was like discussing a research subject, not a human being he'd worked with for years." Maja paused at the building's entrance, watching students hurry past in the gathering darkness. "Makes you wonder what he considers the acceptable cost of knowledge."

"The true predator," she thought, glancing back at the closed door, "often wears institutional credentials like protective coloration." Though in Nielsen's case, she suspected the credentials weren't camouflage. They were the point. The respectability wasn't a mask for his appetites; it was the appetite itself.

The drive back to the station unfolded in November's particular melancholy. The early darkness descended like a blanket over Stockholm, transforming the familiar into something more mysterious. They passed a group of teenagers outside H&M, their conversation a mix of Swedish and English that would have horrified their Swedish teachers. "Fan, det är så cold," one complained, switching languages mid-sentence with the casual bilingualism of Stockholm youth

Even rebellion, Maja thought, followed predictable patterns. The young always believed they were the first to discover that adults were hypocrites. Traffic moved with the resigned patience of a city accustomed to long winters, brake lights reflecting off wet asphalt in patterns that reminded Maja of crime scene photos. Even the windshield wipers seemed to beat out a rhythm of contemplation rather than urgency.

"There's something almost artful about Nielsen's evasions," Maja mused, watching pedestrians hurry past with their collars turned up against the wind. "The way he uses language not to communicate but to create distance. Academic discourse as protective armor."

Her old Mercedes wheezed its familiar protests. The heater that never quite warmed enough, the windows that fogged at the worst moments. Fifteen years of driving this car to crime scenes, interviews, late-night stakeouts. It had become a kind of mobile office, filled with the detritus of police work: empty kaffe cups, case files, the accumulated evidence of a career spent in pursuit of answers that often raised more questions.

"What did you make of his composure?" she asked Sven, genuinely curious about his perspective. In all their years as partners, she'd learned to value his observations. The way he could spot behavioral patterns she might miss.

"Too composed," Sven replied, his breath fogging the passenger window as he spoke. "Most people, when police come asking about their students in connection with murder, they're shocked, defensive, worried. Nielsen was interested. Like we were presenting him with an intriguing puzzle rather than a moral crisis."

They passed a group of university students at a bus stop, bundled in their winter coats, laughing about something only they understood. The normalcy of the scene felt almost surreal after the interview with Nielsen. These young people trusting in institutions, in mentors, in the basic goodness of the academic environment that surrounded them.

"The paradox of police work," Maja reflected, stopping at Sergels torg. "We spend our days with killers and thieves, then go home and worry about whether we remembered to buy milk." She watched a businessman hurry toward T-Centralen, clutching his briefcase against the November wind. "The murderer probably remembered to feed his cat this morning."

"Both, probably," Sven said. "The capacity for evil doesn't eliminate the capacity for ordinary kindness. They coexist. Nielsen can probably discuss his research over kaffe with colleagues and genuinely care about their children's piano recitals."

"There's something particularly chilling about intellectualized cruelty," Maja continued, turning onto their street. "The killer who acts from passion or desperation, I can understand that, even while condemning it. But someone who transforms suffering into data, who approaches human life as a research problem to be solved... that's a different kind of darkness."

She pulled into the parking garage, the familiar concrete walls offering a strange comfort after the day's revelations. Here, at least, was honest ugliness. Institutional architecture that made no pretense of beauty or nobility, unlike the university buildings that draped their secrets in Gothic Revival elegance.

"The question now," Maja said. "Is whether Nielsen sees Erik as a successful experiment or a failure that needs correction."

Maja watched the shadows cast by the garage's fluorescent lights. "Either way, I suspect we've accelerated whatever timeline he's operating on."

They sat in silence for a moment. The case was evolving into something larger than a simple murder investigation.

"Those students we passed," Maja finally said. "They trust their professors completely. Nielsen has decades of students. How many Erik Thoressens might be out there?"

"The institutional investigation will take months," Sven replied. "But right now, we focus on stopping the immediate threat. Erik first, then we work backward through Nielsen's academic career."

As they finally gathered their things and headed for the elevator, Maja felt the familiar weight of responsibility settling on her shoulders. Somewhere in Stockholm, Nielsen was probably finishing his evening routine, perhaps grading papers or preparing tomorrow's lectures. And Erik was out there too, carrying forward whatever lessons he'd absorbed from his mentor.

The elevator climbed toward their floor, carrying them back to the fluorescent-lit world of case files and evidence boards. But Maja's mind remained in Nielsen's carefully curated office, parsing the subtext of their conversation, trying to decode the grammar of academic evil.

"You know what troubles me most?" she said as the elevator doors opened. "The possibility that we're not investigating a crime but participating in a study we don't understand."

The thought followed them down the corridor toward their desks, where the evening's paperwork waited. Reports to file, evidence to catalog, the mundane tasks that transformed human tragedy into official documentation.

"I need to see those participant lists," Maja said, settling at her desk. The institutional machinery around her had settled into its night shift rhythm. Fewer phones, dimmer lights, the building taking on the contemplative quiet that came after the day's urgency had been processed into official reports.

Svensson appeared with a stack of papers. "Every couple who's been involved in Erik's studies," he said, handing them over.

Maja flipped through them quickly, her eyes catching on names that matched the victims. But it wasn't until she reached the bottom of the list that something strange caught her attention. There were handwritten notes at the end. Names crossed out, asterisks next to some entries, and a scribbled name that sent a jolt of recognition through her.

There, scrawled in Nielsen's precise handwriting at the bottom of the page, was an entry that made her blood run cold. Under a section marked "personal subjects" was a single name.

Erik Thoressen.

The implications hit her like a physical blow. The researcher himself as subject. The observer being observed in a recursive loop of experimental design.

"The perfect closed system," she whispered, the pieces falling into terrible alignment. "The scientist who becomes his own experiment."

Her fingers trembled as she scanned the rest of the notes. Erik's name appeared again and again, not as a researcher but as subject. Psychological evaluations, behavioral modifications, something ominously labeled "control protocols." Nielsen's precise handwriting documented it all with clinical detachment, each entry building toward something called "Project Dependency."

"Frankenstein's monster in academic robes," Sven murmured when she showed him the notes. "The difference being that Frankenstein eventually recognized his moral failure. Nielsen seems to see his as a success."

The realization didn't arrive through logic. It came like a shift in light, the way dawn creeps across Stockholm's winter sky. Erik wasn't just the killer—he was Nielsen's creation, molded and shaped through years of careful manipulation. The murders weren't just crimes; they were the culmination of a calculated experiment.

She picked up her phone to call Tobias, but before she could dial, it buzzed with an incoming message from an unknown number:

"Fascinating ideas, Det. Norberg. You still don't grasp dependency. Your view of mentorship? Too narrow. Maybe we need to demonstrate again?"

Maja stared at the screen, her hands trembling. The implications crashed over her in waves—Nielsen hadn't just corrupted Erik, he'd been monitoring their investigation, feeding information to his protégé. The academic's ultimate publication: not in a journal but written in human suffering.

"Sven," she called, her voice tight. "We have a problem."

14
RIKSKRIM

November pressed against the windows of Söderberg's office, weak sunlight struggling through the gray haze over Kungsholmen. Maja watched the afternoon traffic crawl along Scheelegatan below. Her third kopp kaffe sat cooling on Söderberg's desk, leaving a ring on a case file.

The familiar aroma of Gevalia did nothing for her nerves today.

Through the glass, her reflection looked tired. Administrative meetings were theater. Everyone knew their lines, knew how it would end, yet still they gathered to perform. Behind her, the ancient radiator clicked and wheezed, stirring up dust and the smell of old case files. Buildings, she thought, must absorb human disappointment like tobacco smoke in wallpaper. Year after year, until the very walls carried the weight of every bad decision made within them.

Söderberg cleared his throat.

"You're not going to like this, Maja."

She turned from the window. Below, a black Volvo V90 with state police markings was pulling into the restricted lot. Her stomach dropped.

"You're bringing in Rikskrim."

"Helvete." The curse slipped out before she could stop it.

From down the hall came familiar sounds: phones ringing, voices from the break room discussing yesterday's kanelbullar. The normalcy of it felt wrong, like laughter at a funeral.

"...four victims in a month."

Söderberg sounded tired, caught between orders from above and loyalty below.

He gestured to Dagens Nyheter spread across his desk: "*STOCKHOLM'S SERIAL KILLER STRIKES AGAIN*." "The press is having a field day. The Polisöverintendent—"

"We're close," Maja interrupted. The pieces were there, Nielsen's research, Erik's methodology, the careful selection of victims. She could almost see the shape of it, like trying to remember a dream after waking.

"Which is precisely why Rikskrim want in."

Söderberg delivered this with the careful neutrality Swedish bureaucrats perfected when conveying decisions they disagreed with but couldn't change. The institutional equivalent of a shrug.

"Kriminalinspektör Ebba Almqvist is one of their best. Worked with Europol before returning to Sweden. Behavioral psychology specialist."

Another psychologist, Maja thought. As if understanding the mind that created these horrors required the same training. Perhaps it did. Perhaps that was the most troubling part.

A knock interrupted them. The woman who entered moved with practiced authority.

Gray suit, silver hair, age indeterminate in that way of women who'd learned early that competence mattered more than appearance. Everything about her suggested control earned through years of proving herself in rooms where she was the only woman. Maja recognized the armor; she wore a version of it herself.

"Kriminalkommissarie Norberg." Almqvist's handshake was firm, businesslike. Her Stockholm accent was refined, upper Östermalm. "I've read your preliminary reports. Impressive work tracking the academic connections."

Maja almost smiled at the bureaucratic understatement. Academic connections. As if they were investigating plagiarism rather than murder perfected through scholarly methodology. The compliment that preceded being pushed aside.

Maja's jaw tightened. "Tack så mycket. Though clearly not impressive enough."

"Maja," Söderberg warned.

Almqvist's smile remained steady. "I understand your frustration. But this isn't about competence. It's about resources. Rikskrim can provide access to national databases, behavioral profilers, forensic specialists."

"We have forensics," Maja said.

"Not like ours." Almqvist moved to the window, looking down at the same street scene Maja had been watching moments before. "Tell me, what do you see when you look at these murders?"

The question held genuine curiosity beneath its evaluative surface. Maja considered. "Someone conducting a seminar where the only grades are written in blood. The student become teacher, but his audience has already left the lecture hall."

Almqvist's professional mask shifted slightly, revealing something like approval. "Most investigators catalog methods and evidence. You're reading the subtext."

Almqvist studied the evidence board with the calm of someone who'd seen worse. "Your instincts are good. But instincts aren't enough when someone's killing with this level of... sophistication."

"Your killer is escalating. The methodology is becoming more refined, more time-consuming. He's growing confident."

Uppsala. The name surfaced unbidden, bringing with it the weight of failure. She'd been younger then, still believing that determination could substitute for resources. That case had taught her otherwise. Some killers were systems, not individuals, and systems required systematic responses.

"Which means he's more likely to make mistakes," Maja said. "We just need—"

"To work together," Almqvist cut her off. "You know these murders better than anyone. You understand the academic angle, the connection between Erik and Nielsen. I need that expertise. But you need my resources." She paused. "I've seen good investigators destroy themselves trying to solve cases alone. Pride is a luxury we can't afford."

They watched her with the patience of people who understood that some decisions needed to ripen before they could be made. Outside, a siren wailed—Stockholm's eternal soundtrack, the city's way of reminding everyone that somewhere, always, things were going wrong.

This case had gotten under her skin. Four people were dead, and Erik was out there, methodical as ever. She thought about the victims' families, the questions they'd asked her, the promises she'd made. What did her wounded pride matter against that?

"Fine," she said. "Where do you want to start?"

Almqvist turned back to the evidence board. "Tell me about the progression in his methodology. How has it evolved from the first murder to the latest?"

Maja joined her at the board, studying the photos she knew by heart. Each death more elaborate than the last, each scene more perfectly composed. "He's developing a vocabulary," she said slowly. "Learning to speak fluently in a language he's inventing as he goes."

"Or trying to reach someone who finally understands the grammar," Almqvist agreed. "Nielsen?"

The air in the room shifted. Not defeat, but recalibration. Like adjusting your stance before a difficult climb.

She wouldn't let another killer slip away. Inte den här gången. Not this time.

Perhaps wisdom meant knowing when to let others help carry the weight. Even if those others came with state police badges and superior resources.

The radiator wheezed behind them. Outside, November pressed against the windows with the same gray persistence that had marked every winter of her career.

Stockholm in November had its own philosophy: endure, adapt, find light where you can. Even if that light came from unexpected sources.

Maybe Almqvist would see something she'd missed. Maybe that was worth setting aside her ego.

15
KUNGSTRÄDGÅRDEN

The fluorescent lights of Polishuset buzzed overhead, a mechanical drone that seemed to vibrate at the same frequency as Maja's mounting tension. She leaned against the cold metal frame of her window, watching late afternoon deepen toward evening over Norrmalm. November in Stockholm: light didn't so much set as simply give up, exhausted by its own brevity. The melancholy wasn't dramatic—just tired, like everything else by this time of year.

Time had moved strangely since discovering Erik's role in Nielsen's project. Hours felt like interrogations where no one confessed to anything useful.

Her phone buzzed, a text from an unknown number. The message made her blood freeze:

"Fascinating ideas, Det. Norberg. You still don't grasp dependency. Your view of mentorship? Too narrow. Maybe we need to demonstrate again?"

A threat delivered like lecture notes. Some habits, Maja reflected, die harder than their practitioners should.

"Tobias!" Maja called out immediately. "I need a trace on an incoming message." She forwarded the text to their tech team while reaching for her desk phone. "

Kriminalinspektör Almqvist appeared in her doorway, kaffe in one hand, tablet in the other. After three days of working together, she'd already learned to recognize when shit was about to hit the fan. "Our professor again?" Her Norrland accent made everything sound like she had all the time in the world, even when they didn't.

"He's escalating," Maja said, showing her the screen. "And he's got eyes on potential victims."

Below the message was a photo: a young couple walking arm in arm past Kungsträdgården's bare winter trees, completely unaware they were being watched.

The timestamp showed it had been taken less than an hour ago. In the photo's corner, she could just make out the reflection of someone watching from inside a parked Volvo—someone wearing the same wire-rimmed glasses she'd seen yesterday in Erik's office.

"And get me CCTV access for Kungsträdgården, last hour."

Two people walking, thinking they were living their lives. Erik had already reclassified them as data points. The efficiency of it was almost admirable, in a thoroughly horrible way.

"Getting the trace now," Tobias called back. "Number's using an encrypted service, but I can track the location data from the photo metadata. The surveillance request for Erik's apartment is still pending, university lawyers are blocking access."

"Naturally," Maja muttered. Universities defended their faculty the way embassies defended diplomats—on principle, regardless of what the diplomats had actually done.

Almqvist studied the photo the way she studied everything, like it might suddenly reveal the meaning of life if she stared hard enough. "The angle suggests he's been following them for at least twenty minutes. See the reflection in this shop window?" She enhanced a corner of the image. "Same vehicle, three blocks earlier."

"He watches before he moves," Maja noted. "Just like his research papers."

Nielsen's files revealed the usual academic progression: hypothesis, methodology, test subjects. Only the subjects had been people, and the testing had involved rather more suffering than the ethics committee typically approved.

Her phone vibrated again. Another photo from the encrypted number: the young couple now walking past NK's Christmas window displays on Hamngatan. They were heading toward Östermalmstorg. The timestamp showed two minutes ago.

"Signal's moving," Tobias announced, typing fast. "Bouncing between cell towers near Östermalmstorg. Traffic cams show a silver Volvo matching the reflection, but the plates are registered to a scrapped vehicle."

Officially dead but still driving around Stockholm. Erik would appreciate the metaphor.

"I can pull satellite surveillance from Rikskrim," Almqvist offered, already typing. "We've been tracking vehicle movements in that area for another case. Should help."

"Do it," Maja said. At least Almqvist's state police connections were good for something besides making them all feel provincial.

Nielsen's earlier work read like any academic's research notes. Lars Nordfalk, 2018: "Subject displayed unexpected resistance to methodology." Sara Almqvist, 2019: "Relocated after preliminary phase." The bureaucratic language of ruined lives, filed away with the same care as any other failed experiment.

"Sven!" Her voice cut through the precinct's evening quiet. "The background check on Nielsen's Uppsala work just came in. Three more names to cross-reference with missing persons." She gestured to the files Tobias had compiled overnight. "And get me an update on that surveillance request for Erik's apartment."

Sven knocked lightly on her doorframe. "Bergman just sent over her final analysis of the second murder scene. The adhesive modifications show progression—he's perfecting the formula." He paused, glancing at the new photos on her screen. "You think he's accelerating because we confronted Nielsen?"

"He's not just watching them," Maja said, studying the couple's route. "He's herding them. Each photo shows them moving exactly where he wants them to go."

"Free will as performance art," Sven said. "They think they're choosing their evening stroll."

Almqvist looked up from her tablet. "Satellite footage confirms. The Volvo's been positioning itself at key intersections, blocking certain routes. Subtle, but effective. He's been studying traffic patterns."

"Of course he has," Maja muttered. Why kill someone simply when you could turn it into a doctoral thesis?

"Got units in civilian vehicles moving into position," Sven reported, checking his phone. "Keeping their distance like you ordered. But Maja—if we spook him..."

"He might accelerate like he did with Henrik and Maria," she finished. "Where's Nielsen now?"

"Under surveillance since last night," Sven replied. "Hasn't left the university. He's conducting office hours like nothing's happened."

Her phone buzzed again. Another photo: the couple entering a kafé near Östermalmstorg. The message below made her blood freeze:

"Time to begin the next phase, Inspektor. Will you understand this time?"

The pedagogical impulse, apparently, survived even homicidal mania. Stockholm had become Erik's lecture hall.

"Tobias, get me everything on that kafé," Maja ordered, reaching for her coat. "Property records, employee lists, delivery schedules. Erik's had time to prepare, he wouldn't choose that location randomly."

"Already on it," Tobias called back. "Building plans show a service entrance through the basement. Connects to an old storage area."

"He's been planning this," Sven said. "Setting up locations, preparing..."

"The same methodical approach that made him a good researcher," Maja said. "Applied to considerably less socially acceptable pursuits."

Almqvist was already moving, checking her weapon with the automatic movements of someone who'd done it too many times. "I'll coordinate with the tactical unit. We'll need coverage on all exits."

"Quietly," Maja emphasized. "If Erik sees uniforms—"

"He'll adapt," Almqvist finished. "I've read his papers. He treats setbacks as data points for improving methodology."

She was already moving toward her coat when her phone lit up again:

"Kriminalinspektör shows admirable restraint. Training overrides instinct. Noted."

"Fan," Maja muttered, showing the others the message. Even while threatening murder, Erik couldn't resist taking notes on their performance.

"Three minutes to Östermalmstorg," Sven said, checking his watch. "Backup units are in position."

They moved through the precinct toward the stairs, past officers filing reports on the day's ordinary crimes theft, domestic disputes, the usual catalog of human disappointment. How simple those seemed compared to a killer who turned murder into homework.

The November rain had started again, turning the early evening streets into a blur of headlights and wet asphalt. Rush hour traffic moved with the resigned patience of Stockholm commuters, each car carrying people who believed they were going somewhere they'd chosen to go.

"Erik's studying everything," Maja said as they reached her Mercedes. "Our response times, our tactics. We're all subjects in his experiment now."

"The irony being," Sven observed, settling into the passenger seat while Almqvist took the back, "that his academic training makes him both more dangerous and more predictable. He can't help following methodological principles."

"Which is why he'll have contingencies," Almqvist added, still working her tablet, getting her Rikskrim people in place.

"Akademisk jävla tortyr," Maja muttered, pulling into traffic. Academic fucking torture dressed up as research.

Her phone buzzed:

"*Phase two commencing. Your anxiety response is noted for future reference.*"

Still grading their performance. Still the professor, even while orchestrating a killing.

Through the rain-streaked windshield, she could see Östermalmstorg's lights ahead. Somewhere in that evening crowd, two people were living what they thought was their normal life. Erik had other plans for their evening.

The dashboard clock glowed: 17:42. As she reached for her phone to update dispatch, it rang—Söderberg's name lighting up the screen.

16

ÖSTERMALMSTORG

She put him on speaker, hands tight on the wheel as she navigated the rain-slicked streets.

"The university board just called an emergency meeting," Söderberg said without preamble. That careful tone politicians develop when they realize someone's about to make their life difficult. "Where are you?"

"Five minutes from Östermalmstorg. Erik's targeting another couple. Sending photos, positioning them like lab rats."

"Like the Bengtssons and Lindströms?"

"Exactly like. He's documenting everything." She took a sharp left, making Sven grab the door handle. "We've got plainclothes units following at a distance."

Too close and he'd rabbit. Too far and they'd find bodies.

"Nielsen's lawyers are all over this," Söderberg continued. "They're claiming police harassment, threatening academic freedom lawsuits. The university president's worried about losing research grants."

"Academic freedom to commit murder," Sven murmured. "Defending principles while people die."

"Fan ta dig," Maja cut in. "We found Project Dependency in Nielsen's files. The human trials, the psychological conditioning. Erik wasn't just his student, he was Nielsen's primary test subject. They can't hide behind academic freedom when..."

Silence.

"How sure are you about this couple?" Söderberg asked. The sound of a man doing political arithmetic.

"Erik's messaging us directly. Clinical observations, just like in Nielsen's notes. He's not just recreating the experiments, he's documenting our response."

A chair creaked through the speaker.

"You have documentation of this?" The politician giving way to the cop he used to be.

"Erik's sending us clinical observations in real time. Same format as Nielsen's research notes. He's not just recreating the experiments, he's documenting police response patterns."

"Studying the hunters while he hunts," Sven observed.

"Thirty minutes," Söderberg said. "Then I'm sending in tactical teams. Academic freedom ends where public safety begins."

"Understood." Maja ended the call

"He'll be expecting tactical teams," Sven said. "Timing their response, just like everything else."

Maja navigated around a delivery truck. "He knows our protocols better than we do. Academic methods turned to murder."

Through the rain, Östermalmstorg's lights beckoned. People hurrying home from work, shopping bags in hand, no idea they were being catalogued. Somewhere in that glow, Erik was waiting, taking notes.

"What's most disturbing," Sven said, "isn't the killing. It's how he's emptied research methods of ethics and filled them with murder."

The wipers marked time like a metronome. "That's what institutions never grasp—their methods serve knowledge and atrocity equally well."

"He'll be expecting tactical teams," Sven said. "Timing their response, just like everything else."

From the back seat, Almqvist's voice carried that Norrland calm that made everything sound like it could wait until after kaffe. "My people are on foot. Blending with the evening shoppers. Amazing how invisible you become when you're carrying an ICA bag."

Maja navigated around a delivery truck. "He knows our protocols better than we do. Academic methods turned to murder."

Through the rain, Östermalmstorg's lights beckoned. People hurrying home from work, shopping bags in hand, no idea they were being catalogued. Somewhere in that glow, Erik was waiting, taking notes.

"What's most disturbing," Sven said, "isn't the killing. It's how he's emptied research methods of ethics and filled them with murder."

The wipers marked time like a metronome. "That's what institutions never grasp—their methods serve knowledge and atrocity equally well."

"Twenty-eight minutes left," Maja said, checking her watch. "Erik's already factored in our response time."

"Nielsen's perfect subject," Sven said. "A killer who views his own crimes as data."

Almqvist's phone glowed in the darkness. "Uppsala," she said, reading. "Three couples went missing near the university over two years. Rikskrim never connected them." She paused. "Always thought it was strange—couples disappearing during exam season. Assumed they'd run off together."

"The stress of academia," Maja said dryly.

"Or someone studying stress responses," Sven suggested.

They parked a careful distance from the kafé. Through rain-streaked windows, the evening crowd moved between streetlights and shop windows. Every one of them a potential data point in Erik's research.

"What did Nielsen want?" Maja wondered aloud. "A student who could turn theory into violence?"

"Understanding and manipulating," Sven replied.

Almqvist made a sound that might have been a laugh. "The ultimate dissertation defense. Prove your theory by making people dance to it."

Through the windshield, the kafé's warm lights looked deceptively welcoming. Inside, a young couple sat sharing kaffe, probably arguing about weekend plans. No idea they'd been selected for something else entirely.

Twenty-five minutes until the tactical teams arrived. Twenty-five minutes to find Erik before he moved to the next phase of his research.

Erik would be close. Watching. Recording. The good student, applying everything his mentor had taught him about turning people into data.

Maja's radio crackled. "Movement at the service entrance," one of the plainclothes units reported. "Door's propped open."

"One of mine," Almqvist said. "Former reindeer herder from Kiruna. You'd be amazed how patient they can be when they're used to watching animals that barely move."

"Hold position," Maja ordered, already moving. "We go in quiet."

The tactical teams were still twelve minutes out. Through the kafé's rain-streaked windows, she could see the young couple at their corner table, the woman laughing at something on her phone. Normal. Unaware.

Then the lights flickered.

"Sven—"

A shrill electronic wail cut through the evening air. Fire alarm. Through the windows, Maja watched the kafé transform from sanctuary to chaos—chairs scraping, people abandoning tables, the controlled panic of evacuation protocols kicking in.

"Helvete," Sven muttered. "He's flushing them out."

The young couple moved with the crowd toward the service exit, exactly as Erik had planned. Maja saw it all unfold. Like watching a car accident in slow motion.

"All units converge on the service alley," she barked into her radio, but she already knew they'd be too late.

17
KAFÉ

The kafé's windows glowed amber against November's early darkness, a deceptively warm beacon on the rain-slicked street. Tactical team members materialized from doorways and shadows, their black uniforms gleaming wet, weapons lowered in the peculiar silence that followed a near-miss. Three minutes past Söderberg's deadline, and Erik had orchestrated their timing down to the second.

"He timed us perfectly," Maja observed. "Knew exactly how long it would take us to get here."

The kafé's interior hung suspended in the midst of ordinary life interrupted. Steam still curled from abandoned kaffe cups, chairs stood askew where people had jumped up and run. Through windows marbled with rain, Maja counted the remnants of disrupted routines: three half-eaten semla, their cardamom scent still fresh in the air, and a slice of äppelpaj that would never be finished.

A scarf draped over a chair back. Someone's reading glasses left on a folded copy of Dagens Nyheter. All the small things people grab when they have time, leave behind when they don't.

"You never know which kaffe will be your last," Sven murmured beside her. "Makes you think."

The brass bell above the door rang sharply, its cheerful jingle a strange soundtrack to the abandoned scene. "Fan," Maja muttered.

Tactical team members moved through the space with practiced efficiency, checking corners, securing exits—the choreography of armed response played out against a backdrop of pastries and kaffe cups.

Sven's bulk moved with surprising grace through the maze of empty chairs, checking the back rooms. The kitchen lights still blazed, stainless steel surfaces reflecting the fluorescent glare. A pot of lingonberry jam sat uncapped beside half-assembled sandwiches. "Staff's gone too," he called back, emerging with a piece of paper held carefully. "Found this by the register."

The note lay pristine on the counter, its precise Swedish text as clinical as a lab report: "A demonstration of crowd control through induced panic. Note how quickly social norms dissolve when simple variables are adjusted. Data collected. Proceeding to next phase."

"Cold as surgical steel," Sven observed. "Even in criminality, he maintains the posture of the researcher—observing, recording, analyzing."

"Look at this language," Maja replied. "Phrases like 'variables are adjusted' and 'social norms dissolve' transform human fear into abstract data, people into experimental subjects. Nielsen taught him well, how to distance himself from the human implications."

"Gas alarm," one of the patrol officers reported. "Called in to building management." He gestured toward the service entrance . "Standard evacuation - everyone out the back, no electronics, no panic. Perfect cover for moving specific targets."

She moved deeper into the kafé, past the counter where moments ago baristas had steamed milk and ground beans. The abandoned space hummed with absence, business meetings, romantic encounters, friendly catch-ups, all dispersed by the simple trigger Erik had pulled.

Maja's phone buzzed:

"Crowd response as expected. Target couple's reaction promising. Moving to next phase."

"Traffic cameras," she ordered. "Fan," she breathed.

"He's always three steps ahead," Sven said. "Using our own systems against us—emergency protocols, traffic patterns, standard response times. The university taught him to analyze systems, and now he's turning that analysis toward breaking them."

"Or perhaps revealing their inherent fragility," Maja replied. "Maybe that's what fascinates him. How quickly the structures we rely on can be disrupted, how thin the veneer of orderly society really is."

"The most dangerous predators," Sven observed, "aren't those who operate outside the system, but those who understand it intimately enough to use its own mechanisms against it."

Maja nodded, her eyes scanning the scattered personal effects that marked the kafé tables—a pair of gloves here, a shopping bag there, left behind in the sudden evacuation.

"That's what Nielsen created in Erik," she said. "Not just a killer, but an observer of killing, someone who can stand outside the human drama he creates, recording reactions with the detachment of a scientist observing lab rats."

Outside, the tactical team was already dispersing into the rainy evening, their black uniforms melting into the darkness as they established a perimeter.

"We need to stop responding to his script," Maja said turning to Sven. "He's counting on us following procedures, deploying resources in predictable patterns. We need to introduce an element he can't anticipate."

"Become the variable instead of the constant," Sven nodded, understanding immediately. "But how? He's studied police response patterns, knows our protocols..."

"We stop thinking like police," she said. "Start thinking like the ordinary people Erik sees merely as experimental subjects. He's anticipating institutional responses, tactical teams, surveillance perimeters, command structures. But what about responses that don't fit into his academic framework?"

Almqvist's voice crackled through her radio. "Got something from Rikskrim's database. Erik's been using university library cards to access buildings all over Östermalm. The kafé's owner has ties to Uppsala University's alumni association."

"He's using the academic network," Maja said. "Of course he is."

The rain intensified outside, drumming against the kafé windows.

"I'll coordinate with my people," Almqvist said through the radio, her Norrland accent making even urgency sound measured. "We can track those library access points."

The brass bell jingled as they stepped back into the rainy evening. Somewhere in Stockholm's November darkness, Erik was moving to his next carefully planned phase.

"Humlegården," a voice reported through the static. "Possible sighting near the library."

"That's Almqvist's team," Sven noted. "She must have sent them ahead."

Of course. Where else would an academic predator go but to hunt among the books?

18

SÖDERBERG

8:15. The morning's briefing had left Maja's office littered with evidence of their failure: surveillance photos from the kafé evacuation, Tobias's network logs showing Erik's digital footprints, the tactical team's report describing their perfectly orchestrated late arrival. Her fourth kaffe of the day had gone cold, forgotten during the team's dissection of Erik's methodology. The artifacts of police work spread across her desk like a small museum of institutional inadequacy, each document a testament to systems functioning exactly as designed yet failing completely in their purpose.

Her phone sat silent on the desk, his morning threat about Paul a constant presence in her mind; not so much a fear as a weight, a gravitational pull that subtly altered all her movements, her thoughts, her decisions. The boundary between professional and personal dissolving precisely as Erik had intended.

"The peculiar horror," she thought, "of becoming data in someone else's experiment. Of having your fear measured, your love quantified, your reactions noted as variables in a study you never consented to join."

The kafé footage played on endless loop on her screen, each

frame now annotated with timestamps and tactical observations. She watched the scene unfold again and again: police units arriving with textbook precision, deploying according to protocols that had once seemed like protection but now revealed themselves as predictable patterns, easily anticipated by anyone who had studied them.

Steam from the precinct's ancient kaffe maker curled into the stale office air, mixing with the scent of printer toner and damp wool. A shadow fell across her desk as Söderberg appeared in the doorway. His tactical training showed in the way he entered; assessing the space, closing the door with deliberate care. After thirty years running Violent Crimes, he could still move with the quiet precision that had made him legendary in the field, though the administrative weight of his position had added a certain deliberateness to his movements, as if each gesture now carried bureaucratic consideration.

"University board's emergency session starts in an hour." His voice carried the weight of decades managing institutional politics. A particular tone that suggested he was conveying not just information but implications, the subterranean currents of power and influence that flowed beneath official proceedings. "The president's office has been calling since dawn. They're particularly interested in our tactical deployment at the kafé."

"Of course they are. Academic institutions, they'd rather have a serial killer than bad publicity." She gestured at the evacuation photos. "At least killers are discrete."

"Erik didn't just predict the evacuation," Maja said aloud, freezing the footage on a frame that showed the exact moment their tactical teams emerged from cover: too late, perfectly late. "He choreographed it. Response times, deployment patterns, containment procedures, all of it measured and documented." She pulled up Tobias's timeline analysis. "He turned standard police protocols into experiment variables."

"Metodisk som fan—"Methodical as hell" she muttered. "Academic training at its finest; everything becomes data, even murder."

Her hand moved unconsciously toward her phone, still silent after Erik's morning message about Paul. "Now he's expanding his test parameters. Making the experiment personal."

The worn leather of the visitor's chair creaked as Söderberg settled his weight, studying the surveillance photos that covered her wall.

"Looks like a movie," Söderberg said, studying the evacuation photos. "Bad one, where the police arrive just in time to miss everything."

"At least in movies, the incompetence is scripted," Maja replied.

"Nielsen's playing politics," he said finally, his voice carrying a mixture of resignation and calculation that characterized senior officials navigating institutional crises. "His office claims zero contact since the ethics committee rejection. Says Erik's actions have 'deeply shocked the academic community.'"

"Shocked," Maja repeated flatly. "Like discovering gambling in a casino."

"While he's accessing Erik's research files every night," she continued, pulling up Tobias's network analysis. Lines of data scrolled past: login times, document access, download records. "Nielsen's faculty credentials, used between midnight and four AM. Downloading experimental protocols, reviewing old study data." She highlighted a sequence of timestamps. "Each access exactly forty-eight hours before a murder."

"Old habits," Söderberg said, studying the timestamps. "Even when you're helping plan murders, you still work late and check your references."

"Some people are methodical about everything," Maja said. "Filing systems, research protocols, accessory to murder."

"The same Nielsen," Maja confirmed, "who not only chairs the ethics committee but sits on the Nobel selection panel. Who reviews every research proposal in the psychology department." She pulled up Nielsen's faculty profile, his distinguished career filling the screen. "Twenty years of shaping the institution's ethical guidelines while apparently helping Erik refine his experiments."

"The fox designing the henhouse," she said. "Then complaining about all the missing chickens."

Söderberg's expression hardened. The political implications weren't just clear; they were potentially catastrophic. A distinguished professor's connection to murder would do more than shake the institution. It would shatter the carefully maintained facade of academic integrity just weeks before the Nobel ceremonies, that annual ritual where Sweden presented itself as guardian of global intellectual achievement.

"The irony doesn't escape me," Maja thought. "An institution dedicated to recognizing human achievement now potentially harboring those who view humans merely as research subjects. The Nobel ceremonies celebrating knowledge while that same knowledge is weaponized across campus."

Maja spread the seized documents across her desk. Nielsen's red ink annotations covered every margin, creating a map of academic obsession that revealed itself through careful, chronological examination. "Look at the progression in his comments." She arranged the papers chronologically. "'Interesting theoretical framework' becomes 'Consider practical applications.' Then 'Real-world testing essential.'" Her finger traced the dates. "His suggestions getting more specific, more demanding, with each rejection."

"The mentor's influence manifesting in marginal notes," Söderberg observed. "The official documents maintain appropriate language while the handwritten comments reveal the true direction of thought. Institutions function this way too: official policies on the surface, actual practices in the margins."

The chair creaked as Söderberg leaned forward to study the evidence. His decades of experience with institutional politics showed in his grim expression. "The Institute's damage control is already starting. Nielsen's office is calling in favors, activating networks built over thirty years of grant approvals and tenure recommendations." He tapped one of the most recent documents. "They'll claim these are just academic discussions. Theoretical explorations."

"The academic's ultimate defense," Maja noted with bitter irony. "That words remain merely words, that theories don't translate to actions. The peculiar belief that knowledge exists in some realm separate from its applications, that understanding how doesn't imply responsibility for what happens when that knowledge is applied."

Maja's phone vibrated—another message. Her hand hesitated before picking it up, remembering Erik's morning photo of Paul. Instead of Paul, this image showed Nielsen leaving his office, time-stamped ten minutes ago.

"Subject demonstrates consistent behavioral patterns. Institutional loyalty vs ethical obligations. Data collection continues."

"He's watching Nielsen too," she said, passing the phone to Söderberg. "Documenting his mentor's responses just like he documents ours." She gestured at the annotated documents. "Everything's data to him now: the investigation, the university's reaction, even Nielsen's attempts at damage control."

"The perfect academic transformation," she thought but didn't say. "From researcher to research subject, from observer to observed. The student applying to the teacher the very methodologies he was taught."

Söderberg studied the photo of Nielsen, his expression darkening. "He's turning his mentor into another test subject." The leather chair protested as he shifted forward. "Using the same methodology he developed under Nielsen's supervision."

"The student surpassing the teacher?" Maja pulled up the network logs again. "Or proving the effectiveness of Nielsen's training?" The timestamps of Nielsen's late-night access to Erik's files now felt like part of a larger experiment—mentor and student still locked in their academic dance, but with deadly stakes.

"Perhaps the most disturbing aspect," she reflected, "is not that Erik has broken with Nielsen's teaching, but that he's applied it with such terrible fidelity. Not a deviation from his training, but its purest expression: the academic gaze turned toward human connection, but stripped of ethical constraint."

"We've got eyes on Nielsen," Maja said, bringing up Tobias's surveillance grid. Red dots tracked movement through the Institute's corridors, each one tagged with timestamps and location data. "Teams at his Östermalm apartment, his regular kafé, his parking spot. Digital monitoring on every device." She zoomed in on his office location. "But Erik knows all these protocols. He helped design some of them during his research."

"The surveillance expert as subject of surveillance," Söderberg noted. "An irony that would not be lost on him. Our observation becoming part of his data collection, our monitoring incorporated into his experimental design."

"And the Nobel committees arrive Monday." Söderberg's tone suggested this wasn't just another deadline but a confluence of institutional pressures, public scrutiny, and potential catastrophe. "The Institute's hosting the medicine prize announcement. Half of Sweden's academic elite will be there, plus international press." He leaned forward, shadows deepening across his face. "If Erik's planning something public…"

"The perfect laboratory conditions," Maja finished for him. "Maximum institutional pressure, optimal subject density, guaranteed media documentation. If you were designing an experiment to measure institutional response under extreme conditions—"

Her phone vibrated again. Another message from Erik: "*Nobel ceremony = optimal test conditions. Institutional pressure at maximum. Subject response data will be significant.*"

The words felt like a confirmation of her thoughts, as if Erik had been tracking not just her physical movements but her mental processes—anticipating her realizations, measuring her understanding of his methodology. The sensation was unsettling, a reminder that in trying to understand him, she was playing exactly the role he had designed for her in his study.

"And the university administration is still more worried about publicity than public safety," Söderberg added, checking his phone. "The president wants us to keep the investigation 'discreet' during the Nobel preparations."

"Fan ta dig!" The words exploded from Maja before she could stop them. Her outburst hung in the stale office air between them; a momentary rupture in professional composure that seemed to surprise them both.

Söderberg's expression didn't change as he left, closing the door with careful precision—the practiced non-reaction of a career administrator who had learned that visible emotion only complicates institutional machinery.

After Söderberg left, Maja found herself studying the surveillance photos with new intensity. The Institute's buildings rose against the darkening sky, their windows lit from within like rows of clinical observation rooms; each illuminated rectangle containing unknown human activity, any of which might include Erik's preparations or Nielsen's machinations.

"Universities as organisms," she thought, scanning the lit windows. "Complex systems with immune responses designed to protect themselves from external threats—even when those threats emerge from within. The institutional body deploying antibodies against exposure rather than infection."

The November wind rattled her office window, carrying the first hints of snow and the weight of Lars-Erik's impending exposé. Somewhere in those academic halls, Erik was preparing his next experiment, while a former Kriminalinspektör prepared to turn their investigation into literature. Different forms of documentation, different methods of observation; both rendering human experience into narrative, though with vastly different intentions.

Her screen still showed Erik's morning message:

"Your own patterns are particularly interesting."

The photo of Paul and Loki felt like a hypothesis being tested, her personal life transformed into another set of variables. Even her instinct to warn Paul had probably been predicted, measured, noted in whatever records Erik was keeping.

"The terrible symmetry," she realized. "I observe Erik observing others, while he observes me observing him. Layers of surveillance folding back on themselves, each observer simultaneously becoming the observed."

The sun had already surrendered to Stockholm's winter darkness, though her clock showed barely mid-afternoon. Swedish winter's particular melancholy—the premature nightfall, the extended darkness—matched her mood as she contemplated the multiple frameworks closing around her. Her phone sat silent, waiting. Each minute that passed felt like data being collected, her reactions being observed and analyzed. The institutional politics, the Nobel Week pressure, Lars-Erik's book—all of it just more complexity in Erik's experimental design.

Through her window, she watched the university's lights multiply in the gathering dark. Each illuminated window represented someone working late—researchers, students, faculty. All of them potential subjects in Erik's study of human connection. All of them moving through their routines, unaware they were being observed by someone who'd learned to see relationships as laboratory specimens.

"The academic gaze turned predatory," she thought. "Knowledge without compassion, observation without empathy: the perfect intellectual machinery for turning people into data."

The lights of the university glowed against the darkening sky, each one a small point of human activity in the winter gloom. Within those illuminated spaces, knowledge was being created, theories developed, ideas exchanged—the noble pursuit of understanding that justified the institution's existence. Yet somewhere within that same constellation of lights, that same pursuit had twisted into something monstrous: understanding divorced from ethics, knowledge separated from humanity.

The paradox of institutions, Maja reflected, watching the distant windows, is that they simultaneously enable our greatest achievements and our most terrible failures; providing both the structures that advance human knowledge and the systems that can shield its misapplication. The university's lights continued to glow against the gathering darkness, beautiful and terrible in equal measure, much like human knowledge itself.

ACT 2

Method

19
NÄMNDEN

Chapter 18

The emergency board meeting felt like a medical procedure. Everyone wore their institutional masks, speaking in carefully sanitized language that drained the humanity from what they were discussing. Helena Wallin, the Rektor, gripped her Montblanc pen like a lifeline.

"The question," she said, "isn't whether Nielsen crossed ethical boundaries. The question is whether we created the environment that made crossing them seem acceptable."

"This police investigation," Board Chairman Gustaf von Silfverstolpe began, "threatens the very foundation of our academic independence."

Professor Eklund shifted uncomfortably. "Academic independence to do what, Gustaf? To let our faculty treat students like lab rats?"

Dr. Katarina Wahlberg cleared her throat. "We have to consider the implications for ongoing research grants. The European Research Council is particularly sensitive to ethical oversight."

"And Nielsen's role in all this?" Dr. Emma Söderström, Alumni Association President, asked. "He chairs three doctoral committees."

Rektor Wallin's fingers tightened around her pen. "Let's be clear about what we know. The police have no direct evidence linking Nielsen to these incidents. Their interest stems from his role as Erik Thoressen's doctoral advisor."

"A role thoroughly documented and approved by this board," Professor Eklund interjected. "His methods were reviewed by the appropriate committees."

"By Nielsen's committees," Dr. Wahlberg corrected. "The same committees he chairs."

The silence that followed carried weight. Chancellor Björnsson broke it by sliding today's Svenska Dagbladet across the table. "The press is already making connections. This former Kriminalinspektör they're quoting, Gustafsson, specifically mentions institutional oversight failures."

Von Silfverstolpe's color rose. "Perhaps it's time we reminded the police about the importance of discretion in ongoing investigations. I can make some calls."

"Gustaf." Rektor Wallin's tone carried a warning. "The police have a tactical team report showing unauthorized use of university facilities. And now this morning's incident at Östermalmstorg. A public evacuation that the media is connecting to us."

Dr. Wahlberg leaned forward. "There's also the matter of Nielsen's current research grants. Three million kronor from the EU Research Council, plus matching funds."

"Which is precisely why we need to handle this internally," von Silfverstolpe cut in. "The Institute has procedures for reviewing faculty conduct. We don't need police investigators questioning our academic integrity."

"And Erik Thoressen?" Dr. Söderström's question silenced the room. "His doctoral thesis passed through our review process. Under Nielsen's supervision. If the police are right about his involvement in these murders..."

Chancellor Björnsson straightened her papers with deliberate calm. "Perhaps we should discuss Nielsen's temporary leave of absence. Purely administrative, of course. To facilitate the investigation."

"A leave of absence implies wrongdoing," Professor Eklund protested.

"Better a voluntary leave than a public spectacle," Björnsson replied.

Rektor Wallin held up her hand. "There's another consideration. The police Kriminalinspektör leading the investigation, Maja Norberg, is requesting access to all of Nielsen's research documentation. Including sealed ethics committee reviews."

Von Silfverstolpe's face darkened further. "Absolutely not. Those records are protected by—"

"Four people are dead, Gustaf." Dr. Wahlberg's words cut through his bluster. "Fyra döda människor. And if what the police suspect about Erik's research methods is true, there may be other incidents we don't know about. Other students who were... subjects."

Professor Bergström loosened his bow tie. "There's precedent for this. The Uppsala incident in '95. A distinguished professor, allegations of student exploitation."

"That situation was handled appropriately," von Silfverstolpe snapped. "The university's reputation was preserved."

"And the students?" Dr. Söderström's voice carried steel. "What happened to them, Gustaf? After they were quietly transferred abroad with their full scholarships?"

The uncomfortable silence stretched until Rektor Wallin's phone vibrated. She checked the screen, her face paling. "Kriminalinspektör Norberg's team is requesting immediate access to the chemistry building. They've detected unusual electromagnetic signals. They believe Thoressen may have accessed the facility remotely through Nielsen's credentials."

"Call Kriminalinspektör Norberg," Rektor Wallin said, reaching for her phone. "Tell her she has full access to Nielsen's files." She fixed von Silfverstolpe with a stern look. "All of them."

"Helena—" he started to protest.

"Enough, Gustaf. We're not repeating Uppsala. Not this time."

Chancellor Björnsson was already gathering her materials. "Meeting adjourned," Rektor Wallin announced.

Dr. Wahlberg remained seated, watching the old aristocrat's face crumple. Power was like Swedish summer—absolute until suddenly it wasn't.

Fan också.

20

BROMMA

22:30. Rain traced patterns across the windshield of Erik's parked Volvo S90, drops sliding down with tedious predictability. Like human behavior, really. Though at least gravity didn't need committee approval. The car's interior had grown cold, but Erik barely noticed. Cold was data, nothing more.

"Fan," he muttered, watching a police cruiser roll past Biblioteks-gatan. Right on schedule. They'd be coordinating Nobel security within hours, protecting the ceremony's distinguished guests while his real work waited in suburban anonymity. Protecting all the wrong people, as usual.

The third attempt will be perfect. Not a public spectacle, but an intimate demonstration. Djurgården had been too public: couples walking their dogs, joggers, the constant threat of witnesses. The apartment with Henrik and Maria had offered better control. But Bromma. Suburban privacy, predictable routines, neighbors who minded their own business. Perfect Swedish indifference.

Erik opened his notebook. Three weeks of observations on the tennis couple: Monday lessons at Östermalm Racket Club,

Wednesday dinners with his parents in Södermalm, her book club every other Thursday at that pretentious kafé near Stureplan.

"Creatures of habit," he wrote. T-bana schedules with a pulse.

Through the rain-streaked glass, he watched late commuters hurrying toward T-Centralen, umbrellas tilted against the November wind. The wife would be there now, changing from tennis clothes, starting dinner. The husband always arrived thirty minutes later, punctual as a government clerk. Which he was, working at Skatteverket.

Their relationship dynamics were textbook. She deferred to his restaurant choices, adjusted her schedule to his preferences. He guided her with casual touches, ordered for both at restaurants. They believed they had a modern partnership. Living proof of his theories. Swedish equality, achieved through submission.

A text pinged his phone. Nielsen: "Board meeting went well."

Erik smiled. Nielsen knew how to perform for administrators. Nielsen's "worried colleague" performance yesterday had been masterful, expressing just the right concern about Erik's "obsession". In academia, concern and manipulation looked identical.

Academic methodology versus police methodology. Both systems relied on pattern recognition, precedent analysis. Both were blind to genuine innovation.

19:45. Blue dashboard numbers marked time like the lab clock had during those late nights perfecting his formula. The police would be analyzing that space now, studying his deliberately planted notes about ceremonial security weaknesses. Meanwhile, his real equipment waited in the trunk—three weeks of preparation distilled into elegant chemical efficiency.

Swedish police: methodical, predictable. They'd follow the obvious trail, protect the obvious targets. Kriminalinspektör Norberg seemed competent enough, but systematic competence was its own blindness.

He started the engine. Twenty minutes to Bromma through the rain-slicked streets, past Fridhemsplan and out toward the western suburbs where Sweden's middle class lived their orderly lives. The wife would be home now, following her post-tennis routine. Shower first, then kitchen preparations, NPR's evening programming providing background comfort. American radio, Swedish kitchen.

Three weeks of observation had revealed everything he needed: not just schedules but psychology, not just movements but motivations. Academic methodology, finally useful.

The suburbs waited in their November darkness, each house a small fortress of routine and assumption. In one particular house, two people were living their final ordinary evening, unaware that their comfortable patterns were about to serve a higher purpose.

Erik adjusted his rearview mirror and checked his appearance one final time. Tennis club casual—the uniform of Sweden's aspirational middle class. The wife would recognize him from their brief encounters at Östermalm Racket, those three conversations where he'd become just another academic with a weak backhand. Three conversations to invisibility. Swedish politeness as camouflage.

03:17. The S90's engine ticked as it cooled outside Björnsonsgatan 23, a modest villa that embodied Swedish middle-class aspirations —red wooden siding, white trim, the inevitable Volvo in the driveway. Erik sat in darkness, observing the house where Magnus and Vera Strandberg had built their orderly life.

Two weeks of observation had revealed patterns as predictable as the T-bana schedule. She returned from Skatteverket at 17:30, started dinner while he finished client calls in the spare bedroom. They ate watching Rapport, discussed nothing of substance, went to bed at 22:30. Twenty-three years of marriage reduced to routine. Love became habit. Connection transformed into mere proximity.

What fascinated him was their elaborate rituals of avoidance. Date nights every second Friday. Annual trips to the same hotel in Visby. Sunday dinners with her parents where the same stories were retold with diminishing enthusiasm.

Erik collected his materials. The adhesive compound had been refined since the previous attempts. This batch would create truly permanent bonds—a literal interpretation of "till death do us part." Swedish wedding vows. Such beautiful lies people told themselves.

Inside, the house smelled of yesterday's köttbullar and furniture polish. The Strandbergs had achieved the Swedish dream: comfort without meaning, security without purpose. Even their IKEA furniture seemed to judge them—Billy bookcases filled with unread books, a Klippan sofa that had hosted a thousand evenings of parallel silence.

The bedroom door opened silently. Two forms under a duvet from Åhléns, breathing in unconscious synchronicity. Even in sleep, they maintained careful distance—close enough to share warmth, far enough to avoid accidental intimacy.

Erik administered the paralytic with clinical precision. First Vera, then Magnus. Their eyes opened to consciousness without movement, understanding without recourse. Perfect subjects. Aware but helpless.

"Your marriage interests me," Erik said quietly, preparing the adhesive. "Twenty-three years of careful avoidance disguised as companionship. You've already bound yourselves to each other through habit and mortgage payments. I'm simply making the metaphor literal."

He worked methodically, positioning them face to face. The adhesive created permanent molecular bonds between their skin. Soon they would share each breath, experience each heartbeat. All that careful distance, erased.

Magnus's eyes tracked the preparations with growing comprehension. A tax lawyer—he understood contracts, obligations, the weight of permanent commitments. His final contract wouldn't need signatures.

"The question," Erik continued, professional curiosity coloring his tone, "is whether forced intimacy can transform avoidance into actual connection. Or whether proximity without choice simply amplifies the emptiness."

He made the necessary incision—clean, precise, avoiding unnecessary suffering. This wasn't about cruelty. It was about understanding. About what happened when people couldn't look away.

The house settled around them with small sounds—radiators ticking, the refrigerator humming its mechanical lullaby. Outside, November snow began to fall, each flake adding to the silence that would soon blanket everything.

04:02. Erik gathered his materials, leaving the Strandbergs to their final experiment in intimacy. Magnus was fading now, his breathing increasingly labored. Vera remained conscious, experiencing every moment of his departure while unable to move, speak, or look away.

Their vows, finally tested. For better or worse, in sickness and health. Though probably not quite what the Lutheran minister had envisioned during their ceremony at Engelbrekt Church all those years ago.

As he drove back toward the city center, Erik considered the variables. Would Vera find meaning in Magnus's final moments? Would forced proximity reveal hidden depths, or simply confirm the emptiness of their connection? Academic questions required empirical testing.

Behind him, snow continued to fall on Bromma's sleeping streets, covering his tire tracks, muffling sound, wrapping the suburb in its cold embrace. Everything human, eventually erased.

In the quiet house on Björnsonsgatan, Vera Strandberg remained conscious and immobile, discovering what happened when metaphorical bonds became literal ones. When "together forever" transformed from promise to predicament.

The things people said at weddings. If only they knew.

. . .

05:45. Maja's phone buzzed once, then again, the digital pulse of emergency intruding into predawn darkness. She was already awake, had been since the first reports of "suspicious activity" in Bromma started coming across the police band. Sven's message confirmed what she'd been dreading:

"Third couple found. Björnsonsgatan 23. Female subject still alive."

Erik had left one alive. Djävlar. Not mercy—methodology. The researcher's need for complete data sets.

Maja dressed quickly in yesterday's sweater—cigarettes and stale beer from that Södermalm dive where she'd gone to think. Outside, Stockholm's November darkness pressed against the windows like a living thing.

The drive to Bromma took fifteen minutes through empty streets slick with rimfrost. Even the kebab shops on Götgatan were shuttered, a minor miracle in itself. As she pulled up to the villa, the scene was already contained: tactical teams securing the perimeter, forensics setting up their equipment with practiced efficiency.

Competent chaos. Erik would be documenting their response somewhere, adding their predictable procedures to his research notes.

Sven met her at the door, clutching his thermos like a lifeline. Yesterday's kaffe, from the smell of it. "Neighbor called it in at 03:45. Thought they saw someone in the garden." He lowered his voice. "First responders found them twenty minutes ago. Had to step out when they..." He didn't finish.

Some things didn't fit in police reports.

The chemical smell hit immediately—antiseptic, familiar, but stronger. Erik's formula evolving with each iteration.

Upstairs, the bedroom looked like a laboratory experiment. Standard Swedish furnishings turned stage for horror. The couple lay exactly as he'd positioned them, another of his meticulous "experiments" in forced intimacy. The male victim was already gone, but the woman's eyes tracked their movement—fully conscious, just as Erik had intended.

"Ambulans is three minutes out," Sven reported, checking his phone. "But the separation process..." He left the implications unspoken. They both remembered Henrik.

Maja catalogued the differences from previous scenes. The adhesive pattern was more extensive, the positioning more precise. Each murder more refined than the last. She wondered if he'd submitted this for peer review.

"Full forensics workup," she ordered. "I want to know if he's modified the compound. And get me the university's lab access logs for the past 24 hours. He had to mix this somewhere."

Through the bedroom window, she caught movement in the pre-dawn shadows, probably just snow falling on the hedges, but her hand moved to her weapon anyway.

Erik was out there somewhere, watching them work. Observer observing observers. Recursive madness.

Her phone buzzed:

"Subject response = suboptimal. Methodology requires refinement."

She stared at the message, then at the woman's eyes still tracking movement across the ceiling.

"Fan också," she muttered. He was treating them all like lab rats.

21

VERA

08:45. Three hours after leaving Björnsonsgatan, Maja stood in the sterile corridor of Danderyd Hospital. The morning snow had turned to freezing rain against the windows, nature's own commentary on the day's mood, first soft promise, then hard reality.

She'd spent the intervening hours coordinating with the forensics team, but now came the part she'd been both dreading and anticipating—interviewing their first living witness. At least the paperwork would be different. Hospital forms instead of crime scene reports. Swedish bureaucracy adapted to every form of human misery with its own specialized documentation.

"Förstås," she muttered, watching a nurse struggle with a malfunctioning ID scanner. Even in crisis, the machines demanded their rituals. She'd seen it countless times, humanity's faith that proper procedure could somehow contain chaos. As if evil would politely wait while you found the right form.

The konstable posted outside nodded as she approached. Young. Looked like he'd rather be anywhere else. She didn't blame him. At his age, she'd still believed guard duty meant protecting people from danger. Now she knew better, mostly you protected them from reporters. Inside, the hospital's antiseptic smell and fluorescent hum did nothing to ease the tension in her shoulders.

She checked her notes one last time. The medical team had managed to separate the victim from her partner's body, but the psychological trauma was immeasurable. The clinical language made it sound routine. "Separation procedure." As if love could be surgically removed. The doctors had their own defense mechanisms, wrapping horror in Latin terms and medical jargon. She understood. Sometimes language was all that stood between you and the abyss.

Maja paused at the door. In twenty years of police work, she'd learned that survivors often envied the dead. The living had to remember. She wondered sometimes which was crueler, Erik's adhesive or memory's. At least his victims could eventually be separated.

A nurse emerged from the room, her expression professionally neutral but eyes tired from watching pain she couldn't fix. "Hon är vaken," she said. "But be brief. She's still heavily medicated."

"How brief is brief?" Maja asked.

"Long enough to traumatize her again, not long enough to get useful information," the nurse replied. "Standard hospital timing."

Maja almost smiled at the gallows humor. Healthcare workers and police, both professions that taught you to laugh at the absurd or go mad. Sometimes both.

She entered the room with the careful movements of someone approaching a wounded animal. Medical equipment surrounded the bed, monitoring every vital sign. The victim lay motionless except for shallow breathing, her face ashen against white linens, gaze fixed on nothing. Someone had braided her hair. A small kindness that made everything worse. Maja had seen it before—these tiny gestures of care in the face of enormous cruelty. Humanity's stubborn insistence on tenderness, even when it changed nothing.

"Vera," Maja kept her voice low, moving to where the woman could see her without turning her head. "I'm Kriminalinspektör Norberg. I know this is difficult, but anything you can tell us about what happened..."

The steady rhythm of the heart monitor filled the silence. Beep. Beep. Beep. The sound of a life reduced to electronic confirmation. Strange how machines had become our witnesses now, recording suffering in digital precision. More reliable than memory, less complicated than truth.

Maja waited with the patience she'd learned from two decades of listening to the unspeakable. Time moved differently in these rooms; seconds stretched like hours while years collapsed into single moments of horror.

After what felt like minutes, Vera's eyes found hers briefly before drifting away again.

"Vi ska skydda dig,—We will protect you" Maja said. "But we need to find him before he hurts anyone else. Förstår du?"

The monitor's rhythm quickened—technology's clinical translation of human terror. Vera Strandberg's throat worked, each swallow visibly painful. When she finally spoke, her voice was barely a whisper, raw from the screaming that had torn through the villa on Björnsonsgatan.

"He..." The word caught in her throat, her face twisting. "Couldn't.................brea..."

Maja moved closer, feeling that familiar tightness in her chest—the body's involuntary sympathy with another's grief. After all these years, she still hadn't developed complete immunity. Perhaps that was good. Perhaps that was what separated her from Erik.

"Your husband?" she asked, though she knew the answer. Sometimes questions were just handrails, helping people descend into memory.

A slight nod, her eyes still fixed on some distant point. "Couldn't ... move. The glue..." Her voice fractured like thin ice under sudden weight. "I ...him .....dying....."

Here it was—the gap between Erik's academic abstractions and human reality. He studied attachment theory; Vera had lived attachment's ultimate nightmare. In his papers, death was a variable. In her life, it was everything.

The rain intensified against the windows as Maja forced herself to continue. "The man who did this. Did you see him?"

The monitors counted out the seconds of silence. Vera's fingers twisted in the sheets, knuckles white. The body's own language of trauma, more honest than words. Finally, she nodded.

"You...nng ... .polit......" she whispered.

Of course. The banality of evil dressed in good manners. Maja had learned long ago that monsters rarely looked the part. They said "please" and "thank you" while destroying lives.

"Did he speak to you?" Maja asked, already knowing this would be too much.

Vera Strandberg's breathing quickened, the monitor's steady rhythm faltering. Tears welled in her eyes as she tried to form words. Her lips moved, but only a choked sob escaped.

The body had its own wisdom, shutting down when memory became unbearable. She'd pushed far enough for one day. "It's okay," she said. "We can try again tomorrow."

Tomorrow. As if twenty-four hours would somehow make the impossible speakable. But that was the fiction they all agreed to— that time healed, that justice helped, that catching Erik would somehow undo what he'd done. Necessary lies that kept the world turning.

A nurse appeared in the doorway like a guardian angel in scrubs, summoned by the monitor's distress.

The nurse moved efficiently around the bed, adjusting medication levels. "That's enough for now," she said, positioning herself between Maja and her patient.

"Five more minutes," Maja said, though she knew it was futile.

"Five seconds," the nurse replied. "She's had enough interviews for one lifetime."

True enough. How many times could you ask someone to relive the worst moment of their existence? Justice had its own cruelties.

Vera Strandberg's eyes squeezed shut, tears streaming down her face. Her breathing became more erratic, the monitor's warning beep growing more insistent.

"Out. Now." The nurse's voice brooked no argument as she administered a sedative.

Maja retreated, watching chemistry perform its small mercy— not healing, just postponing. Even in drug-induced peace, Vera's face held shadows of what she'd endured. Some things marked you deeper than skin.

Outside in the corridor, Maja leaned against the wall, processing what little they'd learned. No—what they'd confirmed. That politeness could be weaponized. That academic curiosity could metastasize into cruelty. That Erik would continue his experiments until someone stopped him.

Through the hospital windows, she watched the freezing rain turn to snow again, transforming Danderyd's pine forests into a white silence. Beautiful. Indifferent. Nature's own demonstration that beauty and cruelty weren't opposites—just different faces of the same indifferent universe. She needed to get back to the station. Nielsen's research wouldn't wait.

The hospital's automatic doors opened to chaos. Camera flashes turned the falling snow into sparks, reporters shouting questions over each other.

"Inspecktor Norberg! Is it true you have a survivor?"

"Has the Adhesive Killer struck again?"

"Any comment on the university connection?"

Maja paused, observing the media scrum with weary recognition. They were doing their job, just as she was doing hers. Both professions fed on human misery, the difference being that police occasionally prevented some. The reporters just documented the aftermath, turning tragedy into content. Neither role was particularly noble when you examined it too closely.

The TV4 crew tracked her with predatory efficiency, their lights turning the falling snow into a surreal theater. The Expressen reporter she recognized—Björk, who'd covered the Östermalm murders two years back.

"The public has a right to know if they're safe," he pressed, stepping closer. "Three couples now. Is there a pattern?"

Ah yes, the public's rights. Maja had learned that what the public truly wanted was the illusion of safety, not actual information. They wanted to believe monsters could be identified, categorized, avoided. The truth—that evil wore a pleasant face and knocked politely—that would keep them awake at night.

She stopped, considering. The media would run with speculation whether she gave them anything or not. At least this way she could control the narrative—somewhat.

"We're investigating connections between the crimes," she said. "The public should be aware that couples may be specifically targeted."

"University connection?" another reporter called out.

Too close to Erik. "No comment."

"För helvete," she muttered, pushing past the microphones. Behind her, she could hear them already crafting their lead stories. By evening news, Stockholm would be talking about a "Couple Killer." Erik would be watching, taking notes. Perhaps even feeling a twisted pride at his media coverage. Academic recognition by other means.

As she drove away, Maja reflected on the strange ecosystem they'd all become part of. Police, media, killer—each playing their role in a drama none of them had written but all perpetuated. Erik created horror, she investigated it, they reported it, and Stockholm watched from behind locked doors. Modern civilization's way of processing its nightmares.

The snow intensified as she headed back toward the city center. Somewhere in Stockholm, Erik was likely reviewing his notes, analyzing the previous night's "experiment," planning his next demonstration. And somewhere in the university's digital archives, the roots of his methodology lay waiting to be discovered—academic papers and research proposals that had seemed harmless until they weren't.

The wipers fought a losing battle against the thickening snow. She drove on through the white silence, carrying with her the image of Vera Strandberg's braided hair—that small gesture of care in an uncaring world. Perhaps that was all any of them could do: perform small kindnesses while investigating large cruelties, maintaining civilization's polite fiction that justice mattered, that understanding helped, that catching killers somehow balanced the scales.

It was absurd when you thought about it. All of it. The careful procedures, the evidence bags, the investigation boards. As if organization could contain chaos. As if understanding Erik's motivations would undo his victims' suffering.

But what else was there to do? Quit? Let him continue?

No. You did the job not because it fixed things, but because not doing it was worse. Another lesson from twenty years of police work: sometimes the only choice was between different degrees of futility. You chose the one that occasionally, accidentally, saved someone.

The city emerged through the snowfall ahead, Stockholm transforming into a landscape of muted sounds and softened edges. Somewhere in those white streets, Erik was planning his next lesson in attachment theory.

She would stop him. Not because it would bring back the dead or heal the living, but because that's what she did. She investigated. She persisted. She maintained the fiction that justice mattered.

Some days, that fiction was all that separated them from the abyss.

22

PRESSURE

By eleven, Maja was back at her desk on Polhemsgatan. The drive from Danderyd had taken twenty minutes through Stockholm's November gloom, past Haga Palace where the crown princess lived behind walls that couldn't keep out what Erik brought. She'd spent the time mentally sorting through Nielsen's papers, theoretical frameworks, attachment studies, all academically pristine. Nothing that screamed 'I'm creating a killer.' But Vera Strandberg's whispered words ("Young...polite...") suggested the real evidence lay elsewhere.

Her phone rang. Almqvist.

"We should arrest Erik now," Maja said without preamble.

"On what grounds?" Almqvist's voice carried the weight of too many cases lost to proper procedure. "Being Nielsen's student? Having library cards?"

"Fan också." Maja almost smiled at the absurdity. Swedish justice was so careful with rights that sometimes the guilty walked free just to prove the system worked. "What would Prosecutor Lindholm accept? A signed confession? Video evidence? A note saying 'I am the killer' in triplicate?"

"All three, probably." Almqvist's dry humor matched hers. "How's the archive search going?"

"Sven and our analyst Tobias are working through Nielsen's archives. The professor's been guiding Erik's research for years, pushing him toward more extreme methodologies."

"Christ. The mentor and the protégé." Another pause. "I can be there in 10 mins. This feels like it's accelerating."

Her phone buzzed. Danderyd's main number. Hospital protocol demanding its paperwork, even for deaths witnessed firsthand. The nurse confirmed what Maja already knew: time of death 11:12. She hung up and stared at her desk again. No living witnesses now. Just Nielsen's papers and whatever patterns they could find before Erik struck again.

"It is," Maja agreed. "Mrs. Strandberg just died at Danderyd. No witnesses left."

The line went quiet for a moment. When Almqvist spoke again, her voice was harder. "I'm coming down. We need to coordinate before this gets any worse."

The stack of Nielsen's papers occupied half her desk: decades of academic writing about human attachment, all of it reasonable, measured, publishable. Nothing that screamed 'I'm training a killer.' But then, manifestos were so last century. Modern evil hid in foot-notes and methodology sections.

The old radiator clicked in the corner.

Her phone buzzed. Söderberg: "My office. Now."

Almqvist materialized in her doorway like a rumpled angel, snow still on her shoulders. "Already here. Was communing with the archives at Kronoberg." She read Maja's expression. "Let me guess. The brass discovered we exist?"

"Kommissioner's with him."

"Ah." Almqvist brushed snow onto Maja's floor with sublime indifference. "Someone important's complaining. The university?"

"Who else? Murder's acceptable as long as it doesn't affect enrollment."

They found both men contemplating the snowfall like it was a management problem that could be solved with the right Power-Point. The Kommissioner turned first, his face wearing that expression of official concern that probably came with the uniform.

"The Kungsmedicinska connection requires... delicate handling."

"Six bodies," Maja said. "They're past caring about our delicacy."

"The university board is concerned about reputation..."

"Fascinating." Almqvist's tone achieved that perfect Swedish balance of politeness and contempt. "Perhaps they should have considered that before their psychology department started producing killers. Bad for the brochures."

The silence stretched. Finally, Söderberg: "You have forty-eight hours before I have to brief the Justice Ministry."

In the corridor, Almqvist smiled grimly. "Scared brass means resources. I'll take it."

Back at her desk, drowning in academic prose, her phone rang again. The modern condition, always interrupted, never allowed to think.

"Tobias found something." Sven sounded like a man who'd discovered gold in a garbage heap. "Nielsen's comments on Erik's undergraduate thesis: 'Shows remarkable insight into attachment theory beyond standard paradigms.' Then he fast-tracked him into the doctoral program."

"He fast-tracked him," she said aloud.

"More than that," Sven continued. "Nielsen personally amended Erik's ethics applications. Each rejection, he'd add footnotes citing obscure precedents, suggesting 'alternative methodological frameworks.' The progression is documented, from standard behavioral studies to increasingly extreme human subject experiments. He even cited his own unpublished research to justify Erik's protocols."

Nielsen hadn't just supervised Erik's research. He'd systematically guided him toward this outcome.

"Where are these documents now?" she asked, reaching for her coat.

"Secured in Evidence. Tobias's still going through the archive." Sven paused. "Nielsen's working late tonight. His office light's still on at the university."

Maja stuck her head into the interview room where Almqvist was surrounded by boxes of files. "Nielsen's at the university. I'm going to talk to him."

Almqvist looked up sharply. "Alone?"

"He's an academic, not a killer."

"The academic who created a killer." Almqvist stood. "I'm coming with you."

Maja shook her head. "Two cops will spook him. But call me in thirty minutes. If I don't answer..."

"I'll bring the cavalry." Almqvist wasn't happy, but she understood. "Helvete, Maja. Be careful."

———

The drive to Björkbacka took fifteen minutes of controlled sliding through Stockholm's idea of winter. Her Mercedes gracefully handled the snow with typical German competence, not flashy, just functional. Like everything else here. Even the murders had a certain Nordic efficiency.

The Psykologiska Institutionen squatted in the snow like a concrete toad, all béton brut angles and good intentions gone wrong. Only one office showed light, Nielsen's, of course. The man probably slept there, dreaming in citations.

The hallways were dark, her boots loud on the terrazzo floor. She didn't knock gently this time.

Two sharp raps on the dark wood. A pause, then the door opened. Nielsen stood backlit by his desk lamp, silver hair gleaming. His expression shifted from academic irritation to careful neutrality as he recognized her.

"Kriminalinspektör" His voice was smooth as ever, but she caught the tension underneath. "To what do I owe this late visit?"

She stepped past him into the familiar office. But tonight, the large window behind his desk showed only darkness, the campus lights obscured by falling snow.

"Tell me about your early correspondence with Erik Thoressen," Maja said, remaining standing. She'd learned long ago that sitting in academics' offices gave them home advantage with all those books looking down.

Nielsen closed the door with practiced calm, moving to his chair behind the desk. "Ah. You've been through the archives."

"Six years of carefully guided research." She watched his face for micro-expressions. "Each rejection, each revision, pushing him further from standard methodology. You knew exactly what you were doing."

Nielsen's smile carried decades of academic authority. "You misunderstand the academic process, Kriminalinspektör," he said, adjusting papers with the precision of someone who'd never had to clean up actual blood. "We encourage students to push boundaries, to question accepted paradigms. Erik showed... exceptional promise in that regard."

"Yes, I'm sure the Strandbergs appreciated his exceptional promise while they were dying." The words came out drier than she'd intended. Amazing how academia could drain the humanity from any situation.

"The progression in his work is clear." Maja placed both hands on his desk, leaning forward. "Each study more extreme than the last, each methodology pushing further past ethical boundaries. And you signed off on all of it."

Nielsen's smile was pure academia. "A supervisor's role is to guide, to challenge. Erik's theories about dependency were... innovative. Perhaps unconventional. But I hardly see how encouraging academic rigor makes me responsible for his personal choices."

"Three couples, Professor." Maja studied his pelargoner, their leaves reaching toward the window with vegetable optimism. Even plants believed in better outcomes. "Six people learning about attachment the hardest way possible. Your theories made flesh, so to speak."

"Theories remain theories until someone chooses to test them inappropriately." His tone suggested this was all a fascinating but regrettable misunderstanding between colleagues.

The fluorescent light hummed in the silence that followed. Nielsen's hands remained perfectly still on his desk, his posture relaxed. Academic. Untouchable.

"And now people are dying," Maja added, her voice quiet but firm. "Tell us about Erik's role in these experiments, Professor. What exactly was he meant to monitor?"

Nielsen's smile was pure academia, but his eyes had gone cold. "I'm afraid I can't help you with your investigation, Kriminalinspektör. But if you're interested in my published research, I'd be happy to provide citations."

"Of course. When cornered, academics always want to assign homework." She shook her head. "At least criminals are honest about being dishonest."

This time, Nielsen's mask slipped completely, just for a moment, but long enough for Maja to see something dark and dangerous beneath. She had seen that same look in the eyes of killers, not the frenzied ones who stabbed in passion, but the calculated ones who believed themselves beyond ordinary morality. The look of someone who had convinced themselves that their intelligence justified their cruelty. When he spoke again, his voice was measured and precise, a professor addressing wayward students.

"Be careful, Kriminalinspektör. Some lines of inquiry can be... psychologically damaging. We wouldn't want another unfortunate breakdown, would we?"

"Was that a threat, Professor Nielsen?"

"Merely an observation based on empirical evidence." His smile hadn't changed. "Psychological stress can manifest in unexpected ways."

"Like Erik's victims," Maja said. She placed her hands on his desk, leaning forward. "How many more people have to die before you admit what you created?"

Nielsen's eyes met hers, and for the first time, Maja saw pride beneath the academic facade. "Created? You give me too much credit, Kriminalinspektör. Erik's work is entirely his own. Though I must admit, his methodology shows... remarkable precision."

"His methodology shows exactly what you taught him. Right down to the adhesive bonds."

In the ensuing silence, Maja found herself thinking about the strange progression of violence, how it began in minds like Nielsen's, abstract and theoretical, before finding physical expression through hands like Erik's. The professor would never dirty his own hands with actual murder, but he had shaped the instrument that would. It was like those Russian dolls her mormor had collected, each one containing a smaller, more concentrated version of the same thing.

Nielsen spread his hands. "If you have evidence connecting me to these unfortunate events, by all means, present it. Otherwise, I have papers to grade." He gestured to the door with practiced dismissal. "Though I'd be happy to recommend some reading on attachment theory, if you're interested."

"The arrogance of certain men is perhaps the most consistent variable in human behavior. You might consider studying that phenomenon, Professor. Though I suspect introspection isn't your preferred methodology. Too small a sample size, perhaps."

Maja straightened, her jaw tight. They had what they needed. Nielsen's mask had slipped enough to show what lay beneath.

———

Outside Nielsen's office, the fluorescent corridor lights buzzed overhead, some flickering. The antiseptic smell faded as she walked away, replaced by old paper and dust. She'd gotten under his skin at the end there, his mask had slipped, just for a moment. Her phone vibrated. Almqvist's thirty-minute check-in. She answered as she walked. "Still breathing."

"Productive?"

"He's involved. Deeply. But proving it..." Maja paused at the building's entrance, watching the snow fall harder. "We need more than academic arrogance."

"Get some sleep," Almqvist said. "You sound like you've been awake since the Paleolithic era."

Outside, the Swedish winter reasserted itself with horizontal snow and that special Nordic wind that found every gap in your clothing. The birches along Roslagsvägen bent like old women gossiping about the terrible things happening in their university.

In her Mercedes, driving back toward the city center, Maja felt the familiar weight of a case that refused to resolve. Nielsen's careful non-denials, his academic pride, his certainty—it all pointed to guilt, but guilt wrapped in layers of institutional protection and theoretical distance.

Her phone buzzed. Sven: "Go home. That's an order from your partner, not a suggestion from your colleague."

She stared at the text, sitting in traffic near Odenplan. When had she last been home for more than a shower and change of clothes? When had she last thought about anything except Nielsen's methodology and Erik's patterns?

The city lights blurred through her windshield, exhaustion finally catching up with her. Maybe Sven was right. Maybe she needed distance to see clearly. Maybe she'd been staring at the trees so long she'd lost sight of the forest.

Her phone rang. Daniel.

"When's the last time you saw actual daylight?" her brother asked without preamble. "And I mean daylight you weren't using to examine crime scenes."

"Daniel—"

"Ferry to Vaxholm leaves in an hour. You're going to be on it."

"I can't just—"

"You can. You will. Sven already called me. Says you're becoming your own evidence of whatever theory you're chasing." Daniel's voice carried that particular mix of concern and authority that only family could deploy. "One night, Maja. The case will still be there tomorrow."

She found herself driving toward Strömkajen before she'd consciously decided to go.

23
VAXHOLM

The Waxholmsbåten cut through steel-gray waters like a blade through old silk, and Maja stood at the railing contemplating the peculiar human need to flee from what consumed them. Twenty-three minutes from Strömkajen to Vaxholm. She'd made this journey countless times as a child, back when death was merely theoretical, something that happened in her father's carefully sanitized police stories over Thursday fika.

Now the archipelago's islands drifted past like crime scene photographs. Each red cottage and frost-tipped pine another data point in a pattern she couldn't stop seeing. Even with her phone silenced (except for Sven, who'd practically ordered this exile), Nielsen's academic precision haunted her. Six bodies arranged with dissertation-level care. One survivor who'd lasted minutes at Danderyd before the separation proved too much. And somewhere in Stockholm, Erik Thorssen was probably taking notes on her absence, adding it to his research on institutional responses to systematic murder.

November light scraped across the water at an angle that made even beauty feel melancholic. Seabirds wheeled overhead, their cries absurdly melodramatic, auditioning for roles as harbingers of doom. Nature, Maja reflected, had no sense of subtlety.

The wool coat. Paul's attempt at domestic normalcy last Christmas, it scratched against her neck like a guilty conscience. Five victims, then six. She'd been subsisting on Pressbyrån kaffe and swedish determination that confused suffering with virtue. Always one step behind, like a doctoral candidate perpetually failing to satisfy their advisor.

"You're becoming your own crime scene," Sven had said with that mix of concern and irony that only eight years of partnership could produce. "Go see your brother before I have to investigate your psychological autopsy."

Stockholm receded with each throb of the ferry's engine, but distance, she was learning, was more philosophical than geographical. The Bromma scene kept reassembling itself in her mind.

The archipelago's peace felt almost aggressive in its tranquility. Here she was, surrounded by Sweden's picture-postcard serenity, while her mind kept returning to Nielsen's office with its academic certificates and barely concealed satisfaction. Theory to practice, mentor to student, research to murder. The progression was so methodical it felt like parody. Perhaps that's what she'd been missing: the possibility that Erik's precision wasn't just methodology but also commentary. A dissertation written in blood about the absurdity of trying to quantify human connection.

"Jävla helvete," she muttered, then caught herself. Even her cursing had become reflexive, automatic. Another pattern in a case drowning in them. The fortress emerged from the mist like something from a Bergman film, all symbolic weight and historical irony. Built to defend against external threats, useless against the kind of danger that lived in university libraries and methodology sections.

Fresh eyes. As if eyes could be renewed like library books or driver's licenses. But Sven had been right about one thing. She'd been staring at Erik's patterns so long she'd begun to see them everywhere, like a PhD student who starts finding their thesis topic in breakfast cereal arrangements.

The ferry docked with the practiced bump of Swedish punctuality at Söderhamnsplan. Maja's boots found purchase on frozen gravel that crunched with the satisfying predictability of natural phenomena. So unlike the human behaviors she'd been trying to decode. Without summer tourists clogging its arteries, Vaxholm revealed itself as what it had always been: a perfectly preserved specimen of Swedish nostalgia, each wooden house a testament to the national belief that history could be contained in paint choices and gingerbread trim.

The contrast should have been jarring. Vaxholm's postcard perfection against the clinical horror of Erik's crime scenes. Instead, it felt like two sides of the same peculiarly Swedish coin: the compulsive need to impose order on chaos, whether through heritage preservation or methodical murder.

Kaffe and cardamom wrapped around her like a particularly Swedish form of comfort as Maja pushed open the familiar red door. Daniel stood at the counter, two mugs ready, silver threading through his dark hair in the same pattern as their father's had. Genetics as destiny, another pattern she couldn't unsee.

The floorboards announced her arrival with groans that had documented three generations of family dramas. Their mother's copper kettle occupied its eternal post on the stove, dulled with age but maintained with the kind of devotion Swedes reserved for household objects that had survived the fifties.

"There's my favorite sister," Daniel said, but the greeting died as he catalogued her appearance. In the window's reflection, she caught what he saw: the hollow-eyed aesthetic of someone who'd been subsisting on vending machine kanelbullar and existential dread. Christ, when had she started looking like one of Erik's research subjects?

"Your only sister," Maja managed, her bag hitting the floor with the weight of too many case files. The simple act of removing her coat felt like an admission of mortality.

"Kom," Daniel said, pressing warmth into her hands in ceramic form. The kaffe was strong enough to wake the dead. Or at least the emotionally numbed. "When's the last time you slept in an actual bed? And I mean sleep, not that thing you do where you lie down and mentally reconstruct crime scenes."

"Sunday? Fan, I don't even know anymore." She took a sip. "All the days blend together like a bad smoothie from that overpriced place on Östermalmstorg."

Maja collapsed into the chair by the fire with the grace of someone who'd forgotten their body had needs beyond caffeine and determination. Daniel's house existed in that parallel universe where people had time for things like dusting and plant care. He'd always been the steady one, building a life while she chased shadows through Stockholm's streets.

Through the window, magpies conducted their eternal parliament on the frost-covered lawn, debating whatever it was magpies found worth discussing. Probably more productive than most police meetings.

"You want to talk about it?" Daniel asked, settling across from her with the patience of someone who'd waited out her silences before.

The fire crackled between them, marking time in a way that had nothing to do with investigation timelines or coroner reports. She'd promised herself she wouldn't bring the case here, but promises, she was learning, were just another pattern humans created and broke.

"I can't see it clearly anymore," she admitted. "There's something I'm missing with Erik, something so obvious it's probably staring at me from every crime scene photo."

The weight of the admission hung between them. Six dead. Each death a data point in Erik's grand experiment, each victim selected with academic precision.

"I need to end this," Maja said. "Before he completes his research.

Before he proves whatever theory he's trying to demonstrate with other people's lives."

Daniel studied her with the attention of someone who'd known her before she'd learned to compartmentalize. "What worries me," he said, warming his hands on his kaffe mug with the practiced efficiency of someone who'd survived too many Swedish winters, "is how you've started talking about people like research subjects. 'Victim profiles,' 'behavioral patterns,' 'methodological progression.' Soon you'll be requesting ethical approval before having conversations."

Through the window, waves performed their ancient rhythm against the shore, indifferent to human attempts at meaning-making. So different from the precise choreography of Erik's crime scenes, yet both following patterns older than memory.

"Every time I think I understand Erik's pattern, he shifts," Maja said, watching steam rise from her kaffe like souls departing. "The methodology is perfect, precise. Nielsen taught him well. But there's something..." She let the sentence die, another incomplete thought in a case full of them.

"Sometimes being too close to something means missing what's right in front of you," Daniel offered. "Like those old stereograms. You have to unfocus to see the hidden image."

"Sven's been preaching the same gospel. Step back, get perspective, trust the team." The words tasted bitter, like admitting defeat.

"Because it works." Daniel leaned forward with the earnestness of someone who still believed in solutions. "You taught me that, remember? When I was stuck on my dissertation. Sometimes you have to look away to see clearly."

"This isn't some academic exercise, Daniel. Erik's out there planning his next demonstration. I can feel it. Nielsen's been conducting him like a symphony from the start, and now..." Her grip on the mug tightened until the ceramic creaked a warning. "I can't afford perspective. Not when more lives are hanging in the balance of his theories."

Daniel set down his mug with deliberate calm. "You're not alone in this, Maja. You have an entire department, resources, procedures."

"Who aren't seeing what I'm seeing." The fire popped, sending sparks up the chimney like tiny emergency flares. "They're treating this like a normal serial case. But it's not. It's a thesis defense written in blood."

Outside, branches scraped against the windows with the insistence of something trying to get in. The temperature was dropping with the sun, frost forming its own patterns on the glass. Nature's geometry mocking human attempts at order.

"Every victim, every scene," Maja continued, her voice dropping to professorial tones. "It's all so precise, so academic. Like we're all just participants in Erik's grand experiment. And now with Nielsen pulling strings from his ivory tower..."

The silence that followed had weight, substance. The kind of silence that existed between siblings who'd shared too much history to need words for certain truths.

"I need to end this," Maja repeated.

Daniel watched her with careful attention. "Then maybe that's what you need perspective on. Not the case itself, but Erik as a person. What transforms someone from researcher to killer? What makes theory insufficient?"

"It's like..." Maja stared into her kaffe as if it might reveal patterns more useful than tea leaves. "Like I'm peer-reviewing the same paper over and over, but missing the fundamental flaw in its hypothesis."

Daniel had seen her push too far before. During university exams, her first year as a Kriminalinspektör, the case that had nearly ended her career before it began. Always trying to solve the world single-handedly, as if dedication could substitute for human limitation.

"And Paul?" The question landed softly but precisely. "Is he helping you carry this?"

Maja's hands performed a small symphony of tension around

her mug. "Paul thinks I'm obsessed. Says I can't see anything beyond Erik's patterns anymore. That I'm disappearing into the case."

"And?" Daniel pressed with gentle ruthlessness.

"And he's probably conducting his own parallel study on relationship dissolution." The admission stung with truth. "But I can't just switch it off. Not when I know Erik's out there."

"You know what genuinely concerns me?" Daniel said after a pause that felt calculated. "How much you're beginning to mirror Erik's behavior."

Her head snapped up. "Excuse me?"

"The obsession with patterns. The systematic isolation. Living inside the case like it's your own research project." Daniel's voice carried the Swedish mixture of concern and matter-of-factness that made emotional truths sound like weather reports. "You're starting to embody his methodology, Maja. Maybe that's what Paul sees. You becoming your own test subject."

The mug met the table with more force than intended. "That's not... Erik kills people. I'm trying to save them."

"By isolating yourself? Obsessing over every detail? Pushing away anyone who tries to help?" Daniel's eyebrows performed their own subtle critique. "You're both looking for patterns, both creating controlled environments. The only difference is your intended outcome."

"I'm nothing like him." But even as she spoke, Maja felt the uncomfortable resonance of truth. When had she last thought about anything except Erik's methodology? When had she last had a conversation that didn't circle back to the case?

"You used to paint," Daniel said, shifting tactics with the smoothness of someone who'd learned psychology from life rather than textbooks. "Remember? Those oil paintings of the archipelago. You'd spend hours capturing the way light hit water."

The memory arrived uninvited, carrying the smell of turpentine and the feel of brush on paper. She'd packed away her art supplies when she made Kriminalinspektör, telling herself it was temporary. Just like everything else she'd deferred for the job.

"Erik's whole dissertation is about dependency," Daniel continued, warming to his theme. "About control through isolation. Maybe that's what the case is doing to you. Creating its own dependency pattern."

"Paul mentioned you haven't been home in five days. That you're living out of your office, surrounded by crime scene photos like some kind of macabre wallpaper."

The familiar defensiveness flared, then died. They didn't understand. Every hour away from the case was another hour Erik had to plan. Another hour someone's life ticked toward its theoretical conclusion.

But wasn't that exactly Daniel's point? The case consuming her with the same methodical precision Erik applied to his victims.

She studied her hands as if they belonged to someone else. "I keep telling myself it's temporary. That once we catch Erik..."

"And then what? The next case? The next killer?" Daniel's voice carried years of watching her repeat patterns. The parallel hit with uncomfortable precision. She'd memorized those passages, seen how his subjects became trapped in cycles they couldn't break. The bitter irony of understanding the trap while walking into it.

"Look at what isolation did to Erik's test subjects," Daniel pressed. "What it's doing to his victims. To him. To you."

The litany felt like evidence in a case against herself. Two months of declined dinner invitations. Unreturned calls. The growing silence between her and Paul measured in unread messages and empty spaces in their bed. All sacrificed to the pursuit of patterns that kept shifting like smoke.

"Christ," Maja muttered. "I'm becoming my own case study."

"The thing that terrifies me most," she continued, "isn't Erik. It's that I understand his methodology. How isolation becomes a form of control. Over yourself, over others. How it feels like clarity when it's really just another kind of blindness."

"But here's what Erik missed," Daniel said. "You have something he doesn't. People who won't let you disappear completely. Even when you're trying your hardest to vanish into the case."

The fire had died to embers while they talked, casting shifting shadows that looked nothing like crime scene evidence. Outside, Vaxholm continued its eternal Swedish existence. Peaceful, ordered, utterly removed from the darkness she carried.

"I should call Paul," she said finally.

Daniel's hand covered hers with familiar warmth. "Start there. The case matters, Maja. But so do you. And maybe seeing the whole picture means stepping back from the microscope sometimes."

She'd lost track of where kriminalinspektör Norberg ended and Maja began. Just like Erik had lost track of where research ended and murder began. The parallels were becoming their own pattern, recursive and inescapable.

"I'll call him tonight," she promised. Then, softer: "Before I lose myself in the patterns again."

Daniel squeezed her hand with the particular comfort of shared DNA and childhood memories. "Good. Because I think understanding Erik's isolation might be the key to catching him. But living it? That's just another way of letting him win."

Dusk had painted Vaxholm in shades of Swedish melancholy by the time Maja left Daniel's house. The air carried that crystalline edge that preceded snow, each breath a small violence against the lungs. Frost glittered on grass like evidence of nature's crimes against warmth.

Her phone felt heavier than its actual weight. Modern technology's gift for making emotional burdens physically manifest. Paul's contact information waited behind glass and pixels, a few taps away from potential reconciliation or final confirmation of what they both probably already knew.

But something else nagged at her consciousness. Something Daniel had said about patterns and isolation, about understanding Erik's methodology by recognizing it in herself. The therapeutic insight felt too neat, too convenient, like a resolution forced by narrative convention rather than psychological truth.

Maybe that was the key she'd been missing. Not external evidence but internal recognition. Not the pattern itself but the human need to create patterns, to impose meaning on chaos even when meaning was just another form of denial.

She walked down Eriksövägen to the water's edge, past the ICA and the old Hembygdsgård. Across the dark expanse, Stockholm glimmered like a circuit board—all those lives connected by T-Bana lines, each one a potential data point in someone's grand theory.

The wooden pier protested her weight with creaks that sounded almost conversational. She'd stood here as a child, counting ferries and making up stories about their passengers. Now she stood here as an investigator, seeing patterns in everything, unable to turn off the analytical machinery even when it was grinding her down.

The parallel was becoming unavoidable. She'd been following Erik's methodology without realizing it, creating her own controlled experiment in isolation. The Kriminalinspektör becoming the detected, the observer becoming the observed. There was probably a Swedish word for it—the language had a gift for compound terms that captured life's precise ironies.

Her phone buzzed with Sven's message about new case files—urgent, as everything was these days. Below it, Paul's name attached to a message from three days ago, still unread. The two notifications seemed to represent her diverging lives: the case that consumed her and the connections she'd let atrophy.

24

LOST

The dull hum of fluorescent lights mingled with the soft patter of sleet against the windows of Polishuset. Maja's eyes burned from hours of staring at screens, each new document about Nielsen adding another piece to a puzzle she wasn't sure she wanted to complete.

The man's academic record was impeccable—too impeccable, really. Every paper published at just the right time, every career move calculated with precision.

Either extraordinary insight or advanced knowledge of the maze.

Outside, the bare branches of birch trees lining Kungsholms- gatan swayed in the biting November wind. Kriminalinspektör Almqvist sat beside her in the cramped conference room, her own stack of files spread across the table between them.

Maja watched another file load, her mind drifting back to her interview with Nielsen in his meticulously organized office. Every- thing about him had been precisely calibrated—his responses, his body language, even the carefully casual way he'd arranged his books.

"There's something about Nielsen that doesn't sit right," she said, glancing at Almqvist. "His clinical detachment, the way he dodged questions—it's like watching someone perform the role of a prestigious professor rather than actually being one."

Almqvist nodded, her silver hair catching the harsh fluorescent light. "I agree. His responses in the interview transcripts read like someone who's thought through every possible question. Too perfect."

In Maja's experience, perfection was the quality that should make you most suspicious.

Maja sipped her now lukewarm kaffe, grimacing at the bitter taste. Through the window, she watched the sleet turn to wet snow, blanketing the parked police vehicles in the lot below. The sodium streetlights along Kungsholmsgatan cast an eerie orange glow through the thickening flurries.

The case was spinning out of control, with Erik Thoressen growing bolder with each murder. The deeper they dug into Erik's twisted psychology, the more it felt that Dr. Nielsen was somehow pulling the strings.

"Fan ta dig, Nielsen," Maja muttered under her breath. There had to be something. Some hidden link between Erik and Nielsen that went beyond academic mentorship.

Authority made the perfect camouflage.

Her phone buzzed. Sven.

"Put him on speaker," Almqvist said, shoving aside a stack of files and leaning forward.

"What do you have for us?" Maja asked.

"You're both going to want to see this," Sven replied. "I've been digging into Nielsen's personal life like you asked, and... well, there's something odd. He has a son. A son who's been hospitalized for years."

The words hit Maja like a physical blow. She'd been expecting something in Nielsen's past, but this—this was different. Personal. Family.

"A son?" Almqvist asked.

"Yeah. Tor Nielsen. He had a mental breakdown back in 2015. There's not much public information—Nielsen's kept it under wraps. But I found a record from a psychiatric hospital in Stockholm. Tor's been a patient there ever since the incident."

Maja's mind raced through the implications. A son in a psychiatric hospital, hidden away from public view.

"And the mother?" Almqvist pulled out her notebook.

"That's where it gets stranger," Sven continued. "Nielsen's wife, Anna, disappeared from the public eye around the same time as Tor's breakdown. From what I can tell, they're still technically married, but she's been living separately in a small town up north. No official divorce, but definitely estranged."

Maja felt a cold knot form in her stomach, memories of her own family's carefully hidden secrets surfacing unbidden. Every family had its shadows, but Nielsen's cast longer and darker than most.

She moved to the window, watching as the wet snow accumulated on the sill.

"What happened to Tor in 2015?" she asked.

"Records are sealed. I can't get specifics without a court order, but from what little I've pieced together, it seems like Tor had some kind of psychological break during university. He was studying psychology, following his father's footsteps, but something went wrong."

"I can expedite that court order," Almqvist said, reaching for her phone. "Rikskrim has some pull with the medical records department."

Maja turned back from the window, her mind racing through the implications. The pattern was becoming clear, and it chilled her more than the November wind.

"Both Tor and Erik were psychology students. Both connected to Nielsen. Both brilliant minds shaped by his influence." She paused. "He's not just teaching them—he's conducting his own longitudinal study, using his students as subjects. His own son was just the first experiment."

"Sven," she continued, her voice sharp with urgency. "Dig deeper into 2015. I want everything—university records, medical files, anything you can find. Almqvist will get you the clearance you need."

After they hung up, Almqvist stood, moving to the evidence board. "This changes the profile completely. If Nielsen has a history of manipulating students, pushing them to break..." She trailed off, studying the crime scene photos with fresh eyes.

"He's not just Erik's mentor," Maja finished. "He's been perfecting his methodology for years, starting with his own son."

Through the window, they could see the lights of passing cars on Kungsholmsgatan, their headlights diffused by the thickening snow-fall. The case was expanding, revealing darker depths than either of them had imagined.

Maja thought of Nielsen's son, locked away in some sterile hospital room.

"What are you hiding, Dr. Nielsen?" she murmured, catching Almqvist's reflection in the dark window. The older Kriminalinspek-tör's expression was grim, matching her own growing certainty that they were dealing with something far more sinister than a single killer's obsession.

Behind them, the evidence board loomed in silence, its photos and documents telling only part of a story that had begun long before Erik Thoressen had claimed his first victim.

Investigation was archaeology in reverse—digging backward from visible consequences toward buried origins, never certain you'd found the source.

Outside, the snow fell with increasing determination.

"Let's start with the hospital records," Almqvist said, settling into the chair beside Maja. They had moved from the conference room to Maja's office after the call with Sven. The fluorescent lights hummed overhead, a mechanical counterpoint to the silence of concentration.

"Odd," Maja mused, pulling up Tor Nielsen's hospital records, "how madness becomes a series of checkboxes. Admitted, medicated, discharged. As if tragedy follows forms."

The records were sparse—just admission dates and general status updates, clinical words that failed to capture whatever darkness had descended upon Nielsen's son.

Almqvist nodded, making notes in her precise handwriting. "Sometimes what's missing tells us more than what's present," she observed. "Nielsen went to considerable effort to keep this quiet."

Outside, a gust of wind rattled the old single-pane windows of Polishuset, the building creaking like an old Kriminalinspektör's joints. The view across Kungsholmen showed the first Christmas lights appearing in apartment windows, each one a small act of defiance against the approaching darkness.

Maja pulled her cardigan tighter, grateful for the ancient radiator beneath the window.

"A mental breakdown during a research project," Almqvist said, studying her own screen. "And now, years later, Erik Thoressen is carrying out murders that seem almost... clinical."

"Like experiments," Maja finished. "Academia—where you can torture people and call it research."

She leaned forward, typing rapidly as she searched for mentions of Tor in academic papers. A few clicks brought up an old student directory from 2015, listing Tor Nielsen as a postgraduate student in psychology.

"Here," Almqvist said, turning her laptop. "A research grant proposal from 2014. Dr. Nielsen's study on emotional dependency and control. Tor was listed as lead researcher."

They read through the document together, Maja's fingers tightening on the edge of her desk until her knuckles whitened. The buzzing light overhead grew more insistent.

"Fan," Maja muttered. "How many committees approved this? How many eyes read this and saw only 'science'?"

The proposal detailed a study exploring psychological mechanisms behind emotional dependency—how power dynamics influenced attachment, and how those dynamics could be manipulated. Each paragraph felt more sinister than the last, academic jargon barely masking the disturbing implications.

"The word choice is interesting," Almqvist noted, her professional demeanor a thin veil over what must have been revulsion. "'Manipulation of attachment bonds.' 'Controlled dissolution of autonomy.'"

"A manual," Maja finished. "For breaking people systematically. Universities—they'd fund anything if you use enough footnotes."

Almqvist nodded grimly. "And Tor was involved in this research before his breakdown. The timing can't be coincidence. Father designs the experiment, son becomes the subject, student carries out the results." She let the thought hang unfinished.

"What about the mother?" Maja asked, turning back to her screen. "Anna Nielsen."

Almqvist was already typing. "Disappeared from public life around the same time as Tor's breakdown. From faculty wife to ghost—that's quite a career change." She paused, reading. "Wait. Here's something. Local news from 2016—she filed a restraining order against Nielsen."

"Herregud," Maja muttered. "So she didn't just leave. She fled. Smart woman—some people you can only study from a distance." She thought of all the victims who hadn't fled in time, their faces a gallery in her memory.

"And took legal precautions to keep Nielsen away," Almqvist added, her usually steady voice carrying an edge Maja rarely heard. "That suggests she knew something. Something that made her fear him enough to abandon her entire life."

Maja's phone buzzed. A message from Sven: "Found Anna Nielsen's current location. Small village in Hälsingland. Very remote. She's been living under her maiden name."

"Smart," Maja murmured. "Hide in the forest where academics never go—too far from the nearest kaffe shop."

Almqvist leaned back, contemplative. "So we have a son who

breaks down during his father's research project, a wife who flees and legally protects herself, and now a doctoral student recreating Nielsen's theories through murder."

"A family business," Maja replied. "With very specialized services."

"We need to understand what Nielsen did to him," Maja said. "Tor might be the key to predicting Erik's next move. If we can see the pattern Nielsen established..."

Almqvist was already reaching for her phone. "I'll call the hospital. We need access to Tor's records—all of them."

"Agreed." She reached for her coat. "I'll call ahead to the hospital. Rikskrim clearance should get us access despite the sealed records."

As they gathered their things, Maja felt a familiar tension creeping up her shoulders and settling at the base of her neck.

"Ready?" Maja asked, her partner's hand on the door.

Almqvist nodded, shrugging on her wool coat. "Let's find out what Nielsen did to his son."

They stepped out into the bitter evening, snow beginning to fall again. The parking lot of Polishuset was already dusted white, and Maja's Mercedes would need scraping again. Somewhere in a psychiatric hospital, Tor Nielsen held answers they desperately needed.

"At least the car will be warm," Almqvist said, fishing for her keys. "Small mercies."

"In this job," Maja replied, brushing snow from her windshield, "you take what you can get."

25

TOR

The Värmdöleden highway cut through the stark November landscape of Stockholm's eastern suburbs. Bare birch trees lined the road, their skeletal branches reaching into a leaden sky. Maja's hands tightened on the steering wheel as she passed the exit for Gustafsberg. She wondered, not for the first time, how many troubled souls had traveled this same route, carrying their fractured minds to the sanctuary—or prison—that awaited at the end of this road.

Beside her, Almqvist reviewed Tor's files on her tablet, the blue light casting her face in an artificial glow.

"His admission records show a pattern," Almqvist said, breaking the tense silence. "Episodes triggered by any mention of his father's research. Dr. Forsberg notes he becomes particularly agitated when discussing psychological control studies." She paused, looking up from the screen. "Funny how we build entire institutions to contain the damage caused by the very systems we create to understand ourselves."

Maja nodded, appreciating Almqvist's typically philosophical observation. "The psychiatrists study the minds they've helped break. The circle of academic life."

The narrow road to Sankt Eriks Psykiatriska Sjukhuset wound through Ingarö's dense pine forests, the evergreens providing the only splash of color in the monochrome landscape. A biting wind whipped through the trees, carrying with it the crisp scent of impending winter.

"What do you make of the timing?" Maja asked, glancing at Almqvist. "His breakdown coincides with his father's major research grant."

"And with Erik joining the department," Almqvist added, scrolling through her notes. "Three psychology students under Nielsen that year—Tor, Erik, and another who transferred out mid-semester. No record of why." She set the tablet down on her lap. "The bureaucracy's remarkable ability to document everything except what matters most never ceases to amaze me."

They sat in silence for a moment, watching the pines slip by.

The hospital complex emerged from the pines, a collection of austere 1930s buildings. The institutional architecture spread across the grounds in long, gothic wings, their small windows reflecting the gray day.

"The architects were optimists," Almqvist observed dryly as they approached. "They designed it to look exactly like what it is. No pretense. There's a certain honesty in that gothicism."

Maja parked near the entrance, where Dr. Forsberg waited for them, a tall woman with steel-gray hair pulled back in a severe bun. Her white coat was bright against the building's facade, and behind wire-rimmed glasses, her eyes carried practiced caution.

"Kriminalinspektör Norberg, Kriminalinspektör Almqvist," Forsberg greeted them, her expression carefully neutral. "Tor's having a relatively good day, but I should warn you, he's very sensitive to certain topics. Particularly his father's work."

"We understand," Almqvist replied, showing her Rikskrim credentials. "We'll follow your lead."

The hospital corridors were eerily quiet as they walked, their footsteps muffled by thin carpeting. The air carried institutional mix of disinfectant and forced air, and the fluorescent lights buzzed softly overhead. They stopped outside Room 223, where Forsberg turned to face them.

"One thing," she said. "Tor sometimes... fixates on certain ideas. Particularly about control and manipulation. It's hard to tell whether these are delusions or actual memories."

Maja and Almqvist exchanged glances, a chill running down Maja's spine. Given what they knew about Nielsen's research, the line between delusion and reality might be blurrier than anyone had realized. She flexed her fingers, trying to shake off the growing sense of unease.

"In my experience," Almqvist said, "the most troubling delusions often contain seeds of uncomfortable truths. The mind doesn't invent suffering so much as it reinterprets it."

Inside, Tor Nielsen sat by the window, his gaunt frame silhouetted against the falling snow outside. He looked older than his years, his once-sharp features worn by time and trauma. His hands gripped the armrests of his chair, knuckles white with tension.

"Tor," Forsberg said. "These Kriminalinspektörs would like to ask you about your father's research. Would that be alright?"

Tor's gaze flickered between them, settling briefly on Almqvist's Rikskrim badge before darting away. "You're investigating him?" His voice was barely above a whisper.

"We're investigating someone who worked with him," Maja said. "Erik Thoressen. Do you remember him?"

The change was immediate. Tor's breathing quickened, his fingers tightening on the armrests. "Erik," he whispered. "He was... he was supposed to help me stop it."

Almqvist stepped forward, her voice calm and clinical. "Stop what exactly, Tor? What was happening in your father's department?"

"The experiments," Tor said, his hands trembling slightly. "Erik understood at first. He saw what father was..." He trailed off, staring at the falling snow. "After hours. When the building was empty. Testing."

"To the students?" Maja pressed gently.

Tor's breathing became shallow. "We were part of it. The dependency studies." His voice cracked. "Erik was supposed to help me expose it, but instead..."

"Instead what?" Almqvist asked, her tone remaining steady.

"He became fascinated." Tor's gaze fixed on something beyond the window. "Started seeing what father saw. The way people could be... adjusted. Until they weren't people anymore."

Maja exchanged a quick glance with Almqvist before asking, "What happened in 2015, Tor? During the research project?"

Tor's head snapped up, his eyes suddenly sharp with fear. "Father needed proof. Said theoretical work wasn't enough anymore." His breathing became more erratic. "Erik and I... we were supposed to be the control group, but then Erik started helping him instead." He rocked slightly in his chair. "They wanted to see how far... how much someone could take before..."

"Before what?" Maja leaned forward, but Tor was already retreating into himself.

"Runa," he mumbled, his voice dropping to a haunted whisper. "She threatened to report them. Said what they were doing..." He shook his head. "But I couldn't leave. Erik wouldn't let me. Said we had to see it through."

Dr. Forsberg stepped forward. "I think that's enough for today. He's getting too agitated."

As they left the room, Tor's voice followed them, barely audible: "He won't stop until he proves father right. Until he finishes what we started."

In the hallway, Maja and Almqvist stood silent for a moment, processing what they'd heard. The snow fell heavier outside, muffling the world beyond the hospital walls.

Almqvist stared at the institutional green walls, her voice quiet in the empty corridor. "We build places like this to contain what we can't face about ourselves. Then we staff them with people who find academic justification for what they were going to do anyway."

Maja nodded grimly. "The difference between a psychologist and a psychopath sometimes comes down to institutional approval and a good grant proposal."

Almqvist pulled out her notebook, flipping to her earlier notes. "Three students under Nielsen in 2015: Tor, Erik, and this Runa student who 'got out.' That's our next lead."

"If she threatened to report them," Maja said, "she might be our only chance to understand what Erik's really trying to prove." She paused, watching the snow accumulate on the window. "These murders aren't random, they're his attempt to finish what Nielsen started."

They walked back through the quiet corridors, their footsteps echoing softly.

"I'll have Rikskrim pull the university records from 2015," Almqvist said as they reached the car. "A sudden transfer during a research project would have triggered reviews, explanations. The ethics committee would have been involved."

"Especially with Nielsen on the committee," Maja added, brushing snow from her coat. "He would have had to recuse himself. There'll be a paper trail."

"And we need to move fast," Almqvist said, her breath visible in the cold air. "If Erik's trying to finish what Nielsen started..."

They drove back toward Stockholm in tense silence, the windshield wipers marking time against the falling snow.

"People rarely recognize themselves in the mirror of their actions," Almqvist replied, watching the city lights blur through the snow-covered windshield. "Especially those who spend their careers explaining away the behavior of others."

26

NIELSEN

The snow was falling harder as Maja and Almqvist pulled into Kungsmedicinska Institutet's parking lot. Along Roslagsvägen, headlights reflected off the slick asphalt, cutting through the early evening gloom. The concrete mass of the Psykologiska Institutionen loomed before them, its windows glowing with artificial light. Inside one of those offices, Gustaf Nielsen was waiting. He was probably already anticipating their visit after what they'd learned from Tor.

Maja stared at the building for a long moment, watching students hurry past with their bright Fjällräven backpacks and take-away kaffe from Espresso House. Universities were like police stations—both places where people worked very hard to avoid telling the truth.

"He'll try to control the conversation," Almqvist said as they crossed the parking lot, her boots crunching in the fresh snow. "That's his methodology. Shape the narrative, maintain academic distance."

Maja nodded, thinking of Tor's broken testimony, of Anna's fear. "Nej då. Not this fucking time."

Nielsen's office door looked the same as always. Polished wood, brass nameplate catching the fluorescent light. But now Maja knew what was behind it. A man who'd broken his own son to prove a point.

Almqvist knocked, her sharp rap echoing down the empty corridor. A moment passed, then Nielsen's measured voice: "Come in."

He was standing behind his desk when they entered, backlit by the snow-filled window, his silver hair catching the last light of the fading day. His eyes moved between the two kriminalinspektörs, settling on the unfamiliar face.

"Kriminalinspektör Norberg." His tone was perfectly calibrated. Professional interest with just a hint of concern. His gaze remained on Almqvist, waiting for an introduction.

""Kriminalinspektör Almqvist, Rikskrim," Almqvist said, showing her credentials. "I'm assisting in the investigation into the murders of several couples."

Something subtle shifted in Nielsen's posture—a tightening around the eyes, a slight straightening of his spine. Like watching a snake coil before striking, Maja thought. Or perhaps more accurately, like watching a professor realize his lecture had been interrupted by someone who'd actually done the reading.

"Rikskrim? I wasn't aware the case had escalated to that level. Please, how can I help?" His voice carried the tone of academic helpfulness that somehow always managed to suggest superiority.

"Tor Nielsen," Maja said, remaining standing as Almqvist closed the door behind them.

The name hung in the air. Nielsen's hands moved to arrange papers on his desk—a gesture Maja now recognized as one of his tells. "My son's condition is a private matter."

"Not anymore," Almqvist said, her clinical tone a perfect match for Nielsen's academic distance. "Not when his breakdown is directly connected to Erik Thoressen, who we believe is a credible suspect in these murders."

Nielsen's smile was thin. "I fail to see the connection between my son's unfortunate mental health issues and your investigation."

Almqvist glanced around the office—the certificates, the leather-bound journals, the careful arrangement of authority. "Unfortunate issues," she repeated flatly. "That's what we call it when a father breaks his own son." She looked back at Nielsen. "Very professional."

Nielsen's eyes narrowed slightly. A small victory, Maja thought. The first crack in the polished veneer.

"The 2015 experiments," Maja cut in. "The one where you used your own son as a test subject. The one where Erik was supposed to stop if things went too far." She watched Nielsen's face carefully. "But he didn't stop, did he? He watched. He learned. Just like you wanted him to."

Nielsen's hands stilled on his papers. For a moment, the only sound was the soft whir of his computer's fan. When he looked up, his eyes had changed—sharper now, more focused. The academic facade was slipping, revealing something colder beneath, like permafrost emerging as spring thaw strips away softer ground.

"You've been speaking with Tor," he said, his voice carrying a new edge. "I wouldn't put too much stock in his... recollections. His condition makes him an unreliable witness."

"His condition is precisely what we're interested in," Almqvist said. "Along with the experiment that caused it. The one that Erik was supposed to monitor."

A quick blink and tightening jaw betrayed his composure. "You're making assumptions about complex psychological research that you don't fully understand."

Maja watched him with the detached curiosity of someone observing a specimen under glass. There was something almost fascinating about the way he maintained his professional demeanor while everything beneath it shifted and contorted. Like those nature documentaries where the narrator calmly describes a predator's hunting behavior while something dies on screen.

"It's curious," she said, "how often 'complex' is used as a shield against 'unethical.' As if understanding the intricate mechanics of harm somehow justifies inflicting it." She paused. "You know what my farfar used to say? 'En idiot med utbildning är fortfarande en idiot.' An idiot with education is still an idiot." She studied Nielsen's face. "He was a dock worker in Göteborg. Never went to university, but he could spot bullshit from a kilometer away."

Nielsen leaned back in his chair, a calculated movement that Maja recognized as him reasserting control. "The university ethics committee approved all my research protocols. Everything was properly documented."

"Including the experiment that broke your son?" Maja pressed. "The one where Erik was meant to monitor Tor's responses?"

"You're oversimplifying complex psychological research," Nielsen said, his voice taking on a lecturing tone. "Erik was a promising student who understood the importance of proper methodology. The fact that some subjects prove... unsuitable... is simply part of the scientific process."

"The scientific process," Almqvist echoed, her voice carrying just a hint of dark amusement. "A wonderfully abstract term for what is often just the systematic infliction of distress in the name of knowledge. Would you say your son was a successful experiment, Professor, or merely an instructive failure? I assume there's a proper academic classification for destroying one's own child."

"And now people are dying," Maja added, her voice quiet but firm. "Tell us about Erik's role in these experiments, Professor. What exactly was he meant to monitor?"

Nielsen's smile was pure academia, but his eyes had gone cold. "I'm afraid I can't help you with your investigation, Kriminalinspektör. But if you're interested in my published research, I'd be happy to provide citations."

Almqvist made a sound that might have been laughter. "Of course. When cornered, academics always want to assign homework." She shook her head. "At least criminals are honest about being dishonest."

27
RUNA

Back at Polishuset, Maja stared at the ethics committee website.

"Got something," Almqvist said from her desk. She'd been working her Rikskrim connections for an hour. "Transfer records from 2015. Three students left Nielsen's research group that year: Tor Nielsen, Erik Thorssen, and..." She paused. "Runa Törnblom. Complete withdrawal, mid-semester."

The third student. Someone who might actually know what happened to Tor.

"There's more," Almqvist continued. "After Runa left, Nielsen filed a complaint about her mental stability. Called her accusations 'delusional.' But she didn't disappear—she transferred to Uppsala University."

"Where is she now?"

"Publishing papers on research ethics. Particularly experiments involving student subjects." Almqvist pulled up another document. "But here's the interesting part. Runa's emergency contact:" She turned her screen toward Maja. "Anna Nielsen."

Nielsen's wife. The one person who might have seen everything.

"How far is Anna away from Stockholm?"

"Three hours. Säljemar." Almqvist was already shutting down her computer. "We'll need to take back roads—storm's coming in."

They drove north through thickening snow, Stockholm's familiar rhythms fading behind them. The landscape changed gradually— buildings giving way to forests, highways narrowing to rural roads. Another Swedish winter asserting its dominance over human ambition.

"What makes someone disappear like this?" Almqvist asked, studying the transfer records on her tablet.

"Fear," Maja said simply. "Or protection. Sometimes both."

———

Three hours later, they found themselves on a single-lane road winding through pine forests. The village of Säljemar appeared through the swirling snow like something from a fairy tale—if fairy tales included rusted ICA signs and sagging rooflines.

The address led them to a small wooden house at the road's end, pressed against the forest like it was trying to escape notice. Dark siding, thick icicles, smoke rising from the chimney. Everything about it spoke of deliberate isolation.

"Let me lead," Almqvist said quietly as they approached. "She might be more willing to talk to someone with no connection to Nielsen."

The path to the door was treacherous with fresh snow hiding ice beneath. Almqvist's knock echoed through the winter silence, sharp and intrusive.

The door opened just enough to reveal Anna Nielsen's face— silver-streaked hair, features carved by more than just time. Her eyes moved between them with the assessment of prey analyzing predators.

"Who are you?" Her voice was steady despite the slight tremor in her hand on the doorframe.

"Detective Almqvist, Rikskrim." Almqvist kept her distance. "Detective Norberg, Stockholmspolisen."

"Prove it." Anna's gaze hardened. "Both of you."

As they showed their badges, Maja noticed Anna's eyes checking their hands, their shoulders. When her gaze settled on Almqvist's Rikskrim credentials, something shifted in her expression.

"I wondered when someone would finally come," she said quietly, then caught herself. Her gaze darted past them to the road. "Gustaf prefers to pretend I don't exist. Easier that way." She studied their faces. "Why now? After all this time?"

"We're investigating incidents in Stockholm," Almqvist said carefully. "We found transfer records from 2015. Runa Törnblom's name came up. Along with yours, as her emergency contact."

Anna's hand tightened on the doorframe, color draining from her face. But beneath the fear, something flickered—a desperate sort of hope.

She glanced over their shoulders one final time, scanning the darkness beyond their car. "Come inside," she said, stepping back. Her voice dropped to barely above a whisper. "These aren't conversations for doorways."

28

SÄLJEMAR

Inside, warmth and the scent of burning wood wrapped around them, a stark contrast to the biting cold they'd left behind. Anna moved through her practiced routine of securing the door, checking the locks, before leading them into the living room. The space spoke volumes in what it lacked—no photographs on the walls, no academic certificates, nothing to suggest any connection to Gustaf Nielsen or his work. Instead, worn furniture and shelves of fiction lined the walls, carefully curated to erase any trace of psychology or academia.

"The negative space of a life," Almqvist observed quietly, her gaze taking in the conspicuous absences. "Defined by what's been removed rather than what remains."

"Please," Anna gestured to the chairs by the fire, positioning herself with her back to the window. She settled into her own seat with careful precision. When she looked up, Maja saw Nielsen's intelligence there, but without the cruelty.

The silence stretched between them. Maja found herself thinking about the strange ways knowledge could be imprisoned—not just in institutions or books, but in people who carried truths too dangerous to share.

"If you're looking into Gustaf's old research group," Anna said quietly, "you must have seen Tor. When you saw him... was he..."

"He's still at Sankt Eriks's," Maja said gently, watching Anna's reaction. "Still trapped in whatever happened that day."

Anna's face went pale. "And Erik?" The name seemed to catch in her throat. "He was there too, that day. With Gustaf." She looked between them, searching their faces. "Is that why you're here? Has something happened?"

Almqvist and Maja exchanged a glance. It was Almqvist who answered, her clinical tone measured and careful. "We're investigating a series of incidents in Stockholm. Some aspects... remind us of your husband's research methods."

"Gustaf's research?" Anna's voice had gone hollow. "The dependency studies?"

"Yes," Maja said quietly, watching Anna's face. "The ones involving attachment theory and psychological control."

Anna's hands stilled in her lap. "The adhesive trials," she whispered. "Gustaf called them preliminary studies for the ethics committee. But Runa found his private protocols."

"Runa?" Maja asked, her voice steady.

"Runa Törnblom," Anna said, a new tension entering her voice. "She was the most meticulous of Gustaf's graduate students. Worked alongside Erik and Tor, documenting everything."

"Everything?" Maja pressed, watching Anna's face carefully.

What kind of notes?" Maja asked, her voice steady.

Anna stared past them toward the window. "He'd been conducting trials after hours, testing theories about breaking down resistance through enforced proximity. The adhesive was just part of it. When Erik joined the program, he became... fascinated. Started suggesting refinements to the methodology. Ways to make the bonds permanent."

"The student surpassing the master," Almqvist observed quietly. "A perversion of the educational ideal."

Anna moved to the bookshelf near the fireplace, her fingers tracing along the spines until she found what she was looking for—a battered psychology textbook. "Runa Törnblom left this. Said if the right people ever came asking..." She pulled something from between its pages: a small USB drive.

"Everything's here," Anna said, pressing the drive into Maja's palm. "The night Runa finally understood what they were planning —she'd been working late, came back to the lab for her phone. Found Erik and Gustaf testing the compounds on..." She stopped, her voice catching. "On tissue samples. Human tissue samples."

"Erik's suggestions terrified her most," Anna continued. "The modifications he wanted to make. Ways to extend the experiments. Make them more extreme." She turned away from them. "By the time I understood what was really happening with Tor, it was too late. Gustaf had documented everything, made it all look legitimate. When I tried to stop it..." She stopped herself. "He said he'd have me committed. Called me 'emotionally unstable.' Said no one would believe me over a respected professor."

"Runa understood she couldn't trust the regular channels," Anna continued, her voice steady now. "Gustaf had connections every-where—university board, ethics committee, even some people in Polismyndigheten. The first journalist she contacted turned out to be an old colleague of Gustaf's. She knew she had to disappear completely. But she also knew that eventually, someone would need that evidence."

"And now someone does," Maja said quietly.

29
DRIVING

Chapter 28 - Driving

Neither spoke as they made their way back to the car, snow already filling their footprints. Maja's fingers were tight around the USB drive in her pocket, its edges pressing into her palm. She thought about how evidence had changed over the decades—once confined to physical objects, now reduced to microscopic patterns on silicon.

Back on the main road, Säljemar disappearing behind them, Almqvist finally broke the silence.

"What do you make of her story?"

Maja kept her eyes on the road, watching the snow spiral in her headlights. The flakes rushed toward the windshield like stars in a primitive space simulation.

"She's telling the truth. About Nielsen, about the experiments. About Erik."

"Yes." Almqvist's tone had an edge now. "But there's something she's still holding back. Did you notice how she avoided talking about the actual day Tor broke down? She knows more about what happened in that lab."

"She's protecting herself," Maja said. "Or maybe protecting Tor. Some memories you wall off just to survive." She thought of Anna's carefully curated house, stripped of any trace of her old life. "The question is, what else did Erik learn from Nielsen besides the methodology?"

"The art of making people disappear," Almqvist said quietly. "Turning murder into accidents. The most effective control isn't force—it's manipulation of perception."

"Academia's gift to the world," Maja said, watching ice crystals form patterns on the windshield. "Reframing reality until truth becomes subjective interpretation. Like these snowflakes—unique until they melt into sameness."

"We need to get to Runa before—"

The phone's buzz cut through her words—a sound that always reminded her of her father's old Ericsson, back when phones stayed tethered to walls and conversations couldn't chase you into cars on dark highways.

Sven's name on the display. She ignored it.

The windshield wipers marked time in the growing darkness. The drive gave them space to process what Anna had revealed—the methodical horror of Nielsen's experiments, Erik's eager participation, and somewhere in the USB drive's memory, proof of it all.

Maja's phone rang. Sven's name on the display again.

"Where are you?" His voice carried the familiar mix of concern and exasperation. "Söderberg's been asking.

"Heading back from Säljemar with Almqvist." Maja caught the detective kriminalinspektör's glance. They hadn't told anyone about Anna Nielsen yet—not even Sven. Some truths required careful timing.

"We're still three hours out," she said, glancing at the darkening sky. "I'll drop Almqvist at Rikskrim headquarters, then head straight to Polishuset."

"Maja." Sven's voice stopped her. "You're doing it again. The thing where you disappear into the case."

"I'm fine," Maja said, but even she could hear the edge in her voice. The same edge that had been there during the Södertälje case, right before everything fell apart.

"Just... keep me in the loop this time," Sven said quietly. "Whatever you and Almqvist found up there, don't go processing it alone."

The snow was falling heavier now, reducing visibility. Maja thought of what Anna had told them about Runa's evidence, about Nielsen's ways of silencing people. "You know," Almqvist said carefully, "Rikskrim has resources. Witness protection if needed. For Anna. For Runa, when we find her."

Maja's laugh was harsh. "Like the university ethics committee protected Tor? "We should coordinate with local police in Uppsala," Almqvist said, checking something on her phone. "If Runa's been teaching there..."

"You can't do this alone, Maja." Almqvist's voice carried the same concern Maja had heard in Sven's. "That's why Rikskrim assisting in this case."

The words stung more than they should have. Maja stared through the windshield at the snow-swept highway, remembering how the Södertälje case had ended. How she'd tried to handle everything alone then too. But this time was different. This time she knew what they were dealing with.

"I'm not alone," she said finally. "I've got Sven. And you." But even as she said it, she was already planning what she'd do after dropping Almqvist at headquarters.

The snow was falling harder now, forcing her to slow down past Arlanda, visibility shrinking to the reach of her headlights. But somewhere in those cold case files was the pattern they needed. Proof that Nielsen had been conducting his experiments long before Tor, with Erik watching and learning.

. . .

It was past midnight when Maja reached Polishuset. The building stood against the darkness on Kungsholmen, its windows reflecting the sparse city lights along Bergsgatan, the late-night trams still rattling past toward T-Centralen. After dropping Almqvist at Rikskrim headquarters, she'd driven straight to the station. The familiar hum of the nearly empty precinct carried a different weight tonight: the distant ringing of phones, the soft murmur of the night shift, the eternal smell of terrible kaffe from the Norrmalm district's finest vending machine.

Sven looked up as she entered, his desk lamp creating a small island of light in the darkened office.

"You look like hell," he said, which was rich coming from someone who'd clearly been surviving on Pressbyrån sandwiches and spite. A half-eaten semla sat accusingly on his desk, despite it being months past the proper season.

Maja dropped her coat over a chair, snow from the drive north still melting into the standard-issue carpet that had probably witnessed more confessions than most priests. She hadn't told Sven about Anna yet, or what they'd learned regarding Runa's evidence.

"You going to tell me where you disappeared to?" Sven asked, his voice carefully neutral.

"We found Anna Nielsen," she said finally. "Gustaf's wife."

Sven's eyebrows rose. "And?"

"And I think I understand why this case won't let go." Maja swept her hand over the desk, taking in the empty kaffe cups, the silent phone, the evidence of another night lost to obsession. "Nielsen didn't just experiment on strangers. He used his own family. His own son."

She met Sven's gaze. "We found the third student in Uppsala. Runa Törnblom. And Erik's following his mentor's footsteps."

"What's Almqvist's take?"

"Official channels. Uppsala police, surveillance teams." Maja's laugh was bitter. "As if Nielsen's influence doesn't reach into every institution we're supposed to trust."

Through the window, Stockholm's winter dawn crept over Södermalm like an old detective working a cold case—patient, methodical, revealing nothing until every piece aligned. Somewhere between the facts they could prove and the truth they suspected, Erik was continuing his work. The question was whether they'd see the pattern in time.

30
HOME

By the time Almqvist arrived at the station, the morning briefing had devolved into controlled chaos. Word of the cold case connections had spread like Stockholm gossip, and suddenly everyone had theories about Nielsen's methodology. Academic murder apparently inspired academic analysis. Almqvist surveyed the assembled crowd, investigators, analysts, borrowed personnel from other departments, then quietly ordered Maja home.

The drive through Södermalm felt longer than usual, the familiar streets somehow foreign. Maja found herself studying the pedestrians with professional detachment. How many carried secrets that would horrify their neighbors?

She sat in her ancient Mercedes, engine ticking as it cooled. The parking garage felt like a confession booth: enclosed, private, a place for uncomfortable truths. Nielsen's case had taught her something about the observer's paradox: the act of studying something inevitably changed both subject and investigator. She'd spent twenty years hunting killers, and somewhere along the way, she'd started thinking like them.

She tried calling Sven, but it went to voicemail. His recorded voice promised to return her call: mechanical, detached, like Nielsen's academic prose. Everyone hiding behind professional language, institutional distance.

In the parking garage, her footsteps echoed against concrete. Something felt shifted. Not wrong exactly, but rearranged. Like walking into a room where someone had moved a single piece of furniture.

The elevator felt smaller than usual, fluorescent light flickering in an unfamiliar rhythm. She'd been a cop too long to ignore such details, but exhaustion made everything feel slightly surreal. The observer's paradox again: studying her own environment changed how she experienced it.

At her apartment door, she paused. The lock looked normal, the hallway empty, but something nagged at her. A faint smell: cologne, maybe, or cleaning products. Nothing she could identify, just the sense that someone had been here recently.

She almost missed it: her apartment door, slightly ajar. A detail out of place in the ordered world she tried to maintain. The irony was perfect: she'd spent the day studying Nielsen's methodology, and now she was about to become his subject. Academic research had a way of becoming personal. The observer becoming the observed, the hunter becoming the hunted. Some patterns were more circular than linear.

She drew her weapon with practiced ease. The weight of the gun felt solid after hours of abstract theorizing about academic methodology. Strange how physical reality could ground you when intellectual analysis had become too cerebral. She pushed the door open with careful precision. The first thing she noticed was the needle in her neck.

As the sedative took hold, Maja experienced a moment of perfect clarity. They'd been studying Erik's experiments when they should have been studying his teacher. Looking at the events themselves rather than the methodology behind them. Like scientists so focused on data points that they failed to question who designed the experiment. The ultimate academic irony: becoming research subjects in your own investigation.

The room tilted around her, familiar contours dissolving into abstract shapes. Between consciousness and darkness, Maja had one final thought: weren't they all just subjects in someone else's experiment? The observer's paradox made literal. Nielsen had been right about one thing: professional partnerships did make fascinating research subjects. Especially when the subjects were unaware they were being studied

Then darkness claimed her, and even this thought faded into silence.

31
TRAP

The apartment smelled of kaffe grounds and old books—the particular Stockholm scent of a life lived in careful solitude. Maja's head felt filled with cotton, her thoughts moving like honey in winter. Across from her, Sven's eyes tracked the room with professional habit, even as his body remained unnaturally still.

"Ah, you're awake," said Nielsen, arranging instruments on Maja's kitchen table. "I was just explaining to your colleague that you'll both want to remain alert for this."

Erik adjusted something that looked disturbingly like medical equipment. "The compound is derived from an industrial medical adhesives for surgical application," he said, his tone carrying the pride of a student displaying mastery.

Maja tried to speak, managed only a whisper. "Why?"

"Because," Nielsen said, settling into her own armchair with the contentment of a man finally able to demonstrate his life's work, "you represent something unprecedented. The Strandbergs were strong, physically robust enough to test the adhesive's tensile properties, but their mental connection was merely the first phase. Today we complete the circuit."

A flash of clarity cut through the pharmaceutical haze. The Strandbergs their bodies fused together in a grotesque embrace.

"You killed thhhhem," Sven managed, the words slurring together as his tongue fought the chemical restraint.

"Erik did, technically speaking," Nielsen corrected, making a notation in his journal. "Just as he did the Bengtssons and the Lindströms before them. Necessary iterations in the development process."

"Förb... baskad gal... ing," Sven managed. Fucking madman. The Swedish curse fragmented in his mouth, consonants colliding awkwardly against uncooperative lips.

Nielsen smiled. "Language, Inspector. Though I suppose professional vocabulary becomes irrelevant now." He made a note in a leather journal. "Erik, begin with baseline measurements."

The absurdity struck Maja through the chemical haze. Here she was, drugged in her own kitchen on Folkungagatan while the professor they were investigating prepared to make them his next victims. It felt like a particularly dark Astrid Lindgren story. As if Pippi Longstocking had grown up to become a serial killer.

"The timing is perfect," Nielsen continued, checking something on his phone. "Your colleague Nordlund has been calling every thirty minutes since you missed your check-in. She'll escalate to a wellness visit within the hour. That's standard police protocol when detectives investigating serial cases go silent." He'd studied their procedures like a doctoral thesis.

"The previous subjects were merely proof of concept," Nielsen continued conversationally, as Erik attached monitoring devices with clinical precision. "We needed to perfect the adhesive before introducing the neural component. Those earlier pairs, they experienced only physical bonding. But you two..." He consulted his notes. "You'll experience true consciousness sharing. Two minds gradually becoming aware of each other's thoughts. It's the culmination of decades of theoretical work."

Maja's training kicked in despite the drugs. The apartment's layout, the equipment, Nielsen's methodical preparation—all of it registered automatically. Even paralyzed, she was building a case that would never be presented.

"This modified polymer is new," Erik said, holding up a syringe filled with pearlescent fluid. "It's something the Professor and I have been working on for several months courtesy of a government grant meant for studying inter-herd relationships of Uppsalian reindeer." He laughed at his attempt at juvenile humor, the sound jarring and out of character.

"The adhesive contains a cocktail of neurotropic compounds," Nielsen explained, his voice carrying the quiet authority of a professor. "Extracted from certain fungi that grow on Swedish birch trees. Indigenous peoples once used them in shamanic rituals, claimed they could share thoughts with others who consumed the same preparation."

"Pseudoscience," Maja managed, her syllables stretching like taffy.

"Is it?" Nielsen smiled. "The adhesive bonds you physically, but these compounds cross the blood-brain barrier. They enhance neural plasticity, increase sensitivity to electrical fields. When two people are in close physical contact under these conditions..." He paused, consulting his notes. "The brain begins to pick up on the other person's neural activity. Shared sensations, emotions, even fragmented thoughts."

"The neurotropic compounds work gradually," Nielsen explained, as if delivering a university lecture. "First shared sensations, then emotional states, eventually fragmented thoughts. The brain's mirror neurons become hyperactive. What affects one nervous system begins to echo in the other. You'll die experiencing each other's final moments as your own."

"Beginning application," Erik announced. "The compound needs to be applied at matching pressure points," he noted, adjusting his measurements with scientific pride. "Wrists, temples, base of the neck, where the blood vessels are closest to the surface. Maximum absorption into the nervous system."

A strange tingling where the compound touched her skin. Was that merely fear, or the beginning of something else? Maja could swear she felt an echo of pressure on her right wrist, exactly where Erik was applying the adhesive to Sven's left. Mirrored sensation. Impossible. And yet.

She caught Sven's eye across the room. Even drugged, even paralyzed, they maintained their silent communication. This wasn't just another murder; it was experimentation, with a clinical precision that somehow made it more horrifying.

For a moment, Maja thought she felt something, not a voice exactly, but a sensation. A fragment of anger that didn't feel like her own. Was that Sven's frustration she was experiencing, or merely her imagination constructing what he must be feeling?

"Fascinating," Nielsen murmured, watching their nonverbal exchange. "Even now you're coordinating your observations. Your investigative partnership persisting despite chemical and physical constraints. You'll be perfect for observing the integration of consciousness."

She could hear her upstairs neighbor's television—the evening news probably reporting on the weather, maybe another government scandal. Normal Swedish life continuing three meters above her head while she experienced something that would redefine the boundaries of human cruelty.

Nielsen glanced at his watch, a precise, academic gesture. "Nordlund should be arriving soon. She's quite predictable in her concern for missing colleagues. I've studied the response patterns extensively."

"The adhesive will reach full bonding strength in approximately ten minutes," Nielsen explained, consulting his notes. "By then, the paralytic will begin to wear off enough for vocalization and minimal movement. That's when the shared consciousness typically manifests. You'll begin to access each other's thoughts, memories... even sensory experiences."

"How would you know?" Sven mumbled, his consonants soft but his determination hardening through the chemical fog. "If you killed all the... the... others."

Nielsen smiled. "Animal trials, Inspector. Rats, primarily. Though their consciousness is limited, the principles remain consistent. Two rats joined by adhesive demonstrated remarkable behavioral synchronization before expiring."

But Maja found herself oddly calm. Perhaps it was the sedative, or perhaps it was the familiar pattern—another killer who couldn't shut up. How many interrogations had she sat through with perpetrators who couldn't stop talking, couldn't stop justifying their actions to someone, anyone who would listen?

Bastard enjoys hearing himself talk, she thought bitterly.

Always do, came the response in her mind, in what felt distinctly like Sven's sardonic tone.

She froze. Had she imagined it? A trick of her drugged mind, surely. And yet the thought had arrived complete, with Sven's characteristic inflection, his particular way of mental eye-rolling.

"You know," she managed to say, fighting to articulate each syllable through numb lips, "this is the long... longest con... confession I've ever heard."

Nielsen paused in his documentation. "Confession?"

"You're explain..ing every....thing. The method.....ology, the previous victims, your..... motivation....s." She'd hit a nerve. "Classic nar... narcissistic behavior........ You need someone....... to appre....ciate your clever......ness."

"This is scientific research," Nielsen protested, but his academic composure cracked slightly.

"It's murd...errrr with paper....work," Sven added, his words still blurred but his contempt cutting through the pharmaceutical fog. "Dressed up in aca... academic bull... shit to...."

Erik looked uncertainly between his professor and the two detectives. His subjects were refusing to act like victims.

"Continue the application," Nielsen ordered, but Maja caught the slight tremor in his voice.

From outside came the distant sound of a car door slamming, the heavy thunk of a police vehicle. Nielsen's head snapped toward the window, his academic composure fracturing further.

The cold sensation spread up her arm. Heavy footsteps in the stairwell now, Nordlund's distinctive gait, taking the steps two at a time. She and Sven kept gathering evidence. Still building their case. Still refusing to be victims.

Left drawer, kitchen counter. Eight centimeters from edge. Backup service weapon. The thought arrived in her mind with Sven's distinctive tactical precision. She hadn't told him about that hiding place. Couldn't have.

I see it, she thought back, uncertain if the connection was real or merely desperate hope.

The sound of keys at her door. Nordlund had her spare set, standard precaution for single detectives working serial cases.

Her mind kept working even as her body gave up.

It was, she thought with dark Swedish humor, probably the most professional way to die in Stockholm.

32
ADHESION

The ambulans lights flickered against Östermalm storefronts as they headed north toward Danderyd. Morning commuters emerged from the T-Bana clutching kaffe cups, unaware that two police officers were dying six meters away. The city went about its morning business while two cops died in the back of an ambulans. Typical Stockholm. Compartmentalize everything, keep the machinery running.

The medical team worked with precision. Each monitor beep measured her officers' remaining time. Almqvist watched them attempt the impossible: trying to separate two human beings joined by an academic with tenure and a theory about shared consciousness.

The compound had left strange marks on their wrists and temples, discolored patches where Nielsen's neurotropic cocktail had absorbed into their bloodstream. Nielsen's handiwork. In twenty-three years, Almqvist had seen plenty of human evil, but this felt different: murder with footnotes. She'd written off Nielsen's theories as academic bullshit, the kind of nonsense professors debated while real cops handled Saturday night drunks. Turned out the theories had teeth.

"Five minutes out," the driver called.

"How long?" Almqvist asked the medic.

"The compounds are affecting their nervous systems. Respiratory depression, cardiac irregularities. Hour, maybe less."

Fan också. Two cops dying in slow motion, and she couldn't do shit about it.

Nielsen had built a murder weapon with a timer. Neurotropic compounds slowly shutting down their nervous systems. Academic torture. Even killing people required proper methodology now.

Despite sedation, Maja's eyes tracked each medical procedure. Still investigating. Still gathering evidence from her own dying.

Beside her, Sven's breathing had synchronized with hers. Eight years of partnership ending in forced intimacy. Nielsen's theories about professional bonding taken to their logical extreme.

The Bengtsson and Strandberg cases had shown them what the compounds could do: progressive organ failure as the neurotropic substances overwhelmed their nervous systems. Nielsen knew exactly what would happen. Erik had done his homework.

Danderyd's trauma team waited with dialysis equipment and neural monitors. They'd learned from Vera Strandberg that Nielsen's compounds required aggressive treatment to prevent organ failure. Institutional learning. They'd probably write papers about this case later, assuming her officers survived to be case studies.

The ambulans doors opened. The trauma team moved precisely, protective suits rustling.

"We have Nielsen in custody," she told the trauma chief. "And his documentation."

"Good. We'll need the compound formula." The doctor studied the discolored patches on their skin. Medical jargon couldn't hide what they were dealing with. Almqvist recognized the look on the doctor's face. She'd seen it on pathologists examining the worst crime scenes. Professional competence fighting revulsion.

They moved through isolation corridors, each door requiring containment protocols. The hospital had learned from Vera Strandberg: new protocols, neural monitoring, toxicology procedures. Swedish adaptation. They'd be ready for the next professor with a research agenda.

The trauma team moved like people carrying a grudge. They'd lost Vera Strandberg. This time would be different.

"How long were they exposed?" the trauma chief asked.

"Twenty, thirty minutes. Nielsen's assistant documented everything."

The doctor's face darkened. "We'll need those notes. And Nielsen's formula."

"What are their chances?"

"With Strandberg, we waited too long. This time..." He paused. "Maybe."

Maybe. The most honest word in medicine. Maybe they'd live, maybe they wouldn't. Maybe was all anyone could offer.

Through the observation window, she watched her officers dying by degrees.

Maja's breathing was getting worse, the compounds affecting her respiratory center. Sven's lips looked blue. Eight years of partnership, and this was how it ended: poisoned together by a professor's experiment.

They needed the killer's recipe to save his victims. Nielsen would probably find it amusing: his own methodology used against him.

Her radio crackled: forensics had found Nielsen's research journal. Pages of calculations: absorption rates, survival projections, optimal compound concentrations for "sustained viability." and a plastic case with empty test tubes inside. He'd planned their deaths like a dissertation defense. Charts and graphs documenting human suffering. Murder with proper citations.

33
SEPERATION

The emergency surgical center at Danderyd operated with Swedish efficiency. Through the observation window, Almqvist watched the medical team work around Maja and Sven like archaeologists excavating something both fragile and dangerous. Outside, Stockholm lay beneath a slate-gray November sky, the kind that had settled over the city weeks ago and wouldn't lift until March. The overhead surgical lights threw harsh shadows across the scene, turning it into some modern Bergman film about the banality of horror.

"Neurotropic compound cocktail with unknown fungal derivatives," the lead surgeon reported, studying the latest scans. "The compounds have crossed the blood-brain barrier and are affecting multiple neural pathways. We're seeing widespread nervous system disruption."

How easily medical language created distance from atrocity, Almqvist thought. Two human beings slowly poisoned by a madman's chemistry became "nervous system disruption." She'd used similar euphemisms in her own reports over the years. Violence sanitized through professional vocabulary.

Through the window, Maja's eyes tracked every movement

despite the sedation. Even trapped against her partner in this grotesque tableau, she was cataloging, analyzing, building their case from inside Nielsen's experiment.

The security doors opened with a pneumatic hiss. Two officers escorted Nielsen and Erik into the observation area. Even in custody, both men immediately focused on the monitors with unmistakable academic hunger.

"Remarkable neurotropic absorption pattern," Erik murmured, studying the display. "The compound distribution has achieved optimal neural pathway disruption. The partnership dynamic provides fascinating shared consciousness data."

"Håll käften," the lead surgeon cut him off with the bluntness typical of medical staff at the end of a thirty-hour shift. "We need the compound's composition and treatment protocol. Nothing else."

Nielsen approached the monitors with the measured steps of someone approaching a lectern. Even handcuffed, he maintained that academic bearing.

"Standard toxicology protocols won't work," he said, voice carrying the same tone he might use to discuss weather patterns. "The fungal compounds have created novel neurotoxins that resist conventional treatment. Quite elegant, biochemically speaking."

"Sven's showing signs of respiratory depression," the respiratory specialist interrupted. "The compounds are affecting his brainstem. Tidal volume down forty percent and falling."

Numbers that meant death by degrees. Almqvist had seen enough death to recognize its methodical approach, the way bodies began their systematic shutdown.

"The shared consciousness effect adds another complication," Erik added, gesturing at the monitors. "The compounds are creating neural synchronization between them. They're experiencing each other's symptoms, creating a feedback loop that..."

"Fan ta dig," one of the officers growled. "Stop talking about them like lab rats."

But that's exactly what they were to Nielsen: data points in his research.

"The treatment isn't straightforward," Nielsen continued. "Standard detoxification protocols accelerate the compounds' effects. The medical team exchanged glances. They'd lived through Vera Strandberg's death.

"These subjects present different variables," Erik observed. "Their existing professional coordination provides optimal conditions for studying shared trauma response."

"För helvete," Almqvist interrupted. "Give us something we can actually use."

Through the glass, Maja's eyes narrowed. Even sedated, even dying by degrees, she was working.

"The compounds create a three-stage neurological cascade," Nielsen explained, warming to his subject. "Initial absorption occurs within minutes. Then the fungal derivatives begin disrupting neurotransmitter production. The final stage involves permanent neural pathway damage that makes recovery nearly impossible."

"Neurological compromise is worsening," the toxicology specialist reported. "Both subjects showing signs of progressive organ failure. We're looking at maybe ninety minutes before irreversible brain damage."

"The psychological component is equally fascinating," Nielsen continued. "Forced physical proximity between individuals with existing emotional bonds creates unique stress patterns."

The bastard had weaponized their partnership, Almqvist realized. Turned their greatest strength into the perfect trap.

"How do we treat it?" the lead surgeon demanded. "Specifically. Step by step."

Nielsen's expression shifted. Pride mixed with something else. Possessiveness, perhaps. An artist reluctant to reveal his techniques.

"The neurotropic cascade must be interrupted first," he said finally. "Specific enzyme blockers at precisely timed intervals will disrupt the compounds' neural pathway disruption. But the timing is critical. Too fast, and the compounds release secondary toxins."

"Secondary toxins," the respiratory specialist repeated. "You gave your poison a backup killing mechanism?"

A slight smile played at Nielsen's lips. "One must protect one's research from tampering."

Through the window, Maja's breathing had grown labored, but her eyes remained sharp. She was memorizing every word, every gesture, every tell. Building a psychological profile of her torturer even as his creation slowly killed her.

"After the neural cascade is interrupted," Nielsen continued, "the compounds require a specific antidote sequence. Activated charcoal to absorb circulating toxins, followed by targeted enzyme therapy to restore normal neurotransmitter function. But the application must be gradual. Point-five milligrams per minute maximum, or cardiac arrest."

The lead surgeon was taking notes. "What about the areas with highest concentration? The scans show tissue damage where the compounds have accumulated."

"Ah yes," Nielsen leaned forward, genuinely engaged now. "The concentration points. The compounds seek out areas of highest neural density to ensure maximum disruption."

"Herregud," Almqvist said quietly. "You're talking about my officers. Human beings. Not research subjects."

Nielsen tilted his head, genuinely puzzled by the distinction. "The principles remain the same regardless of how we categorize the subjects."

"Sven's oxygen saturation is dropping," someone reported. "Seventy-eight percent and falling."

Through the glass, Maja had noticed too. "Their training is remarkable," Erik observed. "Most subjects panic at this stage, accelerating the compounds' toxic cascade. But these two are managing their stress responses collectively."

"You selected them specifically," Almqvist said. "Their partnership wasn't incidental. It was the whole point."

Nielsen's slight nod was almost approving. "Eight years of professional coordination creates fascinating neural pathways. They've learned to think as a unit, which makes their forced proximity particularly rich in data."

"You hunted them," Almqvist said. "Studied them. Chose them because they trusted each other."

"Trust creates vulnerability," Nielsen agreed. "The stronger the bond, the more interesting the stress patterns when that bond becomes a trap."

The lead surgeon looked up from his notes. "We need to begin the treatment protocol immediately. Even with your instructions, this is going to be extremely risky."

"Previous attempts failed because they treated it as a medical emergency," Nielsen said. "It's really more of a biochemical problem. Each component must be addressed in sequence, or the entire system activates its defensive protocols."

"Sätt igång," the lead surgeon ordered. "Prep for enzyme blocker administration. We'll need precise dosing and monitoring."

The medical team moved with renewed purpose, but Almqvist saw the doubt in their faces. They'd watched Vera Strandberg die attempting something similar.

Through the window, Maja caught Almqvist's eye. A slight nod, barely perceptible but unmistakably deliberate. Still gathering evidence. Still being a cop even as Nielsen's chemistry slowly murdered her.

"Begin setting up the enzyme blockers," the lead surgeon said. "We'll start with interrupting the neural cascade." He turned to Nielsen. "You're going to watch every second of this. If your instructions are wrong, if this fails because you've left something out..."

"It won't fail if you follow the protocol precisely," Nielsen interrupted. "The chemistry is perfect. It's the execution that typically creates problems."

"Jävlar! Sven's going into respiratory distress," someone called out. "We need to reposition them or he'll suffocate before we can attempt treatment."

"Repositioning will trigger the compounds' defensive response," Nielsen warned. "Any stimulation accelerates the toxic cascade."

"Set up for emergency dialysis if the antidote protocol fails," the lead surgeon ordered. "We may have to filter their blood directly and hope we can buy enough time."

"That would be inadvisable," Nielsen said mildly. "The compounds have saturated their nervous systems. Dialysis this late would cause massive organ failure."

"Then we follow your protocol," the surgeon said. "Gud hjälp oss —Gold Help Us"

Even at the edge of death, even trapped in a madman's experiment, they were still partners. Still cops. Still gathering evidence against the monster who'd turned their bond into a weapon.

The medical team began their preparations while Nielsen watched with academic interest.

Ninety minutes until irreversible brain damage.

Ninety minutes to find out if a madman's chemistry was as reliable as he claimed.

In ninety minutes, they'd know.

34
SVEN

Through the observation window, Nielsen leaned forward despite his restraints. There was something almost tender in his attention, like a composer hearing his work performed for the first time. Beside him, Erik had gone rigid, the theoretical suddenly made flesh in neural scans and labored breathing.

"Initial enzyme blocker at 0.3 milligrams per minute," the toxicologist reported. "Beginning neural cascade interruption."

The monitors registered the response immediately. Neural activity spiked in patterns that resembled neither normal consciousness nor standard pain responses. The compounds were releasing secondary toxins.

"Compound showing localized heating at adhesion points," the chemical burns specialist observed. "Temperature rising. 38 degrees, 39, 40..."

Through the sedation, Maja's fingers pressed against Sven's in their old code. Still communicating, even as Nielsen's compounds fought to maintain their grip on their nervous systems. But Sven's responses were weakening, his fingers barely managing to return the pressure.

"His oxygen saturation is critical," the respiratory specialist warned. "68 percent and falling. We're losing him."

"Any movement will trigger the compounds' defensive response," Nielsen said, his academic tone faltering slightly.

"We know," the lead surgeon interrupted. "But he's dying now. Not theoretically. Now."

"Neural cascade showing partial interruption," the toxicologist reported. "Sixty percent of compounds showing neutralization. But the deeper absorption sites are resisting."

On the monitors, Sven's heart rhythm had become erratic. The stuttering percussion of a system failing. The compounds were overwhelming his brainstem, shutting down basic functions one by one.

"V-tach," the anesthesiologist called out. "He's going into ventricular tachycardia."

Through the window, Maja's eyes had opened, aware despite the sedation. She could feel it. Through eight years of partnership, she knew Sven was dying before the monitors confirmed it.

"She's trying to signal something," Almqvist said, watching Maja's fingers move against Sven's still hand. "Morse code."

"G... O... O... D... B... Y... E," the lead surgeon translated, his voice catching. "She's saying goodbye."

"Continue the enzyme blocker sequence," the surgeon ordered. "We can't save him, but we can try to save her."

"But the adhesive bonds," Erik said, pressing against the glass. "If he dies while they're still fused..."

"The adhesive doesn't distinguish between living and dead tissue," Nielsen finished, his voice carrying its first note of genuine concern. "It will maintain the bond regardless."

"V-fib," someone shouted. "He's in cardiac arrest."

The crash team moved with desperate efficiency, but the positioning made everything harder. CPR compressions had to be modified, defibrillation pads placed at awkward angles. They were trying to restart a heart while navigating the geography of chemical bondage.

Through it all, Maja remained conscious despite the neurotropic compounds clouding her awareness. She was watching her partner die from a distance that could be measured in millimeters. The closest observer to death possible, yet utterly unable to help.

"Asystole," the anesthesiologist reported after twenty minutes of effort. "No cardiac activity."

"Continue CPR," the surgeon ordered. "We need to maintain circulation while we dissolve the adhesive bonds. If rigor mortis sets in while they're still fused..."

He didn't need to finish. They all understood. The adhesive would bind living flesh to dead, creating a fusion that might become permanent. Maja trapped not just with her partner's body but with the progressive chemistry of decay.

"Neural cascade disruption at 85 percent," the toxicologist reported, voice tight. "Should we continue?"

"We have no choice," the surgeon said. "Complete the enzyme blocker sequence."

The next minutes unfolded with surreal precision. The medical team performed CPR on a dead man to keep his tissues viable for separation while simultaneously working to neutralize the compounds that bound him to his still-living partner. It was medicine pushed into territories that had no names, no protocols, no precedents.

"Time of death: 14:47," the surgeon finally announced, even as the CPR continued. "Note that mechanical circulation is being maintained for tissue viability during separation attempt."

"Neural cascade fully disrupted," the toxicologist reported. "Beginning solvent application protocol."

"We need to work fast," the burns specialist said. "The adhesive is already responding to the cessation of biological activity. Temperature rising at all fusion points."

Nielsen watched with the intensity of someone seeing their life's work reach its logical conclusion. "The adhesive recognizes death as another form of separation to be resisted," he said quietly.

Through the observation window, Maja's tears weren't just from grief but from the terrible irony. Sven had died from neurotropic respiratory depression, and now mechanical ventilation kept air moving through his dead lungs to prevent the chemistry that would trap her permanently with his corpse.

"DMSO application beginning," the specialist reported. "Two square centimeters per minute. No, we need to go faster. The tissue changes..."

"If you rush, the adhesive will contract," Nielsen warned.

But biology had its own timeline. Even with mechanical circulation, Sven's tissues were beginning their inevitable transformation. The adhesive found itself binding states of being that were increasingly divergent. Life clinging to death, warmth adjoining the creeping cold.

"Multiple application points," the surgeon decided. "We can't wait for sequential separation. Hit every fusion site simultaneously."

The medical team worked with desperate precision, applying solvents at shoulder, thoracic, and hip junctions. The adhesive's response was chaotic. Temperature spikes, localized contractions, chemical burns forming where it fought hardest to maintain its grip.

"She's going into shock," someone reported. "BP dropping rapidly."

"Maintain CPR on the deceased," the surgeon ordered. "And get vasopressors for Maja. We're not losing them both."

Through her tears and the neurotropic fog, Maja's eyes found Almqvist's. Even in shock, even poisoned, even in the midst of unimaginable trauma, she was still a cop. Still gathering evidence. Still documenting Nielsen's crime from inside it.

"Separation at 40 percent," the burns specialist reported. "But the compound is causing severe tissue damage. Third-degree chemical burns at all application sites."

They were trading flesh for freedom, accepting scars as the price of separation. The adhesive extracted its toll in skin and muscle, marking both the living and the dead with the evidence of their forced union.

"Continue application," the surgeon said grimly. "We accept the tissue damage. The alternative is worse."

"Major separation achieved," the specialist announced after what felt like hours but had been mere minutes. "Final adhesion points releasing."

The last bonds yielded with violent reluctance. The adhesive's final protest expressed in heat and chemical burns. Where it had joined them, the damage was extensive. Sven's body bore the marks of their fusion, while Maja's living flesh showed angry wounds that would scar in patterns matching her partner's final position.

"Separation complete," the surgeon said. "Time: 15:03. Moving deceased to preparation area. Patient Norberg requiring immediate burn treatment and psychological support."

As they wheeled Sven's body away, Maja's hand reached out. Not from chemical compulsion but from human need. For a moment, her fingertips brushed his still hand, the voluntary touch a universe away from their forced fusion.

In the observation room, Nielsen watched this final gesture with something that might have been confusion. His adhesive had forced connection, but this choosing to touch, even after experiencing its weaponization, existed outside his calculations.

Erik had slumped to the floor, understanding finally that he had helped murder not just a man but a partnership. The compounds had killed Sven, but they had done something worse to Maja. Forced her to experience her partner's death from zero distance, made her a participant in her own trauma.

The medical team worked on Maja's burns with quiet efficiency, but everyone understood that the visible wounds were the least of it. She had been conscious through it all. Felt her partner die while bound to him, endured the separation of their flesh while knowing his was already beginning its journey toward decay.

"Kriminalinspektör Norberg," Almqvist said quietly, moving to where Maja lay. "You did everything right. You gathered the evidence. You survived."

Maja's eyes held a depth of experience that hadn't been there before. She had seen death from inside its embrace, felt partnership perverted into imprisonment, survived a form of torture that had no name because Nielsen had just invented it.

Her lips moved, forming words almost too quiet to hear: "Did you record everything?"

Still a cop. Still building the case. Even from inside the crime scene.

"Every second," Almqvist assured her. "Nielsen and Erik. We have it all."

A slight nod. Maja had paid the ultimate price for evidence. Experienced the crime from inside, documented torture through endurance. She would carry the scars as proof, her body itself becoming testimony to what human knowledge could become when divorced from human wisdom.

Through the window, they were preparing Sven's body with the same care they would give any officer who had died in the line of duty. Because that's what he was. Killed not by conventional violence but by chemistry weaponized, by knowledge perverted into an instrument of torture.

Nielsen remained at the window, studying the scene with academic interest dimming into something else. His experiment had succeeded perfectly. Demonstrated forced connection, documented stress responses, proved his theories about human bonds.

But in succeeding, it had also revealed the poverty of his vision. He had reduced partnership to proximity, confused connection with adhesion, mistaken the mechanical for the meaningful. His compounds could force bodies together but couldn't touch what actually bound people. The daily choice to face the world together, renewed each morning, resilient even in the face of its own perversion.

Maja would heal, scarred but not broken. She would testify, her body itself evidence. And somewhere in Sweden's justice system, Nielsen would face the consequence of turning knowledge into torture, of forgetting that science divorced from wisdom became just another form of violence.

But for now, in this moment between trauma and whatever came next, Maja grieved. Not just for Sven but for the partnership they'd shared. Poisoned now by its weaponization but not erased. Some things, the best things, survived even their own perversion.

Some knowledge, Maja now knew, came at too high a price. Nielsen had proven his point perfectly. And in doing so, had demonstrated why some points should never be proven at all.

35
FRACTURED

The head of surgery met Almqvist outside the emergency surgical center, his voice low despite the empty corridor.

"We've moved Kriminalinspektör Norberg to intensive care. The coma's keeping her stable, but..." He gestured to the latest scans. "The trauma of separation, combined with experiencing her partner's death through the compound's adhesion..."

He left the sentence unfinished.

Through the observation window, medical staff worked with careful efficiency, preparing Sven's body. The adhesive's residue still marked where they'd been joined, physical evidence of Nielsen's experiment.

"His wife is downstairs," the surgeon said. "And Kriminalinspektör Norberg's brother just arrived."

Almqvist nodded, her mind already composing the impossible conversations ahead. How to explain to Marta that her husband had become part of Nielsen's experiment? How to tell Daniel that his sister had been conscious through every moment of her partner's death?

"I'll speak to them separately," Almqvist said. "Kriminalinspektör

Svensson's wife first. She should..." She paused, searching for the right words. "She should know before she hears anything in the corridors."

The surgeon's expression tightened. "If she wants to see him..."

Sven's body still bore the visible evidence of Nielsen's experiment.

"I know." Almqvist moved toward the elevator. In the ICU, Maja lay surrounded by monitors, her body learning to function alone after being forcibly merged with her partner.

The elevator doors opened onto the main floor with a soft chime. Through the waiting room windows, Almqvist could see Marta Svensson sitting perfectly still, her coat still dusted with snow.

And across the room, Daniel Norberg paced, his eyes fixed on the emergency department doors.

Marta looked up immediately, her eyes carrying that sharpness that comes with hours of anxious waiting. Daniel stopped pacing, his posture shifting to alert stillness.

She would begin with Marta, with the simple, devastating fact of Sven's death. And then, gradually, she would try to help her understand the extraordinary circumstances of that death.

36
SADNESS

Outside, Stockholm's December darkness pressed against windows streaked with melting snow. The city continuing its normal rhythms while inside this building, everything had stopped.

Marta looked up as Almqvist entered, her eyes sharp with the alertness that comes from hours of waiting. Daniel stopped pacing. Both of them reading her expression, understanding that the waiting was over.

"Mrs. Svensson." Almqvist sat beside her, noting how Marta's hands were clasped so tightly her knuckles had gone white. The wedding ring on her finger caught the harsh lighting—a simple gold band that matched the one they'd had to cut from Sven's hand to complete the separation.

Strange how objects outlasted the relationships they symbolized. The ring would survive long after the marriage it represented had been dissolved by Nielsen's compound. This was humanity's real achievement—creating symbols more durable than the feelings they were meant to preserve.

"I saw the news," Marta said, her voice carefully steady. "They said something about an experimental adhesive. That he and Maja were..." She paused, searching for words. "That they were somehow joined together."

Across the room, Daniel had stopped pacing, watching them with the intensity of someone who understood that his sister's fate was being decided in this conversation.

"The suspect we were investigating," Almqvist began, "Professor Nielsen—he developed a compound that..." But the words felt clinical, inadequate. How could she explain what Nielsen had done?

Academic language was designed for academic problems. When professors turned their theories into weapons, ordinary explanations broke down.

"Was he in pain?" Marta asked.

Almqvist hesitated. The truth—that Nielsen's compound had merged their nervous systems so completely that Maja had felt Sven die as if it were happening to her own body—seemed too cruel to share. Nielsen's perfect academic cruelty: ensuring that one partner would carry the physical memory of the other's death.

Nielsen probably saw it as elegance—the beautiful symmetry of his theory made flesh. Academics had such refined capacity for evil. They could torture people with the same precision they brought to peer review.

"The doctors did everything they could," Almqvist said. "The compound's effects were too extensive. When Sven's system began to fail..."

She left the sentence unfinished.

"And Maja?" Marta's voice caught slightly. "They were partners for so long. She must have..." She stopped, perhaps sensing something in Almqvist's expression.

Even in grief, Marta was thinking like a cop's wife—understanding that partners shared more than just professional obligations. Human beings were remarkably consistent creatures. Even when confronted with the impossible, they fell back on familiar patterns of thought and feeling.

"She's in intensive care." Almqvist watched Marta's hands tighten further. "The doctors had to induce a coma when the separation..." Again, the clinical words felt wrong.

A nurse appeared in the doorway, her expression carefully neutral. "Mrs. Svensson? If you'd like to... If you want to see him."

Marta stood with careful control, as though any sudden movement might make this reality more final.

"Will you tell Daniel about Maja?" she asked Almqvist. "He should know what happened to his sister. What they went through together."

Almqvist watched Marta follow the nurse, each step measured and deliberate—a widow's first walk toward a truth she wasn't ready to face. How many such walks happened in hospitals every day? These small processions toward finality, as ritualized as any religious ceremony. Hospitals were secular churches where people witnessed these transformations—the living into the dead, the married into the widowed, the whole into the broken.

Daniel met her halfway across the waiting room, his face tight with questions. Unlike Marta's careful stillness, his body thrummed with contained energy—a brother's need to do something, anything.

"How bad?" he asked.

Almqvist gestured to the chairs, but Daniel shook his head. He'd spent too long waiting already.

When faced with unbearable news, some people sat down while others remained standing. As if physical posture could somehow affect emotional resilience.

"Just tell me. She's my sister..."

"She's alive," Almqvist said, watching some of the tension leave his shoulders. "But Daniel, what Nielsen did to them..." She paused. "The compound merged them completely. Their nervous systems, their blood flow, even their breathing—everything synchronized."

Daniel's hands clenched at his sides. "I saw the news footage. They said something about an adhesive, about them being stuck together, but..."

"It was more than that." Almqvist kept her voice low. "When Sven's system began to fail, Maja experienced everything. The compound forced her to feel her partner die, to share every moment of it through their merged nervous systems."

She watched the horror of understanding cross Daniel's face. Nielsen's experiment hadn't just killed Sven—it had forced Maja to experience his death from the inside, as if it were happening to her own body.

"The doctors had to put her in a coma," she continued. "Her body was fighting the separation, trying to maintain the connection even as..." She stopped, seeing Daniel turn away slightly.

"The human body's remarkable, isn't it?" Almqvist said. She paused, considering this. "Perhaps that was his real experiment— not just to bond people, but to demonstrate that all human connections, once formed, become necessary for survival. A very Swedish approach to psychology, really. We assume people need each other, then we're surprised when they actually do."

"Can I see her?"

"Soon. The medical team is still..." Almqvist hesitated. How to explain that they were still removing traces of Nielsen's compound, still separating what remained of the forced unity?

"And Nielsen?" The question carried an edge of controlled violence. "The news said he was arrested."

"He's in custody." Almqvist watched Daniel's hands clench. "His documentation is helping the doctors treat Maja. The same notes he used to torture them are now being used to save her."

That Nielsen's meticulous academic record-keeping, the very quality that had made his experiment so precise, now made his knowledge indispensable for undoing its effects. Academic thoroughness: it could save you or damn you with equal precision.

"He's probably still taking notes, even now," she added. A nurse appeared—different from the one who'd led Marta away, but wearing the same professional expression. "Mr. Norberg? Your sister's been moved to intensive care. If you'd like to see her..."

Daniel straightened, his posture shifting from anger to something more vulnerable. "Will she know I'm there? With the coma..."

"The doctors think she might be able to hear us," Almqvist said. "But she won't be able to respond. The coma is keeping her stable while her system adjusts to functioning independently again."

Functioning independently—such a simple phrase for something most people never thought about. Daniel nodded once, then followed the nurse. At the doorway he paused. "Tell me we have enough to keep him locked up. That he can't do this to anyone else."

"We have everything we need," she assured him. "Maja and Sven made sure of that. Even at the end, they were still gathering evidence."

She watched Daniel disappear down the corridor. Through the windows, pre-dawn darkness was giving way to grey morning light, Stockholm's winter sky the color of old pewter. The snow had stopped, leaving the world outside as changed as the lives within these walls.

Swedes were particularly good at finding poetry in the most mundane meteorological events. It made tragedy more bearable when it arrived with appropriate atmospheric accompaniment.

Her phone buzzed—the forensics team had finished documenting Nielsen's research materials. Through the hospital's corridors, she could hear the soft sounds of medical equipment, of careful footsteps, of lives being irreversibly changed. The quiet symphony of institutional response to human crisis. Somewhere above, Maja lay in intensive care, her body learning to exist alone after being forcibly merged with her partner.

What kind of therapy could address trauma that lay so far outside normal human parameters? Would therapists need to develop entirely new vocabularies, new frameworks for understanding Nielsen's victims? Another academic discipline would eventually emerge from this horror—the psychology of artificial human fusion. Universities would offer courses. Students would write dissertations. Academic life feeding on its own extremes.

And somewhere in this building, Nielsen sat in custody, probably still analyzing data from his experiment's final demonstration. The academic mind continuing its work even after its methodology had proven catastrophic.

37

KRONOBERGSHÄKTET

The förhörsrum at Kronobergshäktet felt too bright after Stockholm's winter darkness. Gustaf Nielsen sat with perfect posture, his hands folded on the metal table like a professor waiting to begin a seminar at Kungsmedicinska.

Through the observation window, Almqvist watched him adjust his water cup—once, twice, aligning it with the table's edge. Three days in custody, and he still maintained perfect academic standards.

"He hasn't asked about Erik," a constable observed. Snow still clung to his tactical uniform. "Not once since we separated them. Three days, and not a single question about his protégé."

Almqvist pulled her eyes away from Nielsen. Three days of headlines in Dagens Nyheter about the Adhesive Killer. Three days of updates from Danderyd about Maja's condition.

"Of course not." "Erik's just another research subject now. Data to be analyzed. Like all the others."

"The guards say he spends his time writing," Wallin continued. "Page after page of observations about häktet routines, prisoner behavior patterns, institutional procedures. Even in custody, he's conducting research."

Almqvist checked her watch. "How's Maja?"

"Semi-conscious," Wallin said. "The doctors say the adhesive affected her nervous system. She experienced everything. Every moment of Sven's death."

"The worst part?" Almqvist continued. "He's already asked for permission to document her recovery process. Wants to include it in his research about 'survival responses in separated subjects.'"

"Helvete," Wallin muttered. "She felt her partner die, and he wants to turn that into another academic paper."

"Dags att börja—Time to start," Almqvist said. She gathered her evidence folder—photographs and forensic reports arranged with methodical care.

The door clicked open. Nielsen looked up from his notepad, registering her entrance with academic interest rather than concern.

Almqvist took the seat across from him, placing her folder on the metal table. The harsh fluorescent light made everything look clinical, sterile.

"Professor Nielsen," she said. "Let's talk about your research."

The interview room lights cast harsh shadows across the crime scene photographs. Nielsen studied each image with the same careful attention he'd once given to student papers, his hands moving with precise purpose as he arranged them in what he clearly considered proper academic order.

"These interviews are being recorded," Almqvist began, watching him align the edges of a particularly graphic photo with mathematical exactness.

"Fascinating documentation," Nielsen observed, creating his own organizational system. "Though your arrangement lacks proper chronological structure. If we organized them according to the compound's progression through distinct phases..."

His court-appointed lawyer shifted uncomfortably. "Professor, I must advise you-"

"The methodology requires precise documentation," Nielsen continued, as if the lawyer hadn't spoken. "Each phase building on previous observations, creating a complete record of dependency under controlled conditions. See how the adhesive's progression follows predictable patterns?"

"Kriminalinspektör Svensson's death," Almqvist said, placing another photograph on the table. "Explain the compound's role."

"Ah yes." Nielsen's satisfaction was evident. "A remarkable demonstration of complete neural integration. When his system began to fail, Kriminalinspektör Norberg's stronger constitution attempted to compensate through their shared pathways. The monitors at Danderyd documented exactly how-"

"Professor." His lawyer's voice sharpened. "You have the right to remain silent."

"The methodology must be properly explained," Nielsen corrected, still arranging photographs. "Kriminalinspektör Norberg remained fully conscious throughout, documenting every sensation. Perfect data about dependency under extreme conditions."

"Tell me about Tor," she said. "About your first experiment."

Something flickered in Nielsen's expression - not emotion, but academic interest in an unexpected variable. "Anna's emotional response compromised the data collection significantly. Her presence in the lab created uncontrolled variables that affected proper documentation of Tor's psychological progression-"

"Your wife watched what you did to your son," Almqvist cut in. "While you took notes."

"The emotional variables complicated proper documentation," Nielsen replied, adjusting another photograph. "Which is why Kriminalinspektör Norberg's case proved so much more valuable. Her professional detachment provided much cleaner data about dependency under controlled conditions."

"And Erik?" Almqvist placed another photograph on the table, deliberately disrupting his careful order. "Was he a subject or a collaborator?"

Nielsen paused, then began incorporating the new image into his system. "Erik's documentation has been invaluable. His ability to maintain clinical detachment while recording the compound's effects... quite remarkable. Though perhaps we should discuss his methodology separately. The data requires proper contextual-"

"Professor." The lawyer's voice had taken on a desperate edge. "These interviews are being recorded."

"Yes, exactly." Nielsen's satisfaction was evident. "Proper documentation is essential. The psychological impact of institutional intervention... Erik will be quite interested in analyzing these transcripts."

"Interview terminated," Almqvist said into the recorder. She sat back, studying Nielsen's face. He showed no concern about the terminated interview—only mild academic disappointment, like a professor whose lecture had been cut short.

But as she gathered the photographs, Nielsen made one final observation.

"Kriminalinspektör kriminalinspektör." Nielsen's voice stopped her at the door. "When you visit Kriminalinspektör Norberg, do pay attention to her neural responses. The compound's effects on consciousness post-separation... the data could be quite valuable for understanding long-term dependency patterns."

Almqvist turned back slowly. The fluorescent lights reflected off his silver hair, giving him an almost ethereal quality that made his words even more chilling.

"You know what, Professor?" Almqvist said. "I think you're right. I'll be sure to document everything very carefully."

The implied threat seemed lost on him. Nielsen simply nodded with academic approval.

Through the observation window, Wallin watched as the guards led Nielsen away. Even in shackles, he maintained perfect posture—a professor concluding another successful seminar.

38

SKOGSKYRKOGÅRDEN

Snow fell on Skogskyrkogården with the gentle persistence of Swedish winter, each flake adding to the perfect white silence that draped the cemetery in solemn beauty. The ancient pine trees stood like dark sentinels against the pewter sky, their branches heavy with fresh snow, watching over the mourners who gathered in quiet clusters around Sven Svensson's grave.

The snow reminded Almqvist of evidence—how it accumulated gradually, each flake another piece of information until the whole picture changed. She'd seen it happen in investigations, facts layering until familiar suspects became strangers, until certainty became doubt.

Marta Svensson stood with quiet dignity beside her daughter at the polished granite headstone. Her face bore the exhaustion of a woman who had spent twenty-five years as a police officer's wife, who had learned to live with midnight phone calls and missed dinners, who had always known this day might come. Yet there was strength in how she held herself, in how her hand rested protectively on her daughter's shoulder—the same steady presence she had maintained through all of Sven's long cases.

Their daughter stood between them—her and the empty space where Maja should have been—her Uppsala textbooks temporarily forgotten for funeral blacks that seemed to emphasize both her youth and her determination to be strong. She was analyzing everything, Almqvist could see, using her father's methods to keep emotion at bay.

Classic police family coping mechanism, Almqvist thought. Treat grief like a crime scene—observe, catalog, maintain distance. It worked until it didn't.

From her position at the back of the gathering, Almqvist observed how even the press maintained the cemetery's sacred silence. Stockholm's most aggressive crime reporters stood quietly among the snow-laden pines, their cameras hanging unused at their sides.

A small mercy, Almqvist thought. Even vultures understood some boundaries.

Though she noticed Aftonbladet's crime photographer shifting restlessly, probably calculating angles for when the family left. Professional habits died hard—unlike the people they wrote about.

Almqvist watched the medical team from Danderyd—the same doctors and nurses who had worked so desperately to save Sven, who had documented his final moments with clinical precision. Now they stood in unconscious formation, their carefully maintained professional distance beginning to crack. The priest's words about dedication to justice, about protecting others at any cost, seemed to pierce their medical detachment.

They had seen Nielsen's data firsthand—the neural readings, the synchronized responses, the clinical proof of partnership bonds. But standing here in the snow, numbers seemed inadequate. Like trying to capture the aurora borealis with a thermometer.

Or explaining love through tax forms, Almqvist mused. Academia had its limits.

But everyone's eyes were drawn, again and again, to the empty space beside Sven's family—a void that seemed to grow larger with each passing moment. Marta's hand tightened almost imperceptibly on her daughter's shoulder every time someone glanced at that emptiness.

The space beside them should have held Maja, should have contained her steady presence and quiet strength. Instead, she lay in Danderyd's intensive care unit, her nervous system still reeling from Nielsen's and Erik's perfectly designed methodology.

"Akademisk jävel—Academic Bastard," someone muttered behind Almqvist—one of the older Kriminalinspektör's, probably. The sentiment was spreading through the department like winter flu.

The priest's words drifted through the falling snow like a gentle benediction, speaking of dedication and sacrifice, of lives given in service to others. His careful Swedish phrases seemed to settle with the snowflakes on the mourners' shoulders.

Father Nyström Sankt Matteus, Almqvist recognized. He'd buried half the police force over the years, had the funeral liturgy down to muscle memory. Still managed to make it sound personal, though. Professional courtesy.

When Polisoverintendent Fältskog stepped forward, the snow seemed to pause in its descent. Marta met his eyes with the quiet understanding that passed between those who had lived with the weight of police work—he as a commander, she as a wife who had waited up countless nights.

His voice remained steady despite the emotion that tightened the corners of his eyes. "Sven understood what it meant to serve," he said, the words carrying across Skogskyrkogården's winter silence. "Not just the law, but each other. That understanding cost him everything."

Understatement of the year, Almqvist thought. But what else could you say at a funeral?

The snow continued its gentle descent as colleagues stepped forward one by one, each memory adding another brushstroke to the portrait of the man they'd lost. Stories emerged—Sven's dry humor that had kept them sane at crime scenes, his quiet competence, his loyalty that had become legendary in the department.

"Remember that domestic on Södermalm," Kriminalinspektör Eriksson was saying, "husband barricaded himself in the bathroom with a shotgun. Sven just stood outside the door talking about Djurgården's playoff chances until the guy got bored and surrendered." Scattered chuckles, quickly stifled. Even at funerals, cops needed their gallows humor.

Through it all, mother and daughter remained perfectly still, their shared strength evident in every line of their posture. Marta's face softened at the stories of Sven's dry humor—the same wit that had made her fall in love with a young patrol officer twenty-five years ago.

As the ceremony drew to its natural close, Almqvist watched the medical team finally surrender their professional distance. Their heads bowed in unison, white coats exchanged for formal blacks that seemed to absorb the falling snow. They had witnessed too much in recent days—had seen partnership quantified in Nielsen's precise measurements, had watched death transformed into data points.

Dr. Hedberg from emergency looked like she hadn't slept in days. None of them had, probably. Hard to maintain clinical detachment when your patient died for science.

The mourners began to disperse, moving in small groups toward waiting cars, toward lives that would continue despite this rupture. Marta and her daughter remained by the grave a moment longer, their stillness a final acknowledgment.

As Almqvist turned to leave, she noticed a solitary figure at the cemetery's edge—Daniel Norberg, standing halfway between the grave and his car, caught between participation and departure. His sister's absence from the ceremony hung around him like a visible weight. He had come to honor his sister's partner, to witness this acknowledgment of a bond his sister had experienced in ways no one else could fully comprehend.

Poor bastard, Almqvist thought. Probably felt guilty for being here when Maja couldn't be. Survivor's guilt by proxy—if that was even a thing.

As their eyes met across the snow-covered ground, Almqvist saw in his face the same question that had haunted her through the ceremony—what would remain of Maja when she finally emerged from sedation? How would she navigate a world where her partner no longer existed, where the bond Nielsen had forced them to experience in its most extreme form had been irrevocably broken?

The snow continued to fall, covering footprints almost as quickly as they were made, erasing the evidence of passage. Soon there would be no sign that anyone had gathered here. Only the fresh grave would remain, a new feature in the winter landscape, another marker in the geography of loss.

Almqvist pulled her coat tighter against the cold. Time to get back to the station, back to the endless paperwork that followed every tragedy. Nielsen's case files wouldn't process themselves, and justice—such as it was—still required proper documentation.

Even if it couldn't bring back the dead or heal the broken.

Snow fell on Skogskyrkogården with the gentle persistence of Swedish winter, each flake adding to the perfect white silence that wrapped around the mourners like a shroud, like a blessing, like a promise that even grief, in time, could be transformed into something else.

39
GHOST

The first thing Maja became aware of was silence. Not the clinical quiet of hospital machines, but the absence where Sven's body had been bonded to her own. Her hands moved across the starched sheets of Danderyd Hospital, searching for the adhesive residue that no longer existed. Outside, Stockholm's December wind rattled the windows—harsh and solitary after weeks of being physically attached to another person.

The radiator beneath the window ticked steadily against the cold, a sound that reminded her of evidence being catalogued, methodical, repetitive, unavoidable.

The morning shift change shuffled past in the corridor. Fan, even her own movements felt different now— individual again, no longer restricted by chemical bonds to another body.

"Easy," said Dr. Yamamoto, the young resident whose competence reminded Maja of every rookie cop she'd trained. The woman couldn't quite hide her fascination—Maja had become Danderyd's strangest case. "You're at Danderyd, eleventh floor. It's been two months since the compound was neutralized."

Two months since she'd watched Sven die while chemically bonded to his body.

Her Kriminalinspektör instincts kicked in automatically. The tremor in her hands hadn't been there before. The way she startled at unexpected sounds, her body still remembering the constraint of forced physical connection.

"Nielsen," she said. "Is he talking yet?"

Dr. Yamamoto glanced toward the door—the universal Swedish gesture for 'someone else should handle this.' "Polisoverintendent Fältskog has been asking about your condition. Daily."

Of course he had. Maja could picture Fältskog stalking Polhems-gatan, radiating the particular anxiety of a commander whose best Kriminalinspektör had become evidence in Stockholm's most bizarre case.

"Nielsen's compound," Maja said. "I need to review his research notes. The synthesis process."

"Kriminalinspektör,   the   Polisoverintendent   specifically ordered—"

"The Polisoverintendent never watched his partner die while chemically glued to his body." Maja's voice carried the dry patience of someone who'd navigated Stockholm police bureaucracy for decades. "I did. Which makes this medical leave somewhat unprecedented."

She gestured toward the medical chart hanging at the foot of her bed. "Though I'm sure someone's already created the proper forms for it."

Through the window, she could see the Danderydsvägen inter-section. The December light shown Nordic quality—gray and filtered, like looking through frosted glass even when the sky was clear. After weeks of forced physical attachment, the sight struck her as absurd—all these separate people, never knowing what it felt like to be unable to move without affecting someone else's body.

"Kriminalinspektör   Norberg."   Polisoverintendent   Fältskog appeared in the doorway.

"Erik." She'd known him since he was a sergeant in Södermalm. "You look like hell."

"Tack så mycket. You look like someone who got chemically bonded to her partner." His attempt at humor fell flat. "The prosecutors are calling it 'aggravated assault with experimental substances.' Apparently there's no existing statute for what Nielsen did."

"Leave it to Swedish law to find bureaucratic precision even for the unprecedented," Maja said.

"Nielsen's compound didn't just create physical bonding, Erik. It made us unwilling witnesses to each other's responses."

Outside, snowflakes drifted past the window, each following its separate path.

"When can you return to duty?" Fältskog asked.

"When I stop flinching when people stand too close to me," Maja said. "When I stop instinctively checking my peripheral vision for someone who's no longer chemically attached to my side."

Fältskog studied her with the expression of someone realizing his strangest case had become his most complex. Maja watched the February afternoon press against the windows, Stockholm continuing its predictable patterns while she lay here, the only living witness to what happened when two people were forced to witness death while chemically bonded together.

"When you're ready to come back," Fältskog said, "this case is going to require someone who understands what Nielsen's compound actually does."

She met his eyes. Her trauma had become her qualification. The thought should have angered her, but instead she felt the familiar weight of Swedish institutional pragmatism—making use of what you had.

"Erik," she said, watching the December light fade over Stockholm's rooftops. "What Nielsen discovered about human dependency—it wasn't what he expected."

"No?"

"People aren't meant to witness each other's deaths that intimately. We're not built for it." She touched the adhesive residue still visible on her wrist. "But we survive it anyway. Even when we shouldn't."

Fältskog nodded, understanding passing between them. Decades of police work, of seeing what people could endure.

"I'll be back next week," Maja said.

ACT 3

Justice

40

JUSTITIEDEPARTEMENTET

"We've never prosecuted anything like this before." Chief Prosecutor Helena Lindholm spread crime scene photographs across her desk at the Justitiedepartementet. The winter light streaming through the ministry's tall windows caught the edges of each photograph, making them gleam like artifacts from some macabre exhibition.

"Murder, we can handle," Lindholm said, adjusting her reading glasses with the weary precision of someone who'd spent decades translating human horror into legal categories. "But what do we call forcing two Kriminalinspektörs to experience the same death while chemically bound together? There's no precedent for methodically documented torture through enforced proximity."

Almqvist stood by the window, watching snow fall over Gamla Stan's medieval streets. Evidence boxes stacked behind her contained fragments of Nielsen's work—each document part of a larger horror that somehow exceeded the legal framework designed to contain it.

"The technical testimony alone will take weeks," Lindholm continued, lifting another folder thick with expert witness statements. "We'll have the SKL explaining molecular structures, Danderyd's staff describing the adhesive properties, forensics teams analyzing compound composition. Perfect documentation of methodology." She looked up at Almqvist. "But how do we document what Kriminalinspektör Norberg actually experienced? How do we turn the trauma of being physically bound to her dying partner into admissible evidence?"

"We ask her to testify," Almqvist said. "And hope it's enough."

Lindholm held up another photograph—Maja and Sven in Danderyd's emergency room, still bound by Nielsen's adhesive. The image showed two people fused together by chemistry, conscious and separate yet unable to break apart.

"How do we make a judge understand?" Lindholm's voice carried the frustration of a prosecutor who'd built her career on precedent and procedure. "Being chemically bound to your dying partner, unable to separate, unable to help, unable to even look away?"

"And Nielsen himself?" Almqvist turned from the window, watching pedestrians hurry past on Regeringsgatan below. "His lawyer's already building a defense around academic research gone wrong. Trying to frame methodically documented torture as a tragic accident during legitimate scientific investigation."

"Herregud," Lindholm muttered, using the mild oath that had served her through thirty years of prosecuting human stupidity. "As if accidentally creating a compound that bonds people together while keeping them conscious through trauma was just another day in academic research."

More photographs showed Nielsen's previous victims—the Söderberg case, the others.

"The first three couples are the real challenge," Lindholm continued, pulling out another set of files. "Nielsen wasn't physically present for any of those. We have to prove he designed the methodology, provided the compound to Erik, and directed the selection of victims—all while maintaining plausible deniability as the supervising academic."

Almqvist turned back from the window. "What does Erik's testimony give us?"

"Enough to establish Nielsen as the architect, hopefully. Erik's admitted Nielsen provided detailed instructions for compound application, victim selection criteria, documentation requirements. But the defense will argue Erik acted independently—a graduate student who took research too far while his professor was safely in his office at KI."

"Except Nielsen kept copies of everything."

"Ja, including Erik's field reports from each site. Nielsen's handwritten notes in the margins, corrections to technique, suggestions for 'improving data collection.'" Lindholm's voice carried the disgust of someone who'd spent too many hours reading academic discussions of torture methodology. "He was directing every step from his office, just smart enough never to get his hands dirty until the end."

"The Strandberg case gives us precedent. Shows a pattern of deliberate experimentation. And Erik's starting to talk, providing details about their methodology, their selection of victims..."

"But Tor complicates things." Almqvist moved to study the evidence boxes. "His own son. The defense will try to use that to argue against premeditation."

"Except we have his research notes." Lindholm lifted a thick folder filled with Nielsen's architectural handwriting. "Every detail documented with perfect academic precision. How he designed the compound specifically to maintain consciousness throughout the process. How he chose victims based on their existing bonds— family, professional partnerships—to study their reactions to enforced proximity during trauma..."

"We'll need Anna Nielsen's testimony," Lindholm said, opening another file. "She saw him experiment on their son. Watched him document Tor's breakdown like it was just another research project. The boy's still at Sankt Erik's, still dealing with what his father did to him."

"If she'll testify." Almqvist remembered Anna's kitchen in Säljemar, the kaffe pot still steaming on the counter, a mother's hands shaking as she described watching her husband document their son's trauma . "She's spent years trying to escape his methodology. Coming to court means facing it all again."

"We need her." Lindholm's voice carried the steel that had made her one of Stockholm's most effective prosecutors. "The judge has to understand this wasn't just academic research that went wrong. Nielsen deliberately designed that compound to keep his victims conscious and physically bound throughout the entire process. He chose them specifically for their close bonds, documented every moment of their suffering..."

She stopped, studying another photograph—the chemical burns on Maja's skin where Nielsen's adhesive had bound her to her partner. "The defense will try to paint him as a brilliant scientist who lost perspective. But these..." She gestured to the evidence boxes. "These show something else."

"And Kriminalinspektör Norberg?" Almqvist asked. "Will she be able to testify?"

Lindholm's hands stilled on the photographs. Asking a Kriminalinspektör to relive being bound to her dying partner—even veteran prosecutors had limits.

"The doctors at Danderyd say her recovery is progressing. But describing what she experienced to a judge... having to relive those final moments when she was physically bound to Sven, feeling his body fail while being unable to separate from him..."

Through the windows, Stockholm looked peaceful. Nothing in the orderly streets suggested the horrors documented in these files.

Almqvist gathered her coat from the back of the chair.

"I need to get to Danderyd," she said. "Maja's starting to remember more details."

"Good," Lindholm said, though they both knew that "good" was relative when it came to traumatic memories. "We need her perspective on what actually happened in that warehouse.

"Anna Nielsen is going to see Tor tomorrow," Almqvist added.

Lindholm nodded, carefully returning photographs to their evidence boxes. Thirty years of prosecuting human cruelty had taught Lindholm to handle evidence without flinching, but Nielsen's methodical documentation of torture tested even her professional detachment.

41

PSYCHOLOGIST

"So," said Dr. Eva-Lena Nilsson, settling into the visitor's chair beside Maja's hospital bed at Danderyd, "tell me what you remember."

The Polismyndigheten crisis psychologist was younger than Maja had expected—probably fresh from university with theories about trauma recovery that would crumble like day-old kanelbullar when confronted with the reality of Nielsen's methodology. Still, her eyes suggested she'd already begun learning what the textbooks couldn't teach.

Maja watched snow beginning to fall past her window onto Danderydsvägen. Her hands trembled against the hospital's regulation blanket. At least the physical symptoms gave her something concrete to focus on, unlike the bureaucratic maze that would inevitably follow this conversation.

"Everything," Maja said, surprised by how clinical her own voice sounded. "The compound spreading across our skin like some perverted superglue from a children's craft project gone horribly wrong. The way it hardened, binding us together while Sven..." She paused, watching another snowflake drift past. "While Sven died against me, convulsion by convulsion."

Strange how police training prepared you for many things but not for being turned into a living laboratory experiment. Though perhaps that was just another oversight in the curriculum at Polishögskolan, tucked between "Community Relations" and "Advanced Criminal Psychology."

Dr. Nilsson made a small note in her Moleskin journal, probably documenting another case study for her eventual dissertation on law enforcement trauma. The academic food chain, Maja reflected, seemed to extend even into hospital rooms. "And you maintained awareness throughout? Even during the final stages?"

"Nielsen designed it that way." The bastard had thought of everything, really. "Full consciousness throughout the process—can't have proper documentation if the subjects pass out from shock. Very thorough, our university researcher. The kind of methodical approach that would have made him an excellent police Kriminalin-spektör, if he hadn't chosen to become a monster instead."

The Clas Ohlson wall clock ticked, each second marked and measured like evidence in a case file. "You don't have to continue," the psychologist said. "We can take this slowly."

"Slowly." Maja almost smiled. " She shifted against her pillows. "Sven figured it out near the end. We weren't just victims, we were research subjects. Our partnership was the perfect test case for theories about enforced dependency."

Dr. Nilsson made another note. "And now? How are you processing these memories?"

"The doctors at Kungsmedicinska have been very helpful," Maja said dryly. "Apparently my nervous system is still processing phantom sensations from prolonged enforced contact. They have a whole technical vocabulary for it now—Nielsen would be pleased to know his research is advancing medical understanding."

Her hands moved restlessly over the blanket. Even now, part of her expected to feel Sven there, the weight of another person bound impossibly close. Human bodies, it seemed, were remarkably adapt-able to circumstances they should never have to endure.

"Have you been able to sleep?" Dr. Nilsson asked, her Pilot pen hovering above the notebook.

"Sleep comes and goes." Maja watched the snow continue its patient accumulation on the window ledge. "When it does come, I dream about Nielsen's other subjects: Tor, the Lindstroms, the Bengtssons and the Strandbergs.. We're all bound together in some impossible configuration, like a grotesque human puzzle that can't be solved." She paused. "Helvete. At least in dreams, the experience is democratically distributed."

The psychologist studied her carefully over reading glasses. "And during these dreams, what do you feel?"

"Helplessness, mostly. Though I suppose that was the point of his research. Can't study enforced dependency if subjects retain the ability to separate."

"That must be overwhelming," Dr. Nilsson said. "Carrying not just your own trauma, but the memory of being forced to witness his suffering at such immediate proximity."

At least the psychologist wasn't trying to find deeper meaning in Nielsen's experiment. Sometimes trauma was just trauma. No hidden wisdom, no transformative insights, just the raw human cost of someone else's intellectual curiosity.

"I want to see the case files," Maja said, turning from the window. "Nielsen's research notes, the compound's composition—everything. Maybe if I understand the technical aspects, I can make sense of what my body is still processing."

"Kriminalinspektör." Dr. Nilsson set her notebook aside. "Your analytical mind, your need to understand, these are strengths that served you well. But right now, they might be preventing you from processing the emotional impact of what happened."

The afternoon kaffe cart made its rounds in the corridor beyond her door. Some things, at least, remained mercifully unchanged.

"Emotional impact." Maja considered the phrase. "You mean

aside from being turned into a living research apparatus while my partner died against me?" She watched an SL bus navigate the snowy hospital grounds below. "I keep thinking there should be some protocol for this situation in our training manual. Something between 'Officer Down' and 'Unusual Incident Reporting.'"

"By allowing yourself to grieve," the psychologist said, "not just as a Kriminalinspektör analyzing evidence, but as a human being who lost someone important to them. Someone you were forced to watch die in the most intimate, invasive circumstances imaginable."

"Grief," Maja repeated. "Right. I'll add that to my to-do list, right after 'recover from experimental adhesive compound' and 'testify in what will probably be Sweden's most unusual murder trial.'"

"The problem with grief is that my body still thinks Sven is there. The nerve damage from Nielsen's compound... the doctors say some of it might be permanent. So when I try to process his death, my nervous system insists he's still present."

"You're afraid the physical sensations will overwhelm you again," Dr. Nilsson finished. "That memory will become physical experience."

"Exactly." Maja's voice was matter-of-fact. "It's like being haunted by someone who isn't quite dead in your nervous system. Nielsen's final gift, trauma with its own built-in replay mechanism."

Dr. Nilsson leaned forward slightly. "Tell me about Sven. Not about the end, but about your partnership. What kind of police officer was he?"

The question pulled Maja back from darker territories. "Steady. The kind of Kriminalinspektör who brought kanelbullar to morning briefings because he believed sugar helped evidence make sense." For the first time since the psychologist had arrived, Maja almost smiled. "He had this theory that you couldn't properly understand human stupidity on an empty stomach."

"And as a partner?"

"He knew when to ask questions and when to just listen. During interrogations, he'd let me push the technical angles while he watched for the human tells." Maja's hands stilled on the blanket. "We had this rhythm—I'd focus on the evidence trail, he'd focus on the people."

"Until Nielsen turned that partnership into research data," Dr. Nilsson observed.

"Until Nielsen turned it into his personal laboratory." Maja looked back toward the window where snow continued to fall on Danderydsvägen. "

42

ANNA VISITS TOR

Years of forms, and Anna still couldn't say her son's name without tasting copper. The social services reports called it "patient recovery trajectory" and "institutional adjustment metrics." The Swedish state had always excelled at transforming human suffering into manageable categories. It was almost admirable, in its way: this ability to take a father's systematic torture of his own child and reduce it to medical codes and treatment codes.

Ward 3C smelled of institutional kaffe and cheap disinfectant. A nurse with tired eyes and a Kommunal pin checked Anna's credentials against a clipboard. "He's been asking about visitors," she said. Years of silence, then suddenly this.

"Asking what specifically?" Anna said.

"Whether anyone would visit who wasn't from Socialstyrelsen or the prosecutor's office." The nurse's expression suggested this was a reasonable concern. "He's quite articulate about the distinction."

Anna wondered if they taught that at nursing school: how to discuss a boy's terror of authority figures with the same professional detachment used for medication schedules. Swedish healthcare was efficient, comprehensive, utterly committed to treating symptoms while the disease flourished in conference rooms and faculty lounges.

Through the observation window, Anna could see her son sitting by the safety glass. His posture matched what Gustaf had maintained during faculty meetings: back straight, hands positioned with careful symmetry. Even here, locked away from his father's influence, Tor sat like a professor. Some lessons ran too deep to unlearn.

She made a mental note: Subject displays learned behavioral patterns consistent with academic environment. Posture suggests internalized authority structures. The prosecutor would want details like this, evidence of how completely Gustaf had shaped his son, even in captivity.

The nurse unlocked the door with her key card. "Thirty minutes," she said. "Press the call button if you need assistance."

Anna stepped inside. The monthly reports hadn't prepared her for seeing him like this. He was still her boy, but wrapped in institutional quiet like a specimen in formaldehyde.

"Tor."

"Mamma." He didn't turn from the window. "The prosecutor told you to come."

Not a question. Anna settled into the standard-issue chair beside him. "Kriminalinspektör Almqvist said they need testimony about the early experiments. What your father did before he moved to human subjects."

"Human subjects." Tor's laugh held no warmth. "Like I wasn't human when he started documenting my responses to his adhesive."

February light caught his profile through the safety glass. Anna could still see the boy who'd once mixed compounds in Gustaf's lab, back when research meant crystallization patterns instead of... this.

The progression was methodical, she realized. Classic academic escalation: start with voluntary participation, establish trust, then gradually expand the parameters of acceptable research. Gustaf hadn't become a monster overnight. He'd followed a perfectly logical trajectory from respected professor to systematic abuser. The university had probably seen the warning signs and filed them under "academic freedom."

"When did you know?" Tor asked. "When did you realize he'd stopped being a scientist and become something else?"

Anna's hands clenched. "The day he stopped using your name in his research notes. When you became 'Subject A' instead of our son."

"Subject A." Tor finally turned to face her. His eyes carried Gustaf's analytical precision, but the anger was purely his own. "Do you remember what came after Subject A?"

Anna's mouth went dry. "Tor..."

"Subject B was that girl from his undergraduate seminar. The one who thought he was mentoring her academic career." "Subject C was her roommate. They both volunteered, you know. For extra credit."

Three subjects minimum, Anna thought automatically. Sufficient for preliminary statistical analysis. The prosecutor would need this information: the scope of Gustaf's research, the number of victims. She found herself cataloging details even now, her mind falling back into the old patterns of documentation and evidence-gathering. Some professional habits proved more resilient than maternal instincts.

Snow drifted past the window. Anna watched it settle on St. Erik's courtyard, quiet and persistent, burying everything equally.

"You documented everything," Tor said. "Every application of the compound. Every measurement of restricted movement. Every notation about breathing difficulty." His hands gripped the chair's armrests. "Perfect research methodology. Just like he taught you."

"I thought I was gathering evidence," Anna said. "Something to stop him with."

"Evidence?" Tor's laugh was bitter. "His lab notebooks were evidence. The video recordings were evidence. The chemical analysis of his compounds was evidence." His knuckles went white against the institutional furniture. "But you kept writing in your little notebook anyway. Every day. Like any other forsknings assistent."

He wasn't wrong. Anna had maintained her documentation with

the same obsessive precision Gustaf demanded from all his research assistants. Even while watching her husband torture their son, she'd followed proper academic protocol. The Swedish commitment to thorough record-keeping ran deeper, apparently, than basic human decency.

Anna forced herself to meet his gaze. "I was afraid."

"Of him?"

"Of what he was becoming. Of how completely he'd transformed our family into research data." She paused. "Of how easily I'd become complicit."

Tor studied her face. "The night you left for Säljemar, did you consider taking me with you?"

"Every second. But you were already in the system by then. Social services, medical supervision, legal guardianship..." She stopped. It sounded pathetic even to her.

"The system," Tor repeated. "You know what's interesting about Swedish social services? They're designed to protect children from abusive parents. But when the abusive parent is a respected professor conducting 'research,' suddenly it becomes a medical issue requiring institutional supervision." His smile was sharp. "Very efficient. Much easier than admitting they enabled three years of systematic torture."

"I was seventeen," Tor said. "Still legally your son. You could have fought for custody."

"Against the university? Against his research grants? Against the medical establishment that was documenting your 'recovery'?" Anna shook her head. "I barely had money for diesel to get to Säljemar."

"So you ran." No accusation in his voice now, just tired understanding. "Left me here with his methodology and your documentation."

Anna saw their reflection in the window: mother and son, separated by years and a wall of institutional protocol. He looked older, harder. The boy who used to help with chemistry experiments was gone.

This was what the prosecutor needed to understand, Anna realized. Not just Gustaf's methods, but the entire ecosystem that made them possible. The university that prioritized research funding over student welfare. The medical establishment that treated torture as experimental data. The social services that confused institutional authority with professional competence. Her son hadn't just been victimized by his father; he'd been failed by every system designed to protect him.

"The trial starts next month," she said. "Kriminalinspektör Almqvist thinks your testimony could be crucial."

"My testimony." Tor turned back to the window. "About what it feels like when someone you trust transforms you into research data. About the progression from family member to experimental subject. About how academic methodology can consume everything human in its path."

"Will you testify?"

Tor was quiet for several minutes. "Do you know what the worst part was?" he said.

Anna waited.

"Not the compound itself. Not even the physical restrictions." His voice dropped to barely above a whisper. "It was watching you write it all down. Every day. With the same careful precision he used. Like I was just another data point in your shared research project."

The room fell quiet except for the distant sound of institutional life: phones ringing, doors closing, the endless machinery of managed care.

"I'll testify," Tor said. "But not to help the prosecution understand Gustaf's methodology. I think they understand that well enough." He finally looked at her directly. "I'll testify because someone needs to explain how Swedish institutions can systematically fail to protect students while maintaining perfect documentation of that failure. It's quite an achievement, really: creating a system so committed to proper procedure that it can enable torture while keeping impeccable records."

A soft knock at the door. Visiting hours ending with Swedish punctuality. The nurse with the Kommunal badge peered in, her expression suggesting practiced sympathy combined with bureaucratic necessity.

Anna stood slowly. "I'll come back," she said. "If you want me to."

Tor's hands tapped against the chair arms, his father's old nervous habit. "Next time," he said, "try bringing my mother instead of another research assistant."

The door closed. Anna walked down Sankt Erik's corridor, her son's words following her like accusations she couldn't categorize or file away. Today, she'd finally heard her child's voice again, not filtered through monthly reports or clinical observations, but raw and real and unforgivingly human. The voice of someone who'd survived being reduced to data points and case numbers, who somehow remained human despite everything they'd done to catalog him.

Outside Sankt Erik's, the snow kept falling. Anna pulled her coat tight and walked toward the tram stop, past the perfectly maintained grounds and the tasteful signage directing visitors to various departments of managed care. The Swedish welfare state in miniature: clean, efficient, utterly committed to helping people within the boundaries of acceptable institutional behavior.

43
ANGRY SON

"Tor Nielsen spoke to his mother." Almqvist's words cut through the conference room silence. The prosecution team looked up from their files with the alertness that comes when evidence becomes human.

"When?" Prosecutor Lindholm set down the photograph she'd been studying of Nielsen's experiments, clinical precision against documented suffering.

"Yesterday at Sankt Erik's." Almqvist watched snow gather in the ministry courtyard. "All this time, building a case around clinical documentation..." She paused. "Nobody noticed the boy was listening, remembering, thinking."

"It changes everything," Lindholm said. "A coherent witness who experienced Nielsen's early experiments." She shuffled through her notes. "If he's willing to testify."

"He's angry," Almqvist said. "Not just at Nielsen, but at Anna. For documenting everything instead of stopping it."

"Can we use that?" Kommissioner Söderberg leaned forward. "The impact of a son testifying against his father..."

"If we can get him to testify at all." Lindholm spread

photographs across the table. "The defense will argue about his mental state, try to discredit anything he says."

"Nielsen's own damage becomes his shield," Almqvist said. "The man has a gift for irony."

"But combined with Kriminalinspektör Norberg's testimony..." Almqvist paused. "Two witnesses who experienced Nielsen's experiment. Who can describe what it feels like to be bound to another person during trauma."

"And Anna?" Söderberg asked.

"She's still willing to testify. Maybe more so now." Almqvist turned from the window. "Yesterday she faced what that distance cost them both."

"What about Erik?" Lindholm pulled another file from the stack.

"Erik's falling apart," Almqvist said. "Each interview, he's less composed academic, more guilty accomplice."

"Good," Söderberg said. "We need him human, not hiding behind academic jargon."

"And Nielsen himself?" Lindholm asked.

"Still recording everything," Almqvist said. "Even in detention, he's documenting responses, analyzing reactions. His lawyer can't control him."

"The press will be a problem," Lindholm said. "Once they learn Tor can communicate, they'll want interviews."

"We need to protect him," Almqvist said. "He's not just evidence, he's a victim."

Söderberg nodded. "We control the narrative through official channels only."

"Speaking of Norberg..." Lindholm hesitated. "The doctors say she's processing what happened. If she testifies..."

"When she testifies," Almqvist corrected. "She'll tell the judge what Nielsen's methodology does to a body."

The snow fell harder beyond the ministry windows. Somewhere in Danderyd, Maja was learning to live with memories of forced proximity. In St. Erik's, Tor was finally breaking years of silence. In Kronobergshäktet, Nielsen continued his observations, documenting his own downfall.

44

CRACKING

The interrogation room at Kronoberg Prison smelled of disinfectant and fear. Erik's defense attorney Frida Sjögren arranged her files while fluorescent lights hummed overhead, the sound mixing with Stockholm's distant traffic through reinforced windows. Fifteen years of defense work, and she'd never seen a client quite like this one.

Erik traced chemical formulas on the metal table with trembling fingers. His kaffe sat untouched, cold as the February morning outside. Once, she'd seen him deliver a lecture at Kungsmedicinska, composed, precise, every gesture calculated. Now he looked like ice breaking up on Riddarfjärden in spring: all that careful structure coming apart.

"The prosecutor needs your testimony about the compound's progression," she said. "About how Nielsen developed the formula."

"Test subjects," Erik said, and for a moment he sounded exactly like his mentor. "Always subjects. Never victims. Distance maintains objectivity."

Sjögren had heard this before: doctors calling deaths "negative outcomes," police calling murders "incidents." Professional language as armor. But Erik's armor was cracking.

"Even when Tor started screaming, we maintained proper documentation. Recording everything while Anna..." He stopped, hands pressing flat against steel.

"Fan," he whispered. "The sounds they made when the compound started binding them together... when they realized they couldn't separate..." His hands moved faster, sketching molecular structures. "Nielsen said it was necessary. For the research."

"The prosecution needs specific details about the compound's development. About how Nielsen refined the formula between cases." She heard herself retreating into lawyer-speak. Safer to discuss evidence than to think about what the evidence showed.

"Refined?" Erik's laugh was sharp, bitter.

"After each failure, how he adjusted the molecular structure. More permanent."

"After Lindstroms, he knew it needed to maintain consciousness longer. The subjects had to stay awake. Had to experience everything."

The guard behind the observation window shifted in his chair. Probably wondering why this well-dressed academic was falling apart over chemistry equations.

"Helvete!" His hands slammed against steel, the sound echoing off concrete walls. "I filmed it all—the compound taking hold, binding them together while they struggled. Nielsen called it essential data collection." His voice cracked. "Their faces, when they realized... when they understood what was happening to their bodies..."

A bus rumbled past on Kungsholmsgatan, its diesel engine mixing with the prison's ventilation system. The mundane and the monstrous, side by side.

"And Kriminalinspektör Norberg..." His voice fractured. "Nielsen especially wanted her conscious. Made her witness everything, her partner's system failing while she remained physically bound to him, unable to help, unable even to turn away. Perfect data collection."

"Erik." She kept her voice steady, fifteen years of practice with clients on the edge. "The evidence. Tell me what happened."

"Evidence?" He laughed, but nothing about it was funny. "It's all here." His fingers tapped his temple. "Every scream. Every struggle as they realized they couldn't separate."

"The compound's structure..." His fingers traced molecules on steel. "Beautiful, really. Forces two bodies to remain bound together no matter how they struggle. Elegant chemistry for ugly purposes."

Even now, part of him still admired the science. That was the most disturbing thing, how easily brilliance became monstrous when divorced from conscience.

"We refined it after each trial," he continued, slipping back into Nielsen's clinical language. "Strengthened the molecular bonds. Extended consciousness duration." His fingers stilled. "I filmed his son. Recorded Anna begging while Nielsen took notes on optimal stress response."

The corrections officer checked his watch. Almost time. Sjögren gathered her files, but Erik wasn't finished.

"He made me believe it was research." The words spilled out. "Said distance was necessary. Perfect observation.

"He taught me to see data points. Not people." His voice caught. "Not even Tor. Not Anna..."

"But you see them now," Sjögren said.

"I can't testify." His whisper was barely audible. "The way they struggled to separate. Their terror when they realized they couldn't. Norberg's face when she felt her partner die while being physically bound to him..."

Corporate fraud, embezzlement, even murder, those she could handle. But this systematic torture dressed up as research? This was something else entirely.

"Nielsen says I'm contaminating the data with emotion." His voice cracked. "But I keep seeing them. All that precision put to such ugly use."

"You have to testify," she said. "Tell them how Nielsen developed the compound."

He met Sjögren's eyes, something shifting in his expression. "I helped perfect that compound."

The February wind rattled the windows.

"I'll testify," Erik said, his voice raw but steady. "Not for our methodology. For them." His fingers traced one last formula on the steel table. "They deserve to be seen as people. Not subjects."

Keys rattled in the corridor. The corrections officer opened the door, letting in a slice of pale Stockholm winter light.

"Tell them I'm ready," Erik said, standing slowly. "This time I'll document everything as a witness, not an observer."

Sjögren gathered her files, watching her client straighten his shoulders. She'd never seen a transformation quite like this, from clinical detachment to something approaching grace. Not redemption, perhaps. But recognition. It would have to be enough.

45

NIELSEN

March snow fell past the reinforced windows of Kronobergsgatan Prison, each flake distinct before melting into gray slush. Professor Nielsen arranged his papers with the same precision he'd once used to organize lecture notes, a month of custody having done nothing to diminish his certainty.

"They'll seek life imprisonment," Anders Ekman his defense attorney said, the gravity of the moment evident in his voice.

Nielsen's smile carried decades of academic authority. "An understandable reaction to a paradigm shift."

"This isn't theory, Professor." Ekman pushed a photograph across the table, Norberg adhered to Sven long on the floor, her face contorted as Nielsen's experiment took effect. "Erik Thorsessen filmed everything. The judge will see her forced to experience her partner's death."

"Erik documented beautifully." Nielsen studied the image with clinical satisfaction. "Especially Kriminalinspektör Norberg's physical bonding during her partner's bodily failure. Previous subjects lost cognitive function during trauma, but she maintained perfect analytical awareness. Even as Kriminalinspektör Svensson died beside her, their bodies chemically fused by the compound, she continued to provide detailed verbal reports."

The casual satisfaction in Nielsen's voice hit Ekman like a physical blow. "She was screaming."

"Yes, fascinating vocalization patterns. Though her training allowed her to articulate the experience with remarkable precision. 'I can feel his body convulsing against mine,' she said. 'His blood is pooling where we're joined.' Unprecedented documentation of enforced proximity during death."

Ekman had seen the footage. Norberg's tears streaming as the compound bound her physically to her dying partner, her voice breaking as she described each physical sensation Nielsen demanded she report, unable to move away, unable to help, forced to witness his death from inches away.

"The prosecution has Anna's testimony," Ekman tried again. "About how you adjusted the compound dosage while Tor's mind broke."

"Psychological fragmentation under sustained chemical bonding," Nielsen corrected. "Anna never understood she was witnessing breakthrough research. When Tor began experiencing cognitive dissolution, the trauma of being physically fused for hours while conscious, she became hysterical instead of recognizing the theoretical implications."

Ekman gathered the defense files. There was no reaching this man. Nielsen had reduced his son, his wife, two police officers, and God knew how many others to data points in his grand theory of consciousness.

"Court starts at nine tomorrow."

"Excellent." Nielsen's satisfaction deepened. "Kriminalinspektör Norberg's testimony will validate everything. When she describes the physical bonding, perfect awareness maintained even as her partner died against her body, the scientific significance will be undeniable."

The door closed with institutional finality. Through the glass,

Nielsen continued working, his certainty intact and terrible. In the corridor, Ekman heard him speaking to empty air: "Perfect documentation of enforced physical proximity during death. Norberg validates the theoretical framework completely..."

The words faded, but the clinical satisfaction lingered. Even facing life imprisonment, Nielsen remained convinced he'd unlocked the secrets of human consciousness. The cost—his son's sanity, his wife's horror, three couples and two officers' trauma—was simply the price of scientific progress.

Outside, snow continued to fall, each flake separate until it touched the ground and became something else entirely.

46

POLICE DISCUSS MAJA

The Kommissioner's office absorbed sound like fresh snow, leather chairs and dark wood holding secrets. "Kriminalinspektör Norberg's testimony will be crucial," Kommissioner Söderberg said, removing his reading glasses. His office, with its view over Kungsholmen, felt too formal for discussing how completely Nielsen's methodology had altered one of their own. The same room where they debated parking violations now hosted conversations about the dissolution of human boundaries. Helvete, even the forms felt inadequate.

"She's getting stronger," Almqvist replied, knowing this was only partially true. "The physical therapy is helping with the tremors.

Polisoverintendent Fältskog leaned forward. "The defense will try to use her condition against us. Claim the compound's effects on her nervous system make her an unreliable witness."

"That's exactly why her testimony is so powerful," Almqvist countered. "She can explain precisely what Nielsen's methodology does to the human body. How deliberately he designed that compound to maintain awareness while being physically bound to another person during trauma."

"Ah," Fältskog said with dry appreciation. "The perfect legal paradox. Too damaged to be credible, too credible to ignore." Another absurdity for their growing collection.

Söderberg studied Almqvist's face. "In your opinion, Helena... will she ever return to active duty?"

Almqvist thought of Maja's trembling hands at physical therapy, of nerve pathways permanently damaged. The human body wasn't designed for such violations, yet here they were, trying to categorize the uncategorizable. "She's still one of our best Kriminalinspektörs," she said. "Her analytical mind hasn't changed. But what Nielsen's experiment did to her..." She paused. "Some experiences change us permanently. The question isn't whether she'll return to who she was before, but how she'll use what she learned."

"But can she handle crime scenes?" Fältskog pressed. "Carry a weapon with those tremors? Chase a suspect down Drottninggatan if she has to?"

Outside, church bells from Sankt Göran chimed the hour. Three experienced police officers, Almqvist thought, reduced to discussing whether someone could chase criminals when her nervous system still believed it was attached to a dead man. The absurdity would be amusing if it weren't so tragic.

"Dr. Yamamoto says one year minimum for the worst of the tremors," Almqvist said. "But the nerve damage... Her nervous system is trying to process phantom sensations from a physical connection that no longer exists."

"Phantom sensations?" Söderberg frowned.

"She can still feel Sven dying. Months later, and her body thinks it's still attached to his."

The room went quiet. Outside, a tram clanged along Hantverkargatan, carrying people who had no idea what they were discussing in this sealed administrative space. Normal people with normal concerns, their bodies still their own.

"Let's get through the trial first," Fältskog said. "See how she handles testifying. Then we can talk about her future." He smiled wryly. "One impossible situation at a time."

Through the window, snow began falling on Kungsholmen. Each flake separate and distinct, the way human beings were supposed to be.

47
CHILDHOOD

Anna Nielsen's footsteps echoed through Sankt Erik's secure psychiatric ward, a sound she'd never thought to document in all her years of clinical observation. The place smelled of disinfectant and defeat. Today she carried a photo album instead of her usual notes— some things, she'd finally learned, couldn't be measured.

The nurse barely glanced up; Anna had become part of the ward's routine. Through the observation window, she could see Tor by the window, February light making everything look bleached. At least he wasn't sitting with that rigid posture Gustaf had drilled into him. Small victories, she supposed.

"You came back," Tor said when she entered. His voice had lost some of that academic precision Gustaf had insisted on, progress, in its way. The medical reports on his table sat unopened.

"Not reading your files anymore?" she asked.

"Tired of being a case study." He glanced at the album. "Even my own."

Anna set the album on the table. "Thought we could look at some old photos. No analysis, no notes. Just... remembering."

Tor's fingers moved toward the leather binding, then stopped. "You used to document everything. Every birthday, every reaction. Just like him."

"Ja, I did. This is different. These are from before he turned our kitchen into a research lab."

Outside, snow was starting to fall over Södermalm. Even through institutional windows, Stockholm managed to look beautiful in February. Nielsen had always hated winter, said it introduced too many variables into his observations.

Anna opened to the first page. "Your eighth birthday. Look at Dad here, he's actually smiling just... enjoying watching you open presents."

The photo showed Gustaf with his arm around Tor, both of them laughing at something off-camera. No clipboards, no observation sheets. Just a father and son being normal.

"I wanted to be just like him then," Tor said. "The great Professor Nielsen. Students fighting to get into his seminars at Kungsmedicin-ska." His hands were steady now on the photo. "Funny how admiration works. You want to be someone, right up until you realize what they actually are."

"I should have stopped him," Anna said. "When he started timing your emotional responses, measuring your reactions to physical contact. I just... kept taking notes alongside him."

"You were protecting your career."

"I was protecting my cowardice." She turned the page. "Here, summer house in Skåne. You built that sandcastle for hours. He helped you, remember? Just playing."

A nurse glanced through the observation window, making her rounds. Standard procedure, they documented everything here too. But Tor wasn't performing anymore, wasn't sitting with that perfect academic posture Gustaf had demanded.

"The prosecutors want me to testify," Anna said. "About what he did. To you, to our family."

"What will you tell them?"

"The truth. That he turned his own son into a research subject. That I helped him do it." She paused at a photo of the three of them at Gamla Stan. "Kriminalinspektör Norberg will testify too, about what his compound does to the body."

Tor was quiet for a long moment. "The Kriminalinspektör, she was bound to her partner when he died. Couldn't move, couldn't help, couldn't even look away. Just had to experience everything he experienced." His voice was flat. "Dad's methodology worked perfectly."

"That's the goddamn horror of it," Anna said. "It wasn't a failure. It was exactly what he wanted to prove."

"But she survived. And she's fighting back. Like you are." Tor traced the edge of his childhood self in the photograph. "Sometimes I still think in his patterns. Analyzing reactions, measuring responses. Like he rewired my brain."

"Maybe he did. But you're choosing how to use it now." Anna turned to a photo from Tor's tenth birthday. Gustaf was laughing, actually laughing, at something Tor had said. "Look at this. Remember when he could still laugh without analyzing what made something funny?"

"Before he started timing my reactions to his jokes."

"Exactly." She closed the album carefully. "Will you testify?"

"If it helps convict him. If it helps other families." Tor met her eyes directly. "But I want you there. Not as my case manager. As my mother."

Anna nodded, gathering the album. "I'll be there. And Tor... Kriminalinspektör Norberg asked to meet with you, when you're ready. She wants to understand what it was like, growing up as his test subject. It might help her case too."

"The Inspecktor who was bound to her partner?" Tor's voice tightened. "Dad's compound... it was based on what he learned from me, wasn't it? All those years of enforced proximity experiments, measuring my responses..."

"Yes. He perfected it on you first." Anna's hands clenched around the album. "That's why her testimony matters so much. What he did to her partner proves it wasn't just family psychology gone wrong. It was deliberate criminal research."

––––––––

Later that afternoon, Kommissioner Fältskog sat in his office at Polishuset, staring at the medical reports from Danderyd. Söderberg occupied the chair across from his desk, both men avoiding eye contact with the stack of papers between them.

"Helvete," Fältskog muttered, pushing Dr. Yamamoto's assessment away. "We can't put Norberg back on active duty. Look at this, permanent nerve damage, altered pain perception, psychological trauma responses..." He shook his head. "Her nervous system is permanently fucked."

Söderberg lit a cigarette, despite the office smoking ban. Some conversations required nicotine. "What about analysis work? Her experience with psychological manipulation, understanding of enforced proximity trauma..."

"Every case would trigger her." Fältskog pulled out his own cigarettes. "She was bound to Sven when he died, Couldn't move, couldn't help, had to feel everything he felt. Nielsen's compound worked exactly as designed." He flicked ash into his kaffe mug. "Now every case involving physical restraint could trigger those same neural pathways."

"So what do we do? Medical retirement?"

"Probably." Fältskog stared out at the darkening sky over Kungsholmen. "One of our best investigators, destroyed by some academic psychopath's experiment in human bonding."

A truth that would never appear in his meticulously documented observations, his carefully measured variables, his precisely calculated outcomes. A truth about what it meant to be human, separate yet connected, distinct yet related, individual yet part of something larger. A truth that could be approached but never captured, witnessed but never fully understood.

A truth that Maja Norberg now carried within her damaged nervous system, a living reminder that some experiments succeed in ways their creators never intended.

48
OPENING DAY

The oak-paneled courtroom at Stockholms Tingsrätt held the weight of Swedish winter in its silence. Morning light filtered through tall windows, casting long shadows across brass fixtures that had witnessed decades of human folly presented as legal argument.

Almqvist settled into her chair behind the prosecution table, watching the familiar theater of justice unfold. How peculiar, she thought, that humans had developed such elaborate rituals to contain what they couldn't understand. The courtroom transformed murderers into defendants, horror into evidence, incomprehensible cruelty into neat legal categories.

Nielsen sat with perfect academic posture, arranging his papers as if preparing for a faculty meeting rather than facing judgment for methodical horror.

State Prosecutor Helena Lindholm stood before the judge, her voice carrying the weary precision of someone who had spent too many years viewing human cruelty. "This is not a case about academic research gone wrong. This is about a man who deliberately designed a methodology to destroy the most fundamental boundaries between human beings."

"The evidence will show," Lindholm continued, "how the defendant refined his methodology through multiple victims. How he progressed from crude attempts at forced physical bonding to the perfect creation of inescapable proximity during trauma. How he turned his own son into a test subject before moving on to others."

Nielsen's pen moved across his notepad.

Even his own trial had become research material. Almqvist watched him taking notes and felt a strange pity, not for his victims, but for Nielsen himself. Imagine living in a world where every human interaction was merely data to be collected. Even his own prosecution had become another fascinating case study. It was almost zen-like in its complete disconnection from normal human experience.

She wondered if he'd ever experienced a moment of genuine uncertainty, or if everything, even his own death, when it came, would simply be another interesting observation to catalog.

The defense lawyer rose, adjusting his suit with movements that suggested he'd rather be anywhere else. "The evidence will show that my client's research had legitimate scientific purposes. That the tragic outcomes were not intended—"

"Not intended?" Lindholm's voice cut through his careful framing. "The evidence will show how deliberately the defendant designed his compound. How he refined it through multiple victims, documenting every step with perfect academic precision. How he created a methodology specifically to maintain full consciousness while physically binding people together, to force awareness even as one person experienced systemic failure while the other remained helplessly bound to them."

"You will see," Lindholm concluded, "how a respected professor at Kungsmedicinska Institutet turned his academic theories into carefully documented destruction. How he progressed from experimenting on his own son to perfecting a methodology that could force two separate individuals to experience trauma in inescapable proximity, one forced to witness the other's death from inches away, completely unable to help or even turn away."

The defense lawyer tried again, his voice growing thinner with each attempt. "The court must consider the broader context of psychological research. My client's work at Kungsmedicinska represented groundbreaking theories about human connection—"

"The court will consider what he achieved," Lindholm cut in. "Through a mother who watched her child become a test subject. Through a Kriminalinspektör who was physically bound to her dying partner, forced to witness his suffering from inches away with no possibility of escape."

"This was not research gone wrong," Lindholm addressed the judge. "He didn't lose control of his research. He achieved exactly what he set out to achieve."

"When you hear the testimony," she concluded, "you'll understand. This was not an experiment that failed. This was human autonomy itself, methodically destroyed."

The judge called for the first witness.

When Almqvist took the stand, she found herself contemplating the strange rituals humans created to process incomprehensible acts.

"Please state your name and rank for the court," Lindholm began.

"Helena Almqvist, Kriminalinspektör with the National Criminal Investigation Department."

"And when did you become involved in the Nielsen investigation?"

"I joined the case after Kriminalinspektör Norberg identified similarities between the Djurgården victims and Professor Nielsen's academic work," Almqvist replied, aware of Nielsen's growing attention. "By then, we had enough evidence of a serial killer."

"Why was that significant to the investigation?"

The methodical nature of the scenes suggested someone with scientific knowledge, systematically testing and refining a process.

Each new victim showed evidence of learning from previous attempts. It wasn't random violence."

"Walk us through the progression of these cases."

"The Djurgården victims showed his first attempts," Almqvist replied. "A couple found positioned together, crude chemical bonds forcing physical connection. The compound left distinctive traces we'd never seen before."

"And the second scene?"

"At Bromma, Henrik and Maria Bengtsson."

Nielsen's pen moved faster at the mention of names. Still collecting data, she noticed. She wondered if he remembered their faces, or if they'd become abstract variables in his personal dataset by now.

"The compound had evolved. Chemical analysis showed it now affected the nervous system, creating physical bonds that prevented any possibility of separation during trauma."

"In Björnsonsgatan, Magnus and Vera Strandberg revealed his next breakthrough. The compound could now maintain physical bonds longer."

Almqvist found herself thinking about Vera Strandberg. What would she have made of becoming a data point in Nielsen's research? The absurdity of it struck her: a woman who'd dedicated her life to nurturing young minds, reduced to a chemical reaction in someone's methodology. Life had a dark sense of humor.

Lindholm lifted another photograph.

"She survived longer than the others."

"And the attack at Danderyd?"

"His final refinement." Almqvist's hands tightened on the rail.

Kriminalinspektör Norberg survived, but Kriminalinspektör Svensson..." She paused, watching Nielsen's pen move faster. The man was practically vibrating with academic excitement. She wondered if this was how other researchers felt when their work was being discussed at conferences, probably not quite the same context, but the underlying satisfaction seemed identical.

"And this progression," Lindholm pressed, "from crude physical bonds to complete inescapable proximity during trauma, how did it align with Professor Nielsen's research?"

"Each stage matched theories he'd published at Kungsmedicinska. The Djurgården scene reflected his early work on physical dependency. By Bromma, he was implementing ideas from his latest papers on enforced proximity. Danderyd..." She met Nielsen's gaze. "Danderyd proved his theories about maintained awareness during inescapable physical connection while one person dies."

The defense lawyer stood. "

Kriminalinspektör," he began, "you testified that Kriminalinspektör Norberg connected these deaths to my client's academic work. Were other researchers in the field considered?"

"Kriminalinspektör Norberg conducted a thorough investigation," Almqvist replied. "She interviewed researchers at Kungsmedicinska, Uppsala. But Professor Nielsen's theories about forced physical proximity during trauma were unique."

"And yet these theories were published, peer-reviewed. Available to anyone in the field?"

"The compound's chemical structure matched specific modifications he'd proposed in Läkartidningen. Even the victims' positions reflected detailed protocols from his lab work. Each scene showed someone implementing his research with increasing precision."

Nielsen's pen moved steadily, documenting each answer with academic precision. Some people were so completely themselves that even criminal prosecution couldn't shake their fundamental nature. There was something almost admirable about such consistency, if it weren't so terrifying.

"Let's discuss Kriminalinspektör Norberg's focus on my client," the defense lawyer continued. "How many hours did she spend studying his research before the attack?"

"She was building a case," Almqvist replied, sensing the trap. "Following evidence that proved increasingly specific to Professor Nielsen's work."

"Or perhaps finding connections because she was looking for them?" The lawyer lifted a file. "Her case notes show hundreds of hours spent on my client's academic papers. Yet you testified that other researchers were considered?"

"Kriminalinspektör Norberg followed the evidence," Almqvist replied. "Each victim showed increasing sophistication in applying Professor Nielsen's published theories. No other researcher had proposed similar methods."

She paused, watching Nielsen's reaction to his lawyer's strategy. The man looked genuinely puzzled by the suggestion that someone might fabricate evidence against him. Of course he was, in his world-view, the connection between his theories and the murders was simply good scientific observation. Why would anyone need to manufacture such obvious correlations?

"And yet she became so focused on these theories that she continued working the case alone. Even after the Bromma scene showed the killer's growing sophistication?"

Nielsen's pen paused, his attention suddenly more acute. The defense lawyer seemed to register his client's sudden attention. Almqvist wondered if Nielsen was taking notes on his own legal strategy now.

"And why," the defense lawyer continued, "with all this focus on my client, couldn't the investigation prevent what happened to Kriminalinspektörs Norberg and Svensson?"

Almqvist met Nielsen's gaze and felt a moment of unexpected clarity.

"You're suggesting Kriminalinspektör Norberg became obsessed with your client's research?"

"I'm suggesting that when you spend hundreds of hours studying someone's theories, you might see connections where none exist."

Almqvist looked at Nielsen, who had stopped taking notes entirely. For the first time during the trial, he seemed genuinely engaged with the proceedings rather than simply documenting them.

"The connections existed," she said quietly. "Because your client's methodology was designed to be perfect. Each victim refined his process until he achieved exactly what his research predicted. He understood something fundamental about human nature that we didn't want to acknowledge—that our need to help each other, our instinct to comfort the dying, could be turned into a weapon. He weaponized human compassion itself."

Nielsen's pen began moving again, faster now.

"We couldn't prevent Danderyd because we were thinking like police officers, looking for criminals. We weren't thinking like researchers conducting experiments. By the time we understood that this was never about killing people—it was about studying what happens when you force people to experience death together—it was too late."

The defense lawyer sat down. Nielsen continued writing, and Almqvist realized he was probably taking notes on her final answer. Even her insight into his methodology had become data worth preserving.

49
ANNA ARRIVES IN STOCKHOLM

Anna's headlights swept across the E4 as she drove south from Säljemar, snow banking the roadside like courtroom barriers. Three hours to Stockholm. Three hours to prepare for explaining how her ex-husband had turned their son into a research subject.

She'd packed like heading into surgery: dark suit hanging wrinkle-free, testimony notes sorted by date, photos of Tor arranged chronologically in the passenger seat. Old habits from her lab days. Now they served as armor.

The radio crackled with traffic updates. She switched it off. Prosecutor Lindholm had called twice, wanting to rehearse her testimony. Anna had let it ring. She knew what she had to say. How Gustaf's "proximity bonding research" had meant forcing eight-year-old Tor to endure unwanted physical contact while cameras recorded his distress levels.

At the Gävle rastplats, she bought kaffe and checked her messages. Lindholm again, confirming her hotel. The prosecutor wanted dinner to prep. Anna texted back: "No thanks. See you at nine." She needed tonight alone.

Tomorrow she'd face Gustaf across the courtroom. The same Dr.

Gustaf Eriksson, psychologist, published researcher, father of the year according to his university colleagues. They'd see his thin smile when she described what his "methodology" had done to their boy.

Stockholm's lights spread across the winter darkness as she crested Södermalm. Ten years since she'd fled north, leaving Tor with his father. The custody hearing had been brief: distinguished professor versus lab technician dealing with "emotional instability." Gustaf's lawyer had been thorough.

Now she was back. The city looked the same, but she felt like a different person. Someone who'd learned that academia could hide monsters as easily as any other profession.

The Scandic Klara felt sterile as a lab. Anna hung her court suit carefully, placed the photo album on the nightstand like evidence. Room 847 overlooked Vasagatan. She could see the courthouse from her window. Gustaf would be somewhere in the city tonight, probably reviewing his own notes on "maternal hysteria patterns in custody disputes."

She ordered room service but barely touched the salmon. Tomorrow she'd sit three meters from Gustaf and describe his "research methods": the forced hugging sessions, the measured responses to unwanted touching, eight-year-old Tor's tears recorded as "valuable data points."

Sirens wailed down Vasagatan. She'd forgotten how the city never quite slept. Up north, nights were properly dark, properly quiet. Here, even at midnight, traffic hummed like machinery.

She opened the photo album. Tor at seven, gap-toothed and grinning at Skansen. Before Gustaf's "bonding protocols" began. Before their apartment became a testing facility. Before her son learned to flinch when adults reached for him.

The photos were chronological. You could track the change. Tor's smile fading. His posture becoming rigid. His eyes developing that watchful quality, like a small animal expecting pain.

Her phone buzzed. Lindholm again, with tomorrow's timeline. The prosecutor had attached photos from Gustaf's files: clinical shots of Tor during "proximity tolerance training." Anna deleted the message without looking. She'd lived through those sessions.

At the window, she watched traffic move down Vasagatan like blood through arteries.

Sleep wouldn't come. Anna laid out tomorrow's clothes like battle gear. Gustaf would analyze her appearance, looking for signs of "maternal emotional dysregulation." She'd give him nothing to work with.

Lindholm's prep notes sat on the desk. "Stay factual. Don't let him provoke you. Remember: you're not on trial." Easy advice from someone who'd never watched their husband measure their child's distress levels like temperature readings.

The album fell open to Tor's tenth birthday. Their last normal celebration before Gustaf's research grant came through. In the photo, Gustaf's arm was around Tor naturally, protectively. Six months later, he'd be measuring how long the boy could tolerate that same embrace before showing stress indicators.

Tomorrow she'd tell twelve strangers how a father had turned his son into research data. How "proximity bonding therapy" had meant forcing unwanted physical contact while recording the child's autonomic responses. How Gustaf had published papers on Tor's breaking without ever using his name.

But tonight, she let herself remember the before times. When hugs were comfort, not experiments. When her son's laughter wasn't worth documenting because it was simply joy.

Stockholm's lights stretched toward Gamla Stan, each window holding someone's story. Tomorrow she'd add hers to the court record. Not as clinical observation, but as lived truth. Justice wouldn't undo the damage. But it might prevent Gustaf from calling it research.

50
ANNA TESTIMONY

The courtroom at Stockholms tingsrätt smelled of floor wax and old radiators and institutional staleness that came from too many people breathing recycled air. Maja watched Anna Nielsen approach the witness stand, noting the way the woman's shoulders carried themselves. The particular set of someone who'd learned to bear weight they'd never asked for.

"Fan," Almquist muttered beside her. "This is going to be ugly."

Maja had read Anna's statement three times, each pass revealing new layers of methodical horror. Academic precision turned against a child. It was the sort of case that made you question whether intelligence was always a virtue.

At the defense table, Dr. Gustaf Nielsen arranged his papers with surgical precision. "Good morning, Mrs. Nielsen." Prosecutor Lindholm's voice cut through the courtroom's hush. "Please tell the court about your background."

Anna's hands found the witness stand's rail. "I was a research assistant at Kungsmedicinska. That's where I met Gustaf. We married when he became professor, had Tor a year later. I left my position to raise our son."

The familiar story, Maja thought. Brilliant woman supports brilliant husband, sacrifices career for family, discovers too late what kind of man she'd married. Stockholm was full of such women. Accomplished, intelligent, gradually hollowed out by academic husbands who treated everything as a research project.

"Did you remain involved in academic life?"

"Yes. Department functions, faculty meetings. Gustaf insisted on maintaining connections. I helped organize symposiums, took notes at his presentations. Everything had to be documented precisely."

Maja nodded slightly. She'd worked enough domestic cases to recognize the pattern. The gradual normalization of control, obsessive personalities dressing up abuse as intellectual rigor. Gustaf's methodical note-taking even during his own trial suggested a man who'd never met a boundary he couldn't rationalize crossing.

"When did his research interests change?"

"After his papers on human connection were published. He became... different. Started seeing every interaction as data." Anna's fingers traced the wooden rail. "Family dinner became observation time. He'd document how Tor responded to conversations, his interactions. At first it seemed normal. Just an academic father interested in his child."

"But then?"

"He started timing things. How long before Tor would speak. Whether he'd make eye contact. Normal family moments became experiments."

"Christ, Maja," Almquist whispered. "How do you turn a kid into a lab rat?"

"Gradually," Maja murmured, watching Gustaf's pen scratch across his legal pad. "Same way you boil a frog."

"The notes grew more detailed," Anna continued. "Every gesture, every response recorded. He started controlling conditions. Measuring how Tor reacted to different situations."

Lindholm lifted a photograph. The Nielsen family dining room, furniture arranged with geometric precision. Maja had seen similar setups in organized crime surveillance, but this was a ten-year-old's home. The banality of it turned her stomach.

"When did things escalate?"

"Tor's tenth birthday." Anna's voice flattened into the monotone of someone who'd told this story too many times. "We had a small party. Gustaf filmed everything. That wasn't unusual then. Academic families document everything." She paused. "Afterward, reviewing the footage, he said Tor showed 'fascinating patterns of dependency.' That understanding these patterns required more controlled conditions."

Maja felt the familiar chill of recognition. Every case had its tipping point. The moment when bad choices became criminal ones. She'd learned to identify it in witness statements, that precise instant when the speaker's voice changed, when they realized they were describing not just strange behavior but actual crimes.

"What happened next?"

"He turned our basement into a laboratory. Equipment appeared from Kungsmedicinska. Monitors, recorders, metal tables arranged like an operating theater. Our home became his research facility."

"Helvete," Almquist whispered. "A basement lab. In Östermalm."

51
ERIK'S TESTIMONY

February light fell thin and merciless through the courthouse windows on Scheelegatan, cutting Stockholm's winter sky into precise geometric patterns. Even the weather seemed methodical today, Maja observed—snow falling at measured intervals, as if the city itself had been infected by Nielsen's obsession with documentation.

Erik sat waiting to testify, unconsciously arranging his papers in the exact formation Nielsen had taught him. The irony struck Maja as both tragic and absurd: the student using the master's tools to catalogue his own disintegration, like a snake eating its tail while taking notes on the taste.

The gallery had filled with Stockholm's peculiar winter mix—academics from Kungsmedicinska speaking in hushed administrative Swedish, journalists clutching their notepads, and the morbidly curious who found courtrooms warmer than their own thoughts.

Anna sat in the second row, her hands folded in what Maja recognized as Nielsen's documented "optimal neural receptivity position."

Nielsen himself sat at the defense table, Mont Blanc pen poised over his leather notebook.

When Lindholm called him to the stand, Erik's steps followed the careful measurement he'd learned in Nielsen's lab—seven steps from the gallery rail to the witness box. Even approaching his own testimony, he moved like a man navigating by coordinates only he could see, trapped within a methodology that had become both his identity and his prison.

"Please state your name and profession for the record," Lindholm said.

"Erik Thoressen. Former doctoral candidate in neuropsychology at Kungsmedicinska," he replied, his voice carrying the particular tremor Maja had learned to recognize in witnesses caught between confession and recognition.

Nielsen's pen scratched across paper with the rhythm of institutional machinery—one bureaucratic system documenting another.

"How did you first become involved with Professor Nielsen's research?"

"I was his research assistant. He noticed my interest in consciousness studies. Said I had the right kind of precision." Erik's hands moved unconsciously, miming the note-taking gestures Nielsen had drilled into him. Even in confession, he remained trapped within his mentor's system.

"Let's talk about the Lindquists. How were they selected?"

"Professor Nielsen had criteria. Couples with strong emotional bonds." Erik's voice carried the clinical tone of someone who had learned to recite horror as scientific facts. "He said we needed subjects who could maintain consciousness connection during adhesion."

"And how did you find them?"

"Park surveys. We'd observe couples in Djurgården, Humlegården, documenting their interactions like we were studying birds. Professor Nielsen developed a scale for measuring how much couples depended on each other. Marcus and Sofia Lindquist scored

9.7 out of 10." His voice cracked. "They were so connected. Always anticipating each other's movements, finishing each other's sentences. Perfect subjects."

Perfect subjects. They were all subjects in someone's study. She thought of her partnership with Sven—their unconscious patterns, unspoken communication. Would they have scored 9.3 on Nielsen's scale? If you had to be reduced to data, at least let it testify to connection.

"Walk us through what happened that Saturday night," Lindholm said.

"We knew their schedule down to the minute. Every Saturday, dinner at Prinsen on Mäster Samuelsgatan—always the same table, always ordered the same wine. Then they'd walk through Djurgården, holding hands like teenagers."

Erik's clinical detachment wavered. "Professor Nielsen had calculated everything—timing, location, compound dosages adjusted for body weight and estimated alcohol consumption. He approached murder like assembling IKEA furniture: methodical, measured, following the instruction manual to the letter."

"What time did you encounter them?"

"11:23 PM." The palindromic time hung in the courtroom like a prayer or a curse. Nielsen had probably chosen it for its symmetry— the same obsession with mathematical precision that made Swedish design both beautiful and cold.

"How did you approach them?"

"I pretended to be lost. Asked for directions in broken Swedish— played the confused tourist." Erik's voice cracked. "Typical Swedish helpfulness. They couldn't ignore someone who needed assistance, even at eleven at night in a nearly empty park. When they stopped to help..." He swallowed hard. "The compound worked exactly as Professor Nielsen predicted. Fast. Efficient."

Fast, efficient—words that could have described the T-bana or healthcare administration. Instead, they described destroying two people whose only crime was embodying Swedish helpfulness.

Nielsen had weaponized trust itself, turned social cooperation into predation.

"What happened next?"

"I had to work quickly. Remove their clothes—Professor Nielsen's instructions were specific about skin contact being necessary for neural integration. Even in November cold, even with them losing consciousness, I followed the protocol exactly."

Maja watched Erik's hands, understood something fundamental about human nature: how completely people could be programmed, how thoroughly methodology could replace morality. The human capacity for systematic behavior was civilization's greatest strength and most dangerous weakness. Creatures of pattern, and pattern was amoral.

"How did you manage to continue? To complete the documentation while they were..."

"I kept hearing his voice. All the training, all the protocols. Even when they started to understand what was happening, I just... kept taking notes."

"Sofia Lindstrom looked at me. Asked 'Varför?'—why? That single Swedish word, so simple, so profound. And I... I documented her cognitive awareness. Noted the exact time: 11:23 PM. Measured her pupil dilation: 4.2 millimeters, dilating rapidly due to neural integration onset."

Varför? The question that haunted every investigation. Why did people choose destruction over creation? But perhaps Nielsen had found the answer: there was no why, only how. No meaning, only method.

"Jonas tried to reach for her—involuntary muscle response despite paralysis onset. I recorded the attempt, categorized the movement patterns according to Nielsen's motor function assessment scale. Everything they did, everything they felt, became variables in his equation."

"The compound administration?"

"Two doses, precisely timed. First dose paralyzed them but kept them awake. Professor Nielsen calculated exact amounts based on weight, how fast they processed alcohol, even what they'd had for dinner. Everything measured to keep them aware but unable to move."

He paused, catching himself falling into the clinical language that made horror bearable. The pause was telling—even now, part of him sought refuge in methodology.

"Let's talk about the Bengtssons," Lindholm said. "Was the process the same?"

"Professor Nielsen said we needed to refine the process. That the Lindstroms showed promise, but we could do better. He extended the time between doses to thirty-seven minutes," Erik continued, his voice cracking. "Longer fear to make the connection stronger, more time for their minds to overlap before death."

"And the Strandbergs?"

"Final methodology refinement. Forty-two minutes between doses—the Fibonacci sequence applied to neurological trauma." Erik's voice was barely audible. "Professor Nielsen calculated everything based on their forty-year marriage, said their established neural pathways would produce optimal integration patterns."

She almost smiled at the absurdity—mathematical beauty applied to systematic horror. Something deeply human about the impulse to find pattern in chaos, to apply sacred geometry to profane acts.

"I can still hear Vera begging me: 'Snälla, låt mig bara hålla hans hand'—please, just let me hold his hand one last time. I documented her plea as 'subject displaying heightened awareness of partner bond pre-termination' and noted the time: 22:47 PM."

The reduction of human pleading to clinical terminology was the essence of Nielsen's corruption—not just murder, but the systematic dehumanization that made murder possible.

"The Strandbergs' case was different though, wasn't it?

"Magnus started fighting the paralysis—unexpected metabolic

resistance. Kept trying to reach Vera, kept saying her name: 'Vera, Vera, Vera,' like a prayer or a curse." Erik's voice broke completely.

The moment hung in the courtroom like Stockholm's winter silence—that point where methodology fractured against human desperation, where academic language failed to contain love calling out in darkness.

Lindholm lifted a thick folder bearing Kungsmedicinska's letterhead. "The ethics committee approved your research on consciousness integration. But they never saw the real experiments, did they?"

"No. Professor Nielsen had two sets of documentation—the bureaucratic beauty of Swedish institutional deception." Erik's voice carried a bitter edge. "The official research that looked completely legitimate. And the real data. The murders."

The dual documentation was quintessentially Swedish—everything properly filed, including murder disguised as academic research.

"When did you start to doubt the methodology?"

"After the Strandbergs. I couldn't sleep. Kept hearing Vera's voice. But Professor Nielsen said that was just proof of successful neural integration—that their consciousness patterns were affecting mine. He wanted me to document my nightmares."

Even doubt had become data—the way institutions absorb resistance, transform criticism into confirmation.

"What finally made you stop?"

"Maja and Sven. When Professor Nielsen said we needed to test the process on work partners instead of lovers. He showed me their files—how you worked together, how much you depended on each other. You scored 9.3 out of 10 on his partnership scale." Erik looked directly at Maja. "I realized I wasn't doing science anymore. I was just finding new ways to destroy what connected people."

"What happened the night you attacked Kriminalinspektörs Norberg and Svensson?"

"We were watching Sven. He was parked outside Maja's apartment on Upplandsgatan, just sitting in his car. Professor Nielsen noticed him there, said the behavioral pattern was irregular—worth investigating. Nielsen came up with a plan right there on the street. Said we could use Sven's concern for his partner as a vulnerability."

The casual opportunism of it was particularly chilling—not elaborately planned evil, but simply the systematic exploitation of whatever circumstances presented themselves.

"Then what happened?"

"Just what Nielsen predicted. Sven got out of his car when he saw Nielsen heading toward the apartment. I drugged him and we dragged him inside and waited for Maja to come home. Like spiders in a web, except we were documenting the web's construction."

"Professor Nielsen had me inject Sven with paralysis compound. Sven kept asking about Maja: 'Var är Maja? Skada henne inte'— where is Maja? Don't hurt her. Professor Nielsen told me to document his emotional state, said his concern for his partner would enhance the neural integration process."

Maja felt something shift inside her chest—not surprise, exactly, but a deepening recognition of what partnership meant. Sven's reaction under extreme duress revealed the depth of their professional bond.

"What stopped you from completing the experiment?"

"We didn't hear them at first. Professor Nielsen was focused on administrating the integration compound. Then suddenly the door burst open. Kriminalinspektör Almquist and the tactical team were there. Even with guns pointed at us, Nielsen was still telling me to document the interruption, saying it would provide valuable data about consciousness integration under extreme stress."

The institutional momentum had been so complete that even arrest became part of the experiment.

"Looking back now, how do you understand what you did?"

"I used to think I was just following methodology. That somehow the academic framework made it... made it not murder." Erik's voice shook. "But now I understand. Every time I documented their terror, every time I prepared those compounds... I wasn't doing research. I was helping kill people whose only crime was loving each other."

"And Professor Nielsen's influence?"

"I still hear his voice. Still find myself taking notes, documenting everything." Erik looked at his former mentor, who continued writing even now. "He didn't just teach me methodology. He rewired how I think. Even sitting here describing murders, part of me wants to categorize the variables, measure the courtroom's acoustic properties, document the jurors' responses..."

"Just to be clear," Lindholm said, gathering her papers. "The murders of the Lindstroms, the Beengtssons, the Strandbergs—you acted alone?"

"Yes. Professor Nielsen never came to the parks. Never touched the compounds. He just... shaped me. Trained me. Turned me into his instrument. But with Maja and Sven, that was different. He wanted to demonstrate proper methodology himself."

"Final question. You've pleaded guilty to these murders. Why testify today?"

"Because the methodology is still out there. His papers, his theories, all built on what we did. Someone needs to show what that perfect documentation really meant—how many people died to create those precise data points."

Through the gallery, Nielsen's pen moved steadily, recording how his subject continued to provide optimal documentation even while attempting to discredit the methodology. The recursion was both tragic and absurd—the student still serving the master, even in betrayal.

"No further questions, Your Honor." Lindholm returned to her seat.

The judge called for lunch recess. Erik's hands moved mechanically, gathering his notes with Nielsen's characteristic precision. Even in complete breakdown, he maintained the professor's prescribed form.

Nielsen made one final notation before closing his leather notebook: "Subject maintains optimal documentation protocols even during emotional disclosure. Methodology appears permanently integrated. Institutional conditioning successful."

As the gallery emptied, Maja remained seated, contemplating the spectacle she'd just witnessed. Nielsen's influence was still there—in Erik's careful documentation, in the precise horror of his testimony. The courthouse itself had become his laboratory, the trial his final experiment in measuring human response to methodical horror.

The irony wasn't lost on her: in trying to comprehend Nielsen's methodology, they would inevitably employ methodology of their own. Perhaps that was the only way to understand evil—through the same systematic thinking that made evil possible in the first place. Perhaps methodology was both the disease and the only available cure.

The courtroom was empty now except for the bailiff and a few lingering journalists. Maja stood slowly, gathering her thoughts like Erik had gathered his papers. The machinery of justice would continue its methodical work, turning human suffering into legal precedent, transforming individual tragedy into institutional memory.

She was part of that machinery. The question was whether the machinery served justice or simply served itself—whether their systematic pursuit of Nielsen was fundamentally different from his systematic pursuit of victims, or whether they were all just participants in the same larger system of measurement and control.

Outside, Stockholm waited under its methodical snowfall, a city built on systems and procedures, on the faith that sufficient organization could somehow contain the chaos of human nature. It was a beautiful faith, and probably a necessary one. But after listening to Erik's testimony, she wasn't sure it was a true one.

52
COURT

Maja stood at the window of the Prosecution Authority building on Kungsgatan, watching February snow settle against Stockholm's administrative facades. Behind her, Prosecutor Lundqvist arranged crime scene photographs with methodical care.

"The defense will say Erik acted alone," Lindholm said, straightening a photograph of the Strandbergs' final pose. "That Nielsen's influence was purely academic." He paused, studying Nielsen's meticulous crime scene documentation. "Though they might struggle to explain why their client is still taking notes during his own murder trial."

Maja turned from the window. "Did you see him today? Writing down Erik's testimony like he was documenting a particularly interesting lab specimen breaking down." She almost smiled at the absurdity. "Even facing life imprisonment, he can't stop being a researcher."

"The defense attorney noticed something else," Luindholm said. "How Erik still uses academic language to describe the murders. They'll argue his clinical distance proves he acted independently."

"But the judge saw Nielsen taking notes," Maja said. "Recording Erik's breakdown like he was documenting a successful experiment."

————

Two floors below, in a smaller conference room overlooking Klarabergsgatan, Nielsen sat with his defense team, his pen moving with the same steady rhythm Maja had observed in court. Even here, facing a life sentence, he maintained perfect documentation of every interaction.

"You need to stop taking notes during testimony," his lawyer said, watching the familiar precise movements. "The judge sees it as callous, especially when Erik was breaking down."

Nielsen's hand didn't pause. "The behavioral patterns are significant. Erik's retention of academic methodology even during emotional disclosure suggests successful integration of research protocols."

His defense team exchanged glances. "This isn't a research project," the lawyer said, his frustration showing. "Every time you document someone's testimony, the judge sees a man treating murder like an academic exercise."

"Your concern about judicial response patterns has been noted," Nielsen replied. "But proper observation requires consistent methodology."

————

When court reconvened that afternoon, Maja watched from the gallery as the defense lawyer studied Erik's trembling hands, his careful arrangement of papers, the unconscious precision that remained even after his emotional testimony. Here was their strategy: proof of independent action hidden in the very methodical behaviors that proved Nielsen's influence.

"Mr. Thoressen." The formal address carried calculated purpose.

"Let's examine your actual decisions, shall we?" He laid out the laboratory access logs from Kungsmedicinska Institute in careful chronological order. Each page documented Erik's solitary work: timestamps, equipment usage, material requisitions. All bearing Erik's signature alone.

"February 15, 2023. 23:00 hours." The lawyer placed each document with deliberate care. "Your keycard access. Your equipment requisition. Your compound modifications." Each 'your' struck like an accusation. "Professor Nielsen wasn't even in the building."

Erik's hands moved unconsciously, straightening the logs even as he spoke. "He didn't need to be there. The protocols... they were already in my head by then."

The lawyer lifted a bound volume from his evidence cart. "Kungsmedicinska Institute's standard documentation protocols." He opened it to a flagged page. "The same formats used throughout Swedish medical research. Nothing unique to Professor Nielsen."

"But that's exactly the point," Erik said, his voice barely carrying to the judge's bench. "He showed me how to hide murder inside normal The judges leaned forward, watching as Erik's fingers automatically moved to align the paper's edges with geometric precision. At the defense table, Nielsen made another note, his slight smile showing he'd observed the behavior too: one system of documentation observing another, finding confirmation in the patterns.

From the gallery, Maja wondered if Nielsen saw the beautiful absurdity of it: his own methodical training being used to document his methodical training, an infinite loop of Swedish institutional behavior reflecting back on itself like mirrors in a bureaucratic funhouse

Erik's fingers traced his own signature on document after document, the familiar curves of his initials marking each step toward murder. Behind him, a jjudge whispered something to her fellow judge both watching his hands move across the papers with the same telling precision they'd observed in Nielsen.

"You don't understand," Erik said, his voice cracking. "Every signature, every timestamp, every careful note; that was him too. He taught me that proper documentation makes anything look legitimate. Even murder."

The courtroom fell silent except for Nielsen's pen scratching against paper. The lawyer spread out the ethics committee approvals; standard forms bearing the familiar stamps of Swedish institutional authority. "Standard protocols," he said. "Standard academic guidance from a senior professor."

Erik stared at his own neat margin notes, his precise observations, his careful timestamps. "Look at him," Erik gestured toward Nielsen, still writing. "Even now, he's documenting my breakdown. Making notes about how effectively he trained me to follow proper academic protocols for murder."

The judge followed Erik's gaze to Nielsen's moving pen.

"No further questions," the lawyer said, returning to his seat.

But Erik wasn't finished. "The paperwork makes it look right," he said to the courtroom. "Clean. Professional. Until you forget there were actual people dying while you took notes."

Nielsen made one final notation, a slight smile touching his lips. The judges watched him write, then looked back at Erik's trembling hands.

The bailiff called for recess. As the courtroom emptied, Nielsen continued writing, documenting even the silence that followed his protégé's testimony.

53
MAJA TAKES THE STAND

Snow covered the courthouse steps. Maja climbed the steps beside Dr. Yamamoto, who gripped her medical bag with both hands. They'd arrived early, but photographers were already waiting in the shadows along Södermalm. Like ravens, Maja thought. Always gathering where something dies.

She'd spent twenty years watching people destroy each other in systematic ways. Now she was about to testify about being destroyed systematically herself. There was a certain symmetry to it that would have amused her under different circumstances.

Maja wore dark wool that would hide the medical sensors. She'd chosen buttons she could count if her hands started shaking. Even preparing to testify against Nielsen, she was thinking like him. He'd taught her to observe own responses with clinical detachment. Even now, especially now.

"Remember to breathe," Dr. Yamamoto said. "The moment this becomes too much, I pull you out. Medical authority trumps legal procedure. Even in Sweden."

"In Sweden, medical authority trumps everything except academic curiosity," Maja said. "That's how we got here."

Through the windows of Stockholms tingsrätt, the gallery was filling. Journalists, academics, the curious. All of them hoping to witness something extraordinary: a woman testifying about being turned into a research subject.

Lindholm met them in a side room that smelled of instant kaffe. "Anna's here," she said quietly to Maja. "She wants you to know you're not alone."

Maja stopped counting buttons. "He'll try to provoke a reaction," Lindholm said. "He'll want to show the court how well his methods work."

"I know." Maja unbuttoned her coat. "He's already got his notebook ready, hasn't he?"

Lindholm nodded. "Just like in the lab." She paused, considering. "Forty years of academic habit. Put a Swedish researcher in any situation and he starts documenting it."

That was the thing about academics, Maja reflected. They turned everything into data. Even their own trials. Especially their own trials.

Dr. Yamamoto positioned the sensors. "These monitors will tell me things you might not feel yourself. If Nielsen gets too far into your head, I'll know before you do."

"I need to finish," Maja said. "No matter what he writes in that notebook."

But as she said it, she wondered: Was finishing the testimony really about justice? Or was it about proving something to Nielsen?

The courtroom was dark wood and Swedish flags. The architecture of official judgment, designed to inspire respect for institutional authority. It usually worked. Nielsen sat at the defendant's table, and seeing him there—not in his office, not behind his research, but reduced to defendant status—should have felt like victory. Instead, Maja felt only the familiar pull of his methodology, the way her mind automatically began cataloguing his posture, his micro-expressions, his note-taking rhythm.

He'd trained her too well. Even now, preparing to testify against him, she was thinking like him.

She'd seen that smile in lecture halls for forty years. A man who'd spent his career studying human behavior had finally found the perfect subject: himself, being prosecuted for his own methods.

The gallery buzzed. Anna occupied the same seat she'd held during Erik's testimony, her hands pressed flat against the wooden bench rail. A gesture Maja recognized from her own worst moments. They'd all learned to grip things when the world got too strange to navigate normally.

"Kriminalinspektör Maja Norberg."

She stated her name and rank. Nielsen's pen scratched across his notebook. Even her basic identification was apparently worth documenting.

The man was incapable of experiencing reality without taking notes on it. It was almost admirable, in a deeply disturbing way.

Lindholm moved carefully through preliminary questions. Each answer seemed to deepen Nielsen's satisfaction. Behind her, Dr. Yamamoto made small adjustments to her equipment. In the gallery, Anna gripped the bench rail until her knuckles went white.

Her hands began to shake. Nielsen's pen quickened across the page. He'd trained her to observe her own responses, and now he was observing her observing herself. The man had created a perfect feedback loop.

"Kriminalinspektör Norberg," Lindholm's voice softened. "Please describe what happened that night."

Nielsen leaned forward slightly. The posture of a man approaching his life's work. The monitors registered her body's response. She pressed her palms against the witness stand, feeling that terrible pull: the need to slip back into that night, into Sven's dying consciousness.

But before she began, she allowed herself a moment of philosophical clarity. She was about to describe the most intimate violation imaginable to a roomful of strangers who would analyze it, debate it, write papers about it.

"It started..." Maja's fingers found the familiar rhythm of counting buttons. "Like ice in my veins. But that wasn't the worst part. The worst was watching Sven realize what was happening. Seeing him try to fight it."

She could feel Nielsen's clinical vocabulary trying to shape her words even now.

Nielsen's smile carried the satisfaction of a teacher whose student was performing exactly as expected. He'd programmed her to observe with scientific precision, and now she was using that precision to describe his own methods. The man had created his own prosecutor.

"I could feel Sven slipping away. Not just dying. Becoming part of..." The monitors spiked. "Part of me. And I was becoming part of him. Nielsen made sure I felt every moment of it."

"Can you describe the physical sensations?" Lindholm asked.

"Cold," she said, focusing on simple truth rather than Nielsen's terminology. "Like winter in your bloodstream. But underneath that... underneath, there was Sven. His thoughts bleeding into mine. His fear becoming my fear."

Nielsen leaned forward slightly, pen moving.

"The interesting thing," Maja said, surprising herself, "is that I can feel him taking notes right now. Not just see it, but feel it. He's turned note-taking into a physical sensation I can perceive across the room."

The judges glanced at Nielsen, who seemed delighted by this observation.

"What happened when Kriminalinspektör Svensson realized what was occurring?"

"He tried to shield me from it. Even as he was dying, even as we were being forced together, he was trying to protect me from the worst of it."

Nielsen's pen moved faster. The protective instinct, functioning exactly as his research had predicted. Even Sven's love had become data.

"But Nielsen had calculated for that, hadn't he?" Lindholm asked.

"Yes." Maja's voice hardened. "He knew Sven would try to protect me. He'd designed it that way. So I'd have to feel Sven's death and his love at the same time."

She watched Nielsen's pen turn Sven's final act of love into research findings. The man had spent his career studying human nature, and he'd finally found a way to collect data on dying itself.

"What happened after Kriminalinspektör Svensson died?"

"I didn't know where he ended and I began," Maja said. "For weeks afterward, I'd reach for kaffe and taste cigarettes. Sven's brand. I'd wake up knowing things I'd never learned, remembering conversations I'd never had.

"I'd developed his habit of checking the locks twice before leaving. Small things that proved his consciousness was still functioning inside mine."

"The integration was complete," Nielsen said, breaking protocol. "Perfect retention of partner consciousness post-mortem. Unprecedented documentation of..."

"Sustained!" the judge interrupted. "Professor Nielsen, you will not address the witness."

But Nielsen's pen never stopped moving. Even judicial intervention was worth documenting.

She felt a moment of genuine wonder. The man was incapable of experiencing reality without analyzing it. Even his own prosecution had become a research opportunity.

The gallery stirred.

"He can't help himself," Maja continued

."Put him in front of human suffering and he reaches for his pen."

Nielsen glanced up, that familiar smile touching his lips. For a moment, their eyes met. Researcher and subject. And Maja understood something fundamental about Swedish academic culture. They'd created a system where human suffering became publishable research, where systematic documentation justified systematic abuse.

And he was genuinely proud of what he'd accomplished.

"He chose us perfectly," she said. "Two Kriminalinspektörs. Both trained to observe, to document. Even as we died, we kept doing our jobs. Kept collecting data for him."

In the gallery, Anna had closed her eyes, pressing her palms against her ears. Trying to block Nielsen's pen.

"That's enough," Dr. Yamamoto said, moving toward the disconnect switch.

"No." Maja gripped the rail harder. "The court needs to see this. Needs to understand what he is." She turned to look directly at Nielsen. "You're still doing it. Right now. Writing down every word, every reaction."

Nielsen met her gaze, his smile widening. His pen never paused.

"The fascinating thing," Maja said, "is that part of me admires it. The systematic approach. The dedication to observation. He's turned his entire life into a research project, and now he's studying his own trial."

"The subject's awareness of the documentation process validates the methodology completely," Nielsen said. "Even now, she observes her own responses with the precision I trained her to..."

"Professor Nielsen!" The judge's voice cut like ice. "You are warned. Another outburst and you will be removed."

Nielsen nodded respectfully, but his pen kept moving.

"He can't stop," Maja said. "Look at him. Even being threatened with removal, he's still taking notes."

The courtroom had gone quiet except for the scratch of Nielsen's pen and the electronic beeping of monitors. Everyone watching a man who'd spent forty years studying human behavior, now unable to stop studying his own.

"Look at his notes," she said, gesturing toward Nielsen's notebook. "Perfect handwriting. Organized columns. Time stamps. He's turning my testimony into a research paper."

The judges once again craned their necks to observe Nielsen's compulsive note-taking. They were watching Swedish academic culture in its purest form: the systematic documentation of human experience, regardless of ethical considerations.

Nielsen glanced up briefly, his smile carrying genuine academic pride.

"He's proud of it," Maja said. "This isn't horror for him. It's vindication. My testimony proves his theories work exactly as designed."

The scratch of Nielsen's pen seemed to grow louder in the suddenly quiet courtroom.

"Fan," Maja whispered. "He's created the perfect Swedish crime. Systematic. Documented. Peer-reviewed. And the victims participate in their own analysis."

"He's still winning, isn't he? Even here. Even now."

54
THE PROSECUTION RESTS

Kriminalinspektör Maja Norberg sat in the witness gallery, watching Prosecutor Lindholm gather her papers. Twenty years on the force, and this was the strangest case she'd ever testified in: watching a killer turn his own trial into research. Two systems had collided: the human system of justice and the methodological system of Nielsen's documentation. Only one remained intact.

"Does the prosecution have any further witnesses?" The judge's voice carried carefully measured concern: the institutional response to human suffering, packaged in procedural language.

Lindholm stood slowly. From her seat, Maja could see Nielsen's notebook, still open, his pen poised. Even now, he was documenting the prosecutor's movements, her hesitation. Jävlar, the bastard never stopped collecting data.

"No, Your Honor. The prosecution rests."

Fan också, such simple words for such a complex defeat, Maja thought. "And the defense?" The judge turned to Nielsen's lawyer. "Will the defendant be taking the stand?"

Nielsen's pen moved steadily across a fresh page, documenting the procedural interaction. His lawyer glanced at the notebook, then back to the judge. Even in this moment, Maja observed, Nielsen's influence extended to those meant to control him: his lawyer's eyes drawn to the documentation, momentarily captured by its methodical precision. In all her years of interrogations, she'd never seen anything like it. The suspect controlling the room without saying a word.

"No, Your Honor. The defense also rests."

Through it all, Nielsen kept writing: 11:15 - Final procedural observations

- Prosecution strategy concludes as predicted
- Subject responses exceed experimental parameters
- Institutional documentation complete

There was something darkly comical about it, she thought: that in trying to judge Nielsen, the court had become an extension of his laboratory. Even Swedish justice could be gamed by someone clever enough.

Behind her, Anna sat with her hands pressed against her ears, still trying to block out the sound of Nielsen's pen scratching against paper. The futility of this small resistance wasn't lost on Maja: how the sound penetrated anyway, how Nielsen documented even this attempt to escape his documentation.

Twenty years of interrogations had taught her about psychological pressure, but Nielsen had refined it into pure science. The pen was his weapon.

"We'll proceed with closing arguments tomorrow morning," the judge said. Her voice carried the strain of someone trying to maintain procedural normalcy in the face of clinical horror. "Nine o'clock."

Her phone buzzed. A text from her sergeant: "kaffe after? You look like you need it." Even Andersson had noticed. She typed back: "kafé Schweizer at noon. Bring aspirin."

Nielsen made one final notation: 11:17 - Research parameters optimal

- Documentation protocols maintained throughout

• Methodology validated under institutional observation
• Perfect replication achieved in controlled setting

Maja closed her own notebook: neat police handwriting documenting evidence, witness statements, procedural observations. The difference was intent, she realized. Her documentation served justice. His served only itself.

As the courtroom emptied, Nielsen's pen continued its steady movement across the page. Maja lingered, watching him work. She'd always solved cases by getting inside the perp's head, understanding their psychology. But Nielsen's psychology was the crime. His mind was the murder weapon.

Perhaps, she thought, watching from the doorway, that was his final victory: creating a system so perfect it continued documenting itself, even when no one was watching.

Outside, Stockholm's February light was already fading at barely past noon.

55
CLOSING ARGUMENTS

Maja arrived at the courthouse early, her kaffe from kafé Schweizer still warm in her hands. The aspirin had helped with the headache, but not with the persistent sound of Nielsen's pen that seemed to follow her even in sleep.

The gallery filled with familiar faces: Dr. Yamamoto from Danderyd, colleagues from the station, the witnesses who had survived Nielsen's trial-as-experiment. Maja took her usual seat, watching Nielsen arrange his materials with that same methodical precision. Even now, especially now, she was looking for the flaw in his perfect system.

Snow fell steadily outside the courthouse windows. The defense lawyer rose with careful precision.

"What we've heard is emotionally compelling," he said, arranging his notes at measured angles. "But we must look beyond emotion to fact. To documented evidence."

"Professor Nielsen never administered the compound. Never directly participated in the experiments. His role was purely academic— guiding research through proper institutional channels."

Nielsen's pen moved steadily across fresh paper: 09:15— Defense strategy optimal · Institutional framework emphasized · Direct involvement successfully distanced · Documentation protocols maintained

The lawyer lifted each piece of evidence with practiced care. "Every form followed standard procedures. Every protocol matched university guidelines. Nothing unique to Professor Nielsen's methodology."

The snow kept falling beyond the windows, each flake distinct and separate— like consciousness was meant to remain.

"We've heard testimony about emotional trauma," the defense lawyer continued. "But examine the documentation itself." He gestured to the carefully arranged evidence. "Every step followed proper protocols. Every decision made through appropriate channels."

"The prosecution wants you to see monsters," the lawyer said, his gestures measured and precise. "But what the evidence shows is standard academic procedure. Professor Nielsen provided guidance through institutional channels. Nothing more."

Erik's hands moved unconsciously, arranging his papers at perfect angles. Anna's fingers pressed harder against the bench. Even the defense lawyer's careful language carried echoes of Nielsen's methodology— precise, measured, turning human suffering into properly categorized evidence.

Prosecutor Lindholm rose slowly, her movements deliberately imprecise. "The defense speaks of proper channels," she said. "Of standard procedures. Of institutional frameworks."

"But we've seen what those proper channels actually mean. We watched Professor Nielsen document his own student's breakdown. Saw him measure Kriminalinspektör Norberg's testimony. Even now..." She gestured to his moving pen. "Even now, he's turning our testimony into data points."

"Look at him," Lindholm said. "Even now. Even here." She lifted one of his notebooks. "These aren't research papers. They're records of destroyed lives."

Anna pressed her palms harder against the gallery bench.

"We've heard a father describe documenting his son's destruction," Lindholm said, her voice hardening. "Watched a student demonstrate how completely Nielsen reshaped his mind. Saw a Kriminalinspektör forced to relive her partner's death while Nielsen measured her trauma response."

She placed the notebook back on the defense table. Lindholm turned to Judge Andersson. "The defense wants you to see standard procedures. But what have we actually witnessed?" She gestured toward Anna. "A mother watching her child slip away. A student turned into an instrument and a Kriminalinspektör forced to relive her partner's death."

"This isn't about proper channels or institutional frameworks. It's about using those frameworks to hide something monstrous. About turning connection into control. About destroying what makes us human."

The snow kept falling outside, each flake catching the winter light. Like tears. Like trembling hands. Like hospital monitors tracking a damaged mind.

"You've seen what he does to minds," Lindholm said. "What he's still doing. The question now is simple: do we let him continue?"

The defense lawyer rose for his final argument, movements carrying Nielsen's familiar academic precision. "The prosecution speaks of monsters," he said. "But examine the actual evidence. Every form properly filed. Every procedure followed through established channels."

He arranged the evidence files with careful attention to angles. "Professor Nielsen never administered compounds. Never directly participated in experiments. His role was purely academic—providing guidance through established institutional frameworks."

Anna's hands pressed harder against the bench. Several of Nielsen's former colleagues shifted uncomfortably, recognizing in the lawyer's movements that same precise methodology that had once shaped their department. Even here, Nielsen's influence echoed through every careful gesture.

"The prosecution asks if we should let him continue," the lawyer concluded, straightening his papers with familiar precision. "But the evidence shows standard academic procedure. Nothing more."

The snow continued falling beyond the windows, each flake separate and distinct. Like consciousness was meant to remain before Nielsen's methodology turned human connection into something measurable, documentable, controllable.

Judge Andersson addressed the courtroom. "My task is to determine whether Professor Nielsen is guilty of the murders of Jonas and Sofia Lindstrom, Henrik and Maria Bengtsson, Marcus and Vera Strandberg, and Kriminalinspektör Anders Svensson."

"I must also determine his role in the attempted murder of Kriminalinspektör Maja Norberg."

Judge Andersson continued, her voice carrying measured authority. "I must consider each charge separately. For each victim, I must be convinced beyond reasonable doubt that Professor Nielsen bears criminal responsibility for their death."

"The defense argues that Professor Nielsen never directly administered the compound. That his role was purely advisory. I must determine whether his actions— his instructions, his methodology, his documentation — constitute equal culpability."

Several of Nielsen's former colleagues in the gallery looked down at their hands. They'd all used his documentation protocols, praised his methodology. Now they faced what that precision had actually accomplished.

"For the attempted murder charge regarding Kriminalinspektör Norberg, I must determine whether Professor Nielsen's direct participation demonstrates intent to cause death."

Nielsen's pen moved steadily across paper, still measuring, still documenting, even as Judge Andersson and two lay judges prepared to determine whether his perfect methodology constituted murder.

The bailiff's voice carried the formal Swedish procedure: "All rise."

Anna remained seated, hands pressed against the bench, as the judges filed out. Behind her, Dr. Yamamoto's team whispered about Maja's condition. In Kronobergshäktet, Erik waited to face his own judgment for following Nielsen's protocols too completely.

"Court is adjourned until the judges reach their verdict."

The courtroom emptied as snow continued falling beyond the windows. Each flake caught the winter light, separate and distinct. Like minds were meant to remain before Nielsen's methodology turned human connection into something measurable, documentable, controlled.

56
JUDGES CHAMBER

Three hours later, Judge Andersson and her three lay judges sat in deliberation, their notebooks open before them. The courthouse had emptied except for reporters camped near the entrance, but Anna remained in the gallery, hands still pressed against the bench. At Danderyd, Maja's monitors showed the same steady patterns: her mind still processing trauma exactly as Nielsen had trained it.

"The defense argument about indirect involvement," one of the lay judges, a teacher from Östermalm, said. "But we saw him with Kriminalinspektör Norberg. How he chose her specifically. A Kriminalinspektör who could document everything, even while..." She stopped, remembering Maja's testimony, Nielsen's satisfied smile as he kept writing. "Like watching someone dissect their own heart."

Through the conference room windows, reporters gathered near the courthouse steps. Camera flashes caught the falling snow, but in here three people had to determine if academic precision could disguise the oldest crime in Swedish law books.

"The way he shaped minds," the second lay judge said, catching herself arranging her papers at perfect angles. She paused, noting her own compulsive tidying. "Helvete. He's still doing it, isn't he?"

Judge Andersson opened the criminal code. "We've established his methodology. Now we apply Swedish law." She found herself thinking of her grandmother's stories about the occupation: how some people collaborated not from hatred, but from a desperate need for order.

The Östermalm teacher leaned forward. "The Lindquist murders. Direct evidence?"

"Erik Thoressen's testimony," the social worker said. "Nielsen provided the compound formula. Specified the location. Instructed him on documentation techniques." He paused. "But Nielsen never touched the victims."

"Medverkan genom psykiskt bistånd," Judge Andersson said, consulting her notes. "Aiding through psychological assistance. The law recognizes this."

"But this goes beyond typical psychological assistance," the second lay judge observed. "This is systematic mind control over years."

Judge Andersson made a note. "Indirect perpetration. Using another person as an instrument of crime." She looked up. "The prosecution argued Nielsen shaped Erik specifically to commit these murders. The defense claims academic guidance."

"Academic guidance doesn't include compound formulas," the teacher said dryly.

They moved through each charge with methodical precision: the Bergstroms, the Strandbergs. Each murder more refined than the last as Nielsen perfected his control over Erik's mind.

"And Kriminalinspektör Norberg," Judge Andersson said.

The social worker straightened unconsciously. "Direct involvement. He administered the compound himself."

"While documenting her response," the teacher added. "Even in the courtroom, he was measuring the effectiveness of his methodology."

Judge Andersson closed the criminal code. Outside, the Storkyrkan bells chimed nine o'clock. "The evidence supports the prosecution's theory. Nielsen used Erik as an instrument for the first three murders, then demonstrated his methodology directly on Kriminalinspektör Norberg."

"The systematic nature of it," the second lay judge said. "Each step carefully planned, each response measured and documented."

"Like a dissertation defense," the teacher said.

Judge Andersson gathered the files. "Swedish law has provisions for indirect perpetration. Nielsen shaped Erik's mind deliberately, provided the means, specified the methods." She paused. "The fact that he never physically touched the first victims doesn't absolve him. He was the architect of their murders."

"And the attempted murder of Kriminalinspektör Norberg proves his direct capability," the social worker added. "No intermediary. No plausible deniability."

The others nodded. Outside, Stockholm's winter darkness deepened over Riddarholmen and Södermalm, the city lights reflecting off the harbor ice. Tomorrow they would deliver judgment, but tonight they had measured Nielsen's methodical evil against Swedish law and found it wanting.

Some crimes, Judge Andersson reflected, required their own kind of precision to prosecute. Nielsen's perfect methodology had become the instrument of his conviction.

57
VERDICT

Morning came heavy with judgment. Anna had watched the sun rise through the hotel windows, Stockholm emerging from darkness like a photograph developing: first shadows, then shapes, finally the full detail of a city preparing to confront what it had allowed to flourish in its institutions.

She walked through the February morning toward the courthouse on Scheelegatan. The media presence was already building: reporters stamping their feet against the cold, camera crews testing equipment.

Polisoverintendent Soderberg stood near the courthouse steps, watching the crowd. He nodded to Anna as she approached. Two people who'd seen Gustaf Nielsen's methodology up close, from different angles but with similar understanding of its implications.

"How is she?" Soderberg asked.

"Healing," Anna said. "Dr. Yamamoto says her mind is... recalibrating itself."

"Like a computer rebooting?"

Anna almost smiled at hearing her own question echoed. "More like a person remembering who they were before someone else tried to reprogram them."

"The truly disturbing thing," Lindholm murmured, watching Nielsen disappear into the building, "is how normal he looks. How reasonable his methods seemed until you understood their purpose."

Outside the courthouse, Lindholm's phone buzzed with notifications. The case had caught Stockholm's attention in ways that made her uncomfortable. Not just the crime itself, but the way it had become a symbol of institutional failure. He glanced at the headlines scrolling past:

DAGENS NYHETER: Verdict Expected in Nielsen Trial

SVENSKA DAGBLADET: Police Presence Increased Around Courthouse

AFTONBLADET: A Day of Reckoning for Academic Horror

Anna read over her shoulder, recognizing the familiar academic dance of self-protection. One quote caught her attention: *"The truly frightening thing is how close Nielsen's methodologies were to our accepted practices. Only the slightest deviation separated his work from ours."* An unnamed professor, probably someone she'd shared dinner with, someone who'd praised Gustaf's "rigorous methodology" over wine and cheese. Now they were all discovering how thin the line between research and cruelty could be. "Academic horror," she murmured. "As if we haven't been horrifying each other in faculty meetings for decades."

"Look at this," Lindholm said, scrolling to a Reddit thread. "They're discussing whether his documentation protocols are still being used in labs across Sweden. The comments..." He paused, reading. "Someone wrote: *'We follow procedures to feel safe from our own instincts. Sometimes the procedures become the instincts.'*"

Anna felt the familiar chill of recognition, followed by something that might have been dark amusement. "Kafka would have appreciated the irony," she said. "We create systems to protect us from ourselves, then discover the systems have become ourselves."

The social media posts painted a picture of a city trying to process what it had witnessed. Police union statements about wounds that methodology couldn't measure. Students questioning their own institutions. Academics wondering how close they'd come to crossing similar lines.

The gallery had filled early: police officers from Polishuset station sitting with the particular stillness of those who had seen institutional failure from within, medical staff from Danderyd who understood how easily bodies could be broken, academics who had once praised Nielsen's research and now contemplated their own complicity. Anna sat in the front row, hands steady now against her knees, her posture suggesting acceptance rather than resolution.

Nielsen sat at the defense table, pen moving across fresh paper with the steady rhythm of a metronome. Even awaiting judgment, he maintained perfect academic precision. His lawyer had stopped trying to prevent the constant documentation. Perhaps understanding that Nielsen's note-taking was less about legal strategy than about maintaining his identity as the observer rather than the observed. Even now, he refused to acknowledge his transformation from researcher to subject.

"All rise."

Judge Andersson entered with her lay judges. Their faces carried the weight of what they'd witnessed, what they'd had to measure against Swedish law. The Swedish legal system, with its carefully balanced blend of professional and civilian judgment, had never been designed to categorize crimes like Nielsen's. The law, like all human systems, struggled when confronted with behavior that exploited its own foundational assumptions.

"In the matter of the State versus Gustaf Nielsen," Judge Andersson began, her voice clear in the hushed courtroom. "We have considered each charge separately, as the law requires."

Through the gallery, Anna's hands remained steady. At the prosecution table, Lindholm watched Nielsen's pen still moving, still recording, even now. The Kriminalinspektör felt a strange, detached appreciation for the man's consistency. A trait they might have admired in another context, another life. The qualities that made good researchers often made good Kriminalinspektörs: attention to detail, methodical thinking, persistence. The difference lay not in the methods but in what one hoped to illuminate with them.

"For the murders of Jonas and Sofia Lindstrom, Henrik and Maria Bengtsson, Marcus and Vera Strandberg, and Kriminalinspektör Sven Svensson," Judge Andersson continued, "we sentence the defendant to life imprisonment."

From where he sat, Lindholm could see a muscle working in Nielsen's jaw. Not fear or anger, but perhaps frustration that the system's response was so predictable, so lacking in original insight. Even in judgment, Nielsen seemed to be evaluating the court rather than the other way around.

Judge Andersson turned to the final charge. "Regarding the attempted murder of Kriminalinspektör Maja Norberg, where the defendant chose to demonstrate his methodology himself..." She paused, watching Nielsen's pen still moving. "We find the defendant guilty. A sentence that will run concurrent with the life term."

"This court has seen how academic authority can hide systematic horror," Judge Andersson said. "How proper channels can enable deliberate destruction. The sentences reflect not just the murders themselves, but the calculated way human connection was turned into something to be destroyed."

Through the gallery, police officers from Polishuset station sat straighter. For Sven. For Maja. For what Nielsen had done to their partnership. The bonds between officers were something Nielsen had studied but never understood: how two people could work together day after day, seeing the worst of humanity, yet maintain their separate selves while developing a connection that transcended mere professional courtesy.

"The defendant will begin serving his sentence immediately."

Nielsen made one final notation, his pen moving with the same precision he'd used to document Sven's death, to measure Maja's collapse. His lawyer touched his arm as Kriminalvården officers approached, but he continued writing until the last possible moment. A researcher completing his documentation even as the experiment ended.

Through the courthouse windows, snow kept falling on medieval Stockholm, covering ancient streets and modern buildings alike. Anna's hands remained steady in her lap, neither clenched in triumph nor trembling with emotion, simply present, like the moment itself. The bailiff's voice carried the formal Swedish procedure: "All rise."

But Nielsen's notebook remained open on the defense table, its final entry still visible:

09:47 - Judgment rendered

- Institutional response as predicted
- Methodology validated
- Research complete

Lindholm, rising with the rest of the court, glanced at those final notes and felt a strange combination of professional recognition and existential unease. Even in defeat, Nielsen had maintained his observer's stance, as if the entire trial had been merely another experiment, with the legal system as his subject. The Kriminalinspektör wondered, not for the first time, how narrow the gap might be between Nielsen's coldly academic approach to human behavior and the detached analysis police work sometimes required. The thought would follow him out into the snowy Stockholm afternoon, a question without methodology to resolve it.

58
EPILOGUE

Late spring had arrived in Djurgården with typical Swedish reluctance, patches of snow still clinging to the shadows beneath the oaks, as if winter were a bureaucrat refusing to file the proper paperwork for seasonal transition. Maja sat with Daniel on a park bench near where the Lindstroms had been found, watching morning mist rise from the damp earth. The same paths she'd walked as a Kriminalinspektör, documenting death with professional precision, now transformed by time and truth and healing. Six months after Nielsen's conviction, the location remained identical in its coordinates, yet entirely different in its meaning: a paradox that police work had taught her to accept rather than resolve.

"Strange," she observed, "how places hold memories but don't actually remember anything themselves."

The park was quiet this early. Daniel sat quietly beside her, steady as always. Her brother understood the difference between useful silence and bureaucratic speechmaking: a distinction lost on most institutions, which generated reports the way trees shed leaves: automatically and without much consideration for who might have to rake them up afterward.

"I brought kaffe," he said, reaching into his bag. He handed her a thermos. "Still too hot to drink."

"Like justice," Maja replied, then caught herself. "Listen to me. Six months of civilian life and I'm still making police analogies."

Loki, the German Shepherd lay at her feet watching joggers.

"He would have made a good police dog," Daniel observed.

"Too independent," Maja replied. "Questions authority too much. Like his owner."

Somewhere in Kronobergsgatan Prison, Nielsen still wrote in his precise hand, still measuring institutional patterns. The same system that had failed to recognize his methodical madness now contained it. Irony that would have delighted Nielsen if he'd possessed the capacity for irony.

"Do you ever wonder," Daniel asked, breaking their comfortable silence, "if he's still taking notes? Still seeing everyone as subjects?"

She watched a young couple walk past, leaning into each other against the morning chill. "Nielsen will die believing he was conducting legitimate research. Some delusions are too perfectly constructed to abandon."

The thought troubled her sometimes: whether Nielsen's immovable certainty made him more or less human than the rest of them.

Morning light gathered strength, illuminating Stockholm's careful choreography: joggers following predetermined routes, maintenance workers beginning their documented tasks, birds building nests without filing environmental impact reports. Life continuing its beautifully unmeasured flow.

"You know what I don't miss about police work?" she said, opening the thermos. Steam rose like the morning mist, carrying the aroma of good kaffe. "The paperwork. The endless documentation."

Daniel nodded, understanding the deeper meaning beneath her simple observation. "Some things shouldn't be measured."

"Most things," Maja corrected, feeling Loki shift against her feet as a squirrel darted across their path. The dog glanced up at her, seeking permission to pursue. She shook her head slightly, and he settled back with a sigh of resigned acceptance.

"Good dog," she murmured. "Understanding boundaries without needing a manual."

Steam rose from her kaffe cup, dissipating into the spring air. Unmeasured. Undocumented.

Free.

Printed in Dunstable, United Kingdom

65871540R00198